Lock Down Publications and Ca$h
Presents

GANGSTERS BLEED BLUE

SUBTITLE

Written By
NAIM "GUTTA" WILLIAMS

First Edition 2025

Printed in the United States of America

Lock Down Publications
P.O. Box 944
Stockbridge, GA 30281
www.lockdownpublications.com

Like our page on Facebook: Lock Down Publications
www.facebook.com/lockdownpublications.ldp

Stay Connected with Us!

Text **LOCKDOWN** to 22828 to stay up-to-date with new releases, sneak peaks, contests and more…

Like our page on Facebook:
Lock Down Publications

Join Lock Down Publications/The New Era Reading Group

Visit our website:
www.lockdownpublications.com

Follow us on Instagram:
Lock Down Publications

Email Us: We want to hear from you!

Prologue

MENARD CORRECTIONAL CENTER
CHESTER, IL

Hakeem "Star" Cross stared at himself in the stained piece of steel that hung from the wall disgusted. The shell of his former self that stared back at him made him want to vomit. His once vibrant eyes were lined with bags, while his usual wavy hair was in a tangled mess on top of his head. His body was littered with tattoos and stab wounds, but toned to perfection. His mind was on the verge of crumbling and was beyond tired. But then again fifteen years in one of the country's worst prisons would do that to almost anybody. His case was constantly being shot down in the appellate court, and almost everybody he loved or cared about died or left him to rot. He gave himself one more hard look in the mirror, trying to decipher whether he wanted to keep living or not… And his tired eyes gave him the answer he was looking for.

"Just do it! Hell no! Just don't think about it! Stop, Star! What the fuck are you think'!" He battled with himself mentally as he pulled the sheet of his bed. Thankfully his celly was gone on a visit or it would have been impossible. He had way too much love and respect for Star.

Clang! Clang! "Cross!" An overweight Officer Jones yelled, banging on the bars. "Mail!" He tossed a single envelope through the bars and continued down the gallery.

"Fat, funky bitch!" Star mumbled, tossing the sheet aside to retrieve the letter. He flipped it over and read it out loud. "The appellate court," he whispered.

This was his fourth time opening a letter from them, and just like the first there times before, he had butterflies in the pit of his stomach. It reads: *Effectively immediately that you've been awarded a new trial*. He reread the letter there times just to be sure. Tears welled up in his eyes and he didn't bother to wipe them… After all they were tears of joy.

"Here comes the King." He smiled.

CHAPTER 1
THREE WEEKS LATER
CHICAGO, IL

Star stepped through the county's double doors and nearly broke down crying. It had been fifteen long years, and he truly thought he would never see the city again. He looked around through teary eyes, and a smile spread across his handsome face. The city looked completely different, it even smelled different. It was a crisp September day with a light breeze that made the beaming sun bearable. He looked up to the sky and thanked the man responsible for setting him free before starting his march to the bus stop to hell by looking back. The way he saw it, he would never see the inside of a jail, prison, or station again. He would literally lay down and die first. At thirty-two years old he didn't have the luxury of wasting time. It was now or never for him, and for him it was definitely now. As he casually strolled down 26th Street with both of his hands jammed in the pockets of the tattered sweatpants the county donated him he couldn't help but marvel at almost every new car and woman he saw.

"The city changed a lot," he mumbled, staring at a group of Latina women that were walking on the other side of the street. One of them was so thick he couldn't stop rubbernecking until he collided with someone in front of him. "Damn my bad," he said locking eyes with the man in front of him.

He was a tatted-up, mean-muggin' Mexican flanked by four others. Neither of them had to say a word for Star to know they were part of a deadly street gang known as Latin

Kings. The crowns tattooed on all of them spoke for themselves. Plus, he always heard the stories about how they harassed anybody that left the county on foot.

"Watch where da fuck you going homie." The short and stocky man Star bumped into spat.

"I just said my bad," Star repeated, trying to slide past the group, but they formed a wall, blocking his path.

"Whachu was looking at our girls for, Dawg," a tall, skinny King said from the back.

Right then and there Star knew exactly where this was going. He was no stranger to violence, and definitely had his fair share of run-ins with the kings during his bid. If it was about to go down, then he was striking first. He knew he was outnumbered so he had to use the element of surprise to gain the upper hand. His eyes quickly scammed the ground until he zeroed in on what he was looking for.

Bingo, he thought.

"This nigga GO," another one called out pointing at the pitchfork that was tattooed in the middle of Star's neck.

It was GO time. Star cocked back and hit the man he bumped into with a vicious straight left-right hook combo that sat him on his back pockets. He had no time to admire his work though, he was on the move again. He ran and scooped up the beer bottle he spotted earlier. Star sprung into action so fast that the four remaining were still frozen in place and completely caught off guard.

"Kill his ass, King," the tall one yelled, motivating the others again.

They all took slow, cautious steps towards Star trying to surround him, but he peeped the play and took off again. He lunged forward, bringing the bottle down on top of the tall king's head, breaking it in the process.

"Arrrhhh-shiit," he cried, flailing his arms in sheer agony.

A big piece of glass lodged in the middle of his forehead while blood spurted into the air. The man wisely turned on his heels and bolted down the street crying bloody murder.

"Which one of you Latin Queens wants it next?" Star growled still wielding the broken beer bottle.

The remaining three looked at each other then rushed him all at the same time. It was a smart play, but one of them probably wouldn't live to tell about it. Star wasted no time driving the broken bottle in the first man's neck and twisting it. His eyes widened with fear as both his hands immediately reached for his neck. He tried to speak but only managed a low gurgling sound before blood spewed from his mouth and he collapsed to the ground. Before Star could attempt to make a move on the others… They were already on top of him, raining down blows. He managed to block a few, but the majority of them snuck through knocking him into the wall. They rushed again, but this time he was ready. The first one therw a wild haymaker that he easily ducked, and returned two of his own that staggered the King. His comrade however saw his opportunity and swung for the fences. The wild hook landed flush and sent Star skidding to the payment. He followed up with a kick that caught Star directly in the stomach, knocking the wind out of him. By now the other King recovered and joined in stomping Star out.

"Bitch ass!"

"Brick," they yelled as they beat him.

The only thing Star could do at this point was ball up and pray that they got tired. His head felt like it was going to explode, and he had already almost blacked out twice. Then out of nowhere, they stopped and took off running up the street.

Star peeked up from his protective ball and had never been so happy to see the police in his life.

***

Tacarra "TT" Riggens sat on the living sofa of her one-bedroom apartment, annoyed beyond words. Her low down, good for nothing boyfriend forgot to come home last night, and to top it all off he had the nerve to keep her car. She was thirty minutes late for work, and the good lord knew she couldn't afford another write-up. Her obese pissant boss would surely demote her, or worse.

"C'mon, where da fuck is this nigga at," she mumbled out loud checking the time on her phone for the sixth time in seconds. "I'm sick of this broke bitch ass nigga!" She roared, jumping to her feet. This was most definitely the straw that broke the camel's back. She stormed to the bedroom and found the closet and immediately began tossing his clothes out. "Scrub ass nigga gone take my muthafuckin car." She huffed, stomping to the kitchen to search for garbage bags. "Got me all late and shit," she snapped.

BEEP! BEEP! BEEP! The honking car horn in the distance caught her attention. She peeked through the blinds, and there was Tito sitting in her car with Tre and Twan. His two best friends that she couldn't stand to be around.

"No the fuck this scrub ass nigga didn't," she spat, grabbing the biggest knife she could find and trotting downstairs. She flew down the stairs and popped out of the lobby doors like a woman possessed. "Nigga get da fuck outta my car," she snapped, banging on the hood of the car with the knife.

Tito and company damn near jumped out of their skin at the sight of TT with the Michael Myers knife in her hand.

"Tito, boy control yo bitch." Tre said from the back seat.

"Bitch?" She roared, sprinting to his side of the car. "I got yo bitch," she yelled yanking on the door handle.

"Aye get this bitch G," Twan yelled from the passenger, locking the doors.

Hearing Twan yell snapped Tito out of his daze, he was completely thrown off by TT's actions. Normally she was the sweetest person in the world, now she was acting like the Bride of Lucifer. He jumped out of the car and grabbed her by the arm. “Why da fuck you out here tweakin’,” he asked, spinning her to face him.

“You my fuckin’ problem!” She screamed, swinging the knife this way and that.

“Aye watch that shit,” he warned leaping backwards, avoiding the knife by inches. “You gone make me show my ass out here,” he claimed.

“Nigga, try me. And watch how fast I have my brother and his fiend fuck you up.”

At the mention of her brother and his friend Tito slowed his roll. Sure, he was a gangster, but her brother and his friends were on a different level of crazy. “Chill out bae, damn. Why you tweakin’ so hard,” he asked.

“Fuck boy, don’t call me that. You ain’t shit to me so get you and yo broke ass friends outta my car,” she hissed while shaking her neck hood-rat style.

“Damn G. You let her tweak with you like that?” Tre asked.

“Broke niggas don’t get to run shit. Remember that,” she answered. Something inside of TT had snapped, and it felt good to let him know exactly how she was feeling. Plus, she got to do it in front of his friends. She loved Tito, but she was tired of providing for a grown ass man. Tired of coming second to the streets and every skank it had to offer. She was done.

“C’mon baby don’t do this. Let’s just go in the house and talk,” he begged.

“Talk,” she repeated, scrunching her face up as if something stunk. “Now you wanna talk? I been trying to talk when I had to go to the clinic. I was tryna talk when I had to bond yo broke ass outta jail. I was tryna talk when I lit up your phone last night cuz you ain’t come home last night. I’m done fuckin’ talkin’. Now, get the fuck on before I call my brother.” She warned.

Tito swallowed the little pride he had left and dropped his head in defeat. “C’mon y’all. We out,” he said heading towards the bus stop.

“And you got till tonight to come get your shit or it’s going in the dumpster,” she yelled at his back.

He didn’t even turn around to acknowledge her, he just continued up the street with his homies in tow. She plopped down on the hood of her car and burst into tears. Another failed relationship. She was 33 years old with zero kids and lonely as ever. Was love ever coming her way?

***

Star half-walked, half-limped down 71st Street. His ribs were killing him, and the back of his skull pulsated as if it had a mind of its own. He was positive he had a concussion or two. His lip was busted and he could feel his left eye swelling. Yet he still felt like he was on top of the world. After briefly speaking with Chicago’s finest, to his surprise, they let him walk scott free. They explained to him that they knew all about the Latin Kings and their illicit deeds outside of the county, and how they were happy somebody finally gave them exactly what they deserved. They were so glad that they even offered him a ride, which he politely denied. No way was he pulling up to the hood on his first day out in a police car.

As he limped up the block he looked around his old stomping grounds with mixed feelings. On one note he was happy to be home, but on the other he was disgusted at how rundown and dead the block was. Almost every other house was abandoned with the front yard littered with garbage. Crack heads and dope fiends got high on stoops right in the open. Aside from a woman crying in her car, and a group of dudes on the corner nobody was out. The block was as dead as a graveyard.

"Damn. What da fuck happened to my hood," he asked out loud as he spun around, taking in the whole block.

"Star?" A feminine voice called out from behind him.

He spun around and locked eyes with the woman that was crying. "Who wanna know," he asked squinting for a better view.

"TT," she screeched, popping up off the car and zooming into his arms. She ran into him at full speed almost knocking him to the ground. "Oh my gawd," she said, stepping back and gazing into his eyes. "It really is you."

At first Star didn't even remember who TT was, until he locked in on the tattoo on her collarbone. It read "R.I.P. Buckwild". This was his right-hand man's older sister. The funny looking girl who had a crush on him back in the day. "Damn, TT, you done grew up," he chimed, spinning her around. She was mocha chocolate with full lips and big eyes. She was 5'4, and even through her work scrubs he could tell she was thick in all the right places. Most people said she looked like Regina Hall from "Girls Trip".

"Boy, shut up! You know I'm older than you."

"Girl, you know what I mean. You look nice."

"Aww, thanks boo. What the hell happened to you though? You look like you just went toe to toe with Mike Tyson," she joked, throwing jabs at the air.

"Shit." He shrugged. "You know how them kings be outside the county. Why you tryna be funny and shit, why were you crying in your car," he asked making the crybaby face with his hands.

"Nothin' fa' real. I just got into it with my mama and she said all types of hurtful shit," she lied. No way was she about to tell her old crush that she just broke up with her ex, and she was scared she'd never find love.

"Damn, Ms. Riggins still be on that," he asked in disbelief.

"Some things never changed. But what about you? What you about to do now that you a free man? I know after a lotta time you got some type of plan."

"Something like that," he replied, flashing her his pearly whites. "But right now I was 'bout to pop up on my sister."

"Pu-lease! She so far up that nigga Gotti's ass she could tell you what he ate for lunch." She huffed. "Me and her don't even kick it no more behind that fat fuck."

"Gotti? Gotti? Gotti," he asked trying to put a face to the name but came up emptyhanded. "I don't think I know him."

"Most likely you don't. He from Terror-Town."

"Terror-Town? He a Stone," he asked, his smile instantly dropping into a frown.

"Yup."

"And that nigga over here?" Star spat, marching up the street.

The Black P Stones were sworn enemies of the Gangster Disciples, or GDs. The two organizations had been clashing since the early 80's and still clashed to this day. Star was a diehard GD and would lay down his life for the nation, but times were way different now. Nowadays it really didn't matter what you claimed, it only mattered where you were from. Since the F.B.I killed or locked away all the founding members or leaders of every street gang in Chicago… It was nothing but chaos. GDs killed GDs and Stones killed Stones and Vice Lords killed 4 Corner Hustlers. All that mattered now was what clique you were from and how much clout you had. As the saying goes cut the head off and the body will fall.

"Star, hold up," she said grabbing his arm. "Look, shit ain't like it used to be; a lot has changed. Come upstairs with me. I'll fill you in. Plus, I know you hungry and ya girl can throw down in the kitchen." She added, pulling him towards her apartment.

Star reluctantly followed her. He had always heard the stories from the younger guys that came through, but somehow thought his area was exempt… How wrong was he?

CHAPTER 2

THE NEXT MORNING

Star sat up and looked around TT's living room confused until last night's events came rushing back. TT had made fried chicken, Macaroni and cheese with collard greens and cornbread. After devouring his meal, they stayed up into the wee hours of the morning drinking. She then filled him in on the last fifteen years of who, what, when, and where. She even told him about Tito, Twan, and Tre, conveniently leaving out the part that he was her ex. Star didn't remember Tito anyway and certainly wasn't trying to. The only thing on his mind was collecting the check that the state would soon have to pay due to the fact that he served 15 years for crimes that he was acquitted for. He was looking at a good $250,000. Once he secured his bed, he would set out to reunite every hood that was banging D.O.N. One of the most powerful gangs back then. He felt they lost their way, and it was his duty to restore order to the "Glory Days"… or Die trying.

Rubbing the sleep out of his eyes, he swung his legs over the couch and stood up. The soft hum of the shower could be heard, so he knew exactly where to find TT. He still couldn't get over how good she looked. The pimple-faced, malnourished teenager was gone, and in her place was a full-blown woman. He definitely had to tap that.

Knock! Knock! Knock! Beating on the front door interrupted his perverse thoughts.

"Can you get that for me," she yelled from the shower.

"Uhh… Yeah, I guess," he replied really not wanting to answer her door. For all he knew it was her boyfriend, or worse— a crazy ex, which was the last thing he wanted. He hadn't even been out of jail 24 hours and already almost killed a man and had a run in with the police. The door swung open, and he found himself staring at three men who looked not a day over 21. They all just sat there staring at each other, until the one standing in the middle spoke up.

"TT here," he asked with a hint of aggression lacing his tone.

"Yeah. Hol'on," Star said swinging the front door halfway closed. "It's three niggas. You want me to let them in?"

"Yeah," she yelled.

Without waiting on his permission the trio stormed the apartment as if they owned it. Two of them found a home on the couch while the third headed straight for the kitchen.

That must be her nigga, Star thought, sizing the man up. He was a lanky 6'1" with shoulder length dreadlocks that hung loosely. He had a high yellow complexion and tattoos littered his body. The pitchfork tattooed in the middle of his neck caught Star's attention like Randy Moss diving for a touchdown pass in the Superbowl. Not only was it similar to Star's, it was the Gangster Disciples insignia. His lackeys had the same pitchfork tattooed as well. One in the middle of his forehead, and the other right under his eye. There was no doubt in Star's mind these men were G.D.

After securing a cold piece of chicken, the man came back into the living room and stood next to Star. "Wassup? What they call you," he asked in between bites.

"What they call you?" Star asked.

"Pap," he responded.

"I'm Star."

"Where you from, Star," he asked. Staring at the fork on Star's neck.

"Right here. What about you?"

"From 71st?" the man with the pitchfork in the middle of his forehead interjected. His name was Crazy G. He was brown skin with beady eyes and a full goatee.

"71st and Jeffery. Wabash Cottage. I'm all through here. Why?" Star asked amused.

"Cuz we from 71st and Jeffery. Wabash and Cottage but we don't know you," the third man said. His name was LayLow. He was a frail 5'8" with mocha skin and a baby face. He reminded everyone of the actor Idris Alba.

"You 7-4?" Pap asked, using the chicken bone to point at his pitchfork.

"Until the world blows." Star shot back, finishing the G.D.'s famous saying. *"7-4 till the world blows."*

"Pap, what da fuck I tell you 'bout fuckin' wit' my company?" TT asked, interrupting their showdown.

"Nah it's cool, T. We were just getting to know each other, that's all," Star claimed, smiling at her.

"Yeah, ain't nobody fuckin' wit your company. I'm just tryna see where he from since he G.D," Pap said.

"Cuz he sholl ain't from 71st." Crazy G snickered.

"Boy, shut yo dumb ass up!" TT barked. "This was Buck Wild's best friend. The one that's been locked up." She explained.

Star could see the light bulb go off in Pap's head almost instantly. "Damn, I remember you now. You used to be at our crib all the time. You used to give me dollas when I was like six or seven," Pap said.

"Damn, that's our bad, big homie," LayLow said.

"Naw, that shit ain't 'bout shit," Star assured, waving off the situation.

"Damn, TT why you ain't tell me he was out," he said, shooting a confused glance her way. "You straight? You don't need shit," he asked, reaching out to shake Star's hand.

Star grabbed his hand and they performed the Gangster Disciples handshake. It was done by taking both of their forefingers and intertwining, then twisting them up. If done properly it would look as if two pitchforks were crossed.

"I'm straight G, I appreciate it though."

"You sure? It don't look like it." Crazy G said, pointing at Star's black eye.

"Nah, this ain't shit," he said, tapping his eyes. "I had to fuck a couple Latin Queens when I got out."

"Damn true. But shit crazy out here… So, I want you to have this," Pap said, pulling his Glock 9 and extending it towards Star, who stared at the gun as if it was dipped in shit.

The way his first couple days were going, Star was sure he would end up on the first train smoking back to Menard. "Thanks, but I'm good my G," he said.

"It's like the wild-wild west around this bitch. I wouldn't feel right knowing somethin' happened to you," Pap claimed still extending the gun Star's way.

"Shit goes down 'round this muthafucka every other day, and with that *rake* on yo neck niggas gone try it no matter what." Crazy G co-signed.

Star knew Crazy G's words were the absolute truth. The pitchfork on his neck had been causing unwanted attention since the day he got it. After a brief pause, he recanted and took the Glock. The second the cold steel was in his hands, the feeling of power immediately coursed through his veins. A feeling that was all too familiar to Star. "Good lookin' out," he said tucking the compact 9 into his pants pocket.

"That's lil' shit. Look, if you need anything let us know. These my niggas Crazy G and LayLow."

"Say less. I'll grab your info from TT."

"Bet. Just hit me," he said, reaching for Star's hand. He performed their signature handshake, then repeated the process with LayLow and Crazy G as they filed out the door.

"Sorry. My lil' brother somethin' else sometimes," TT said, nervously shifting her weight from foot-to-foot. She had on her work scrubs with her hair straight but slightly curled at the end.

"Nah, I actually like the lil' nigga. Reminds me of Buck when we was comin up."

"True. Well I'm 'bout to head out to work in a few minutes but we can kick until then."

"I would love to but I gotta holla at my sister," he said, slipping on his jail work boots. "You know she really the only family I got left."

"Hmph! We gone see 'bout that," she mumbled.

"You know I can hear yo lil' ass, right?"

"Aanndd," she snapped playfully, rolling her eyes and shaking her neck.

"Same ole TT." He laughed, closing the distance between them.

"I need you to do me a favor though."

"What's that? I just want you to know I'm not givin' you no pussy if you ain't finna wife me." She blurted out crossing her arms.

"What the hell you talkin' 'bout? I was just finna ask you to put this up for me," he said pulling out the Glock. "I would have did it at my sister's house but she got too many kids."

"Awe, I knew that," she claimed. Had her skin not been so dark he would have been able to see her cheeks flush with embarrassment.

"Sure you did." He teased handing her the Glock

"Look, if I ain't here when you get back, I'ma leave a spare key for you with my girl Ke-Ke. She stays downstairs in apartment 1-C."

"Aight, thanks, but I might stay at sis crib for the night."

"Bet you won't. But anyway, I know you got plans to take ova, so remember every gangsta needs a gangsta ass bitch," she said with a wink.

"I'll keep that in mind," he replied before walking out the door.

THREE MINUTES LATER

Star stood on his old porch and so many memories flooded his brain. This was the very house where it all started. As he knocked on the front door, mixed emotions swirled around in his head. Part of him was happy to reunite with the only sibling he had left, but another part despised her for leaving him to rot in a cell. The sounds of children laughing playfully could be heard, making him smile. Even if he wasn't messing with his sister like that, he would be there for his niece and nephew.

Knock! Knock! Knock!

"Who dat?" A deep voice boomed from behind the door.

"Star," he yelled back.

The door swung open, and he found himself staring at the man he assumed was none other than Gotti. He was a chubby 5'9" with a full beard and a bald head. He rocked an all-black Nike jogging suit with a pair of all-white retro Jordan 11's. A platinum chain with a five-point star pendant hung at the center of his chest. Star could instantly tell he was a dope boy. They mean mugged each other for almost a full minute before Star finally spoke up.

"Christina here," he asked.

"Who da fuck is you," he spat, staring at the rake on Star's neck.

"Her brother, nigga! Is she here or not?" He shot back. He could feel his blood begin to boil.

"Brother?" He scoffed curling his upper lip. "Nigga, she only got one brother and you ain't it," he yelled.

Star was glad he left the Glock at TT's because he would have shot the clown in front of him in his big mouth.

Before Star could respond, Christina emerged from the back to see what all the commotion was about. "S-Star?" She stuttered. She was almost sure her eyes were playing tricks on her.

"The one and only." He smiled.

"Bitch! You got five seconds to get this fuck nigga off my porch! I don't give a fuck who he is!" Gotti barked without thinking or hesitation. Star lunged, but Gotti was prepared. He stepped back and pulled out his XD40. "Wassup, bitch?"

He taunted, leveling the gun with Star's face. "What happened to all'at froggy shit?" He laughed

"Gotti, please stop." Christina begged, grabbing his arm. Star could literally see the fear in her eyes, and it made him see red.

"Fuck all'at," he spat, shrugging her off. "Tell bro-bro it's time to go and never show his face here again." He stated hoping that Star would try him so he could smoke him. Truth be told, Gotti knew exactly who Star was the moment he opened the door. Christina always prattled about her savage brother who ran most of the eastside at 17 years old. Everybody from 71st to 79th talked and reminisced about the man named Star who killed two police officers, and how everything was good when he was out. Gotti couldn't wait until he could prove everybody wrong… But he failed to realize Star was the real deal.

"I'm sorry, Star, please just go," she said barely above a whisper.

Star didn't even respond, he just turned on his heels and started his march.

"Psst! And they said you were a gangster. I been bitchin' hoe ass bricks like you my whole life. *Gok! Gok! Gok," he yelled* at Star's back.

Gok meant Gangster Disciple killer, and it was complete disrespect to the nation. Star was fuming. As soon as he was able to support his sister and her kids, Gotti's head was on the chopping block. He would let the light skin Rick Ross win this battle, because he would definitely lose the war.

SEVERAL BLOCKS OVER

"It costs to be alive. I won't say I'm King of the jungle but I survived. Watch the cookie crumble in front of me, at least I tried. You know whatcha called robbed watcha called at least he died." lil' Baby's "Cost to be Alive" pumped from the speakers of Pap, LayLow, and Crazy G's stolen Jeep Grand Cherokee. LayLow navigated the truck with ease.

Driving was like riding a bike to him which is why he always found himself behind the wheel. Pap was posted in the passenger. Strapped with a Glock 17 equipped with a switch. Capable of turning the hand cannon fully auto, and a 33 shot extended magazine. Crazy G occupied the back seat clutching a mini Draco fully loaded with deadly .762s. It was a hot September day, so they knew the opps would be out. The Black P. Stones on 79th and Kingston that went by "OTM", or "Only The Moes", were sworn enemies of Pap and almost every GD on 71st for almost five years.

"You ready, nigga?" Pap asked as LayLow brought the car to a halt at the end of the alley. This had almost become a routine for them. He would drop them off at the end of the block or alley. Then once the shots rang out, he would circle around and scoop them at the other end of the block.

"C'mon, nigga, you know I was born B.P.S.N.K," Crazy G claimed chambering a round in the Draco. It was brand new, and he couldn't wait to see what it could do.

They both exited the Jeep and crept down the alley as quietly as possible until they reached a gate with a hole cut in the middle. As they slid through the gate, they came to a pause in the rundown backyard. The hustle and bustle of fiends coming and going could be heard.

"C'mon, nephew, don't do ole Jim-Jim like that. I'm only short 3 dollas." They heard a raspy voice say.

"Nigga, yo ass been short the last three days. I ain't taking no shorts today. That shit dead," another man said.

"They on the porch," Pap whispered

Crazy G nodded at Pap, and they both darted from behind the house guns blazing.

Ffddddttt! Ffddddttt! With two squeezes of the fully auto Glock, Pap shredded the first man's face and emptied his clip, at the same time sending the man's mutilated corpse flying over the porch banister.

The block was fuller than usual, but as usual, at the sound of gunshots people scattered like roaches when the lights came on.

"Aww shit!" Jim-Jim said before bolting up the block.

Crazy G ran in the middle of the street and took aim. *Blocka! Blocka! Blocka! Blocka! Blocka!* The Draco rattled in his hands sending a deadly barrage of .762s into the crowd. Three of the bullets found home in one man's leg and another's back and shoulder, sending them both twisting to the ground violently.

Scccuuurrrtt! LayLow brought the Jeep to a screeching halt at the opposite end of the block.

"C'mon! C'mon," he yelled, waving his hand frantically, but he may as well been talking to a brick wall.

Crazy G was on a mission and wasn't stopping until he spilled blood. He jogged over to where both men were turning to crawl away and let the Draco speak one last time, spraying blood and brain matter everywhere. He quickly sprinted back to the Jeep where Pap and LayLow were waiting. Before he could even get both feet in the truck, LayLow mashed the gas pedal.

Sccouurrttt!

***

BACK ON 71ST

Star only half listened as Kierra yapped about this and that. After his little clash with Gotti and his sister, his thoughts were all over the place. He had gone back to TT's, but found she wasn't home. Remembering what she said, he stomped down to Kierra's. To his surprise she remembered almost everything about him, and invited him in for lunch. A sucker for a pretty face and a home cooked meal, he gladly accepted. Even though he hardly remembered anything about her. What he did know though… Home girl was stocked. At 5'10" she stood only a couple inches shorter than him. Her peanut butter complexion seemed to glow, while her chinky brown eyes gave her an exotic look. Her long natural curly hair was pulled back into a messy ponytail, but it somehow added to her beauty. Perfect B-cups filled out into a slim waist, pLump thighs, and a round bottom. She wasn't sluggin' like one of those video vixens, but she could hold her own.

Damn! She a sexy ass Amazon, he thought as he watched her dance around the kitchen. He looked around her nicely decorated apartment and nodded his approval. An expensive love sac cotton sectional occupied the middle of the floor on top of snow-white carpet. A sixty-inch LG smart TV was mounted on the wall directly in front of him with a Bose stereo attached. A 7-gallon glowing fish tank sat catty cornered to the far right, giving the living room an exotic setting. It was clear she was doing well for herself.

"Did you hear what I said, boy," she asked, snapping him out of la-la land.

"I ain't even go lie. I zoned out for a minute," he replied looking up at her.

She was standing right in front of him with her hands fisted at the hips. The tight-fitting leggings and tank top she wore clung to every crevice of her body as if they were made especially for her, while her heat perfume by Beyonce intoxicated him. "I said what type of tacos you want? I got chicken and steak."

"Uuuhh, it really don't matter. Whateva you think you make the best."

"I do *everything* the best," she said seductively while staring into his eyes.

Star had heard everything he needed to hear. He grabbed her hand and pulled her towards him, and she didn't resist.

She mounted him cow-girl style, and their lips instantly met. Their tongues danced for almost two full minutes before Star picked her up by her plump cheeks and laid her down on the couch. He grabbed her leggings and relieved her of them, effortlessly revealing her freshly waxed kitten.

"Damn girl!" He huffed, taking a second to admire her body. He could tell she put in some hours at the gym. He quickly shed his tattered attire and began stroking his member to full length.

"Come get this pussy." She moaned, spreading her legs wide, her pussy soaked in anticipation at the sight of his 8-inch monster.

However, Star had other plans. It had been 15 and a half years since he'd been with a woman, so he was going to take his sweet time exploring every inch of her body. He grabbed her foot and began kissing up her thigh until he was face to face with her pussy. He covered her love button with his mouth and expertly swindled his tongue in figure eights while his fingers dipped in her honey pot.

"Ssss! Oooohhh." She moaned, arching her back and palming his head.

He sucked and swirled his tongue around her clit as if his life depended on it, making sure to show her lips some attention every now and then.

"I-I-I-I'm cumin'," she whispered as she humped his face, releasing her creamy juices all over his mouth and chin. She laid back on the couch trying to catch her breath, but Star was all over her.

"*Turn over*." He demanded, stroking himself.

She gladly obeyed his commands and hiked her perfect round ass in the air, making sure to arch her back.

As he eased into her tunnel, he had to will himself not to explode. She was soaking wet and her walls gripped him like a pair of needle nose pliers. "Damn girl." He grunted. He started off with a slow, long stroke and gradually picked up the pace.

"J-Just like that." She moaned, throwing her ass back, matching him stroke for stroke as he pumped in and out of her mercilessly.

"Starrrr! Ahhh-ANNN-OOOO," she cried out in a mixture of pain and pleasure.

"You like that shit."

"I like it! I like it," she yelled holding on to the couch for dear life.

"Naw. Tell. Me. You. Love. It!" He huffed, spreading her cheeks so he could go as deep as possible.

"Uhhh, I-I-I love-lo-love it!" She screamed as her legs began to shake violently. "Uuuhhhh-uh-aahhn, I'm C—" She whispered, coating his pole in a thick white glaze. Before she could even process her second orgasm, he pulled out and buried his face in her ass crack. "Star w-wait. Ooohhh shiiit."

He slurped and licked from her ass down to her pussy, then back up to her sass. The way he licked her you would've sworn she was made out of sugar.

"Fffuuckk." She cried on the brink of another breathtaking orgasm.

"Damn you taste good as fuck," he claimed licking her juices from his fingers. "*Turn back over.*"

Kierra lazily turned back over, her body was tingling all over. She had never had her ass ate or cum so many times in one session in her life. He took both of her legs and tossed them over his shoulder before he slammed his missile home. "Ooohh!" She yelped, closing her eyes.

"Now look at me!"

Her eyes popped open and looked into his. For a second it seemed as if they were staring into each other's soul.

"Damn. You so fuckin' wet."

Kierra could feel his missile swelling and knew he was close. She rolled her hips in rhythm with his strokes while never breaking eye contact.

"Where you want this shit at?"

"Where eva daddy. Oohh shit where eva."

"Arrgggh fffuuuck," he growled as he released 15 years of frustration deep into her abyss before collapsing on top of her.

She was officially hooked and had no plans on letting Star out of her sight.

"Uh-uhn don't be going to sleep. I thought you were cookin'." He teased with his throbbing member inside of her.

"I ain't going to sleep," she said through half-opened eyes.

"I'm lookin' at you."

"Well, you shoulda thought 'bout that before you did all'at." She shot back before drifting off to sleep.

CHAPTER 3
THE NEXT MORNING

"How da fuck y'all let them niggas get up on lil' cuz?" Trindog questioned as he paced the rundown carpet of the traphouse's living room floor. He had his Smith and Wesson .40 out dangling at his side, with the meanest mug plastered across his face. His shoulder length dreads were freshly twisted and seemed to blend in with his pitch-black skin.

"I-I don't know, big bro, it happened so fast. We were in the trap counting money when we heard shots lettin' off. We thought niggas was tryna rob us. So, we packed the money and dope and jetted out da back like you said," Pewee explained with his eyes glued to Trindog's .40. He was exactly what his name spelled. Most people joked about how much he resembled Chris Rock.

"Them niggas had something big too." Ray Moe, Pewee's right-hand man, co-signed. Unlike Pewee, he was 6'3" with muscles bulging from everywhere and was dumb as a box of rocks.

Trindog stopped his husky 5'6" frame in front of both men. Even though he was small, Trindog was as deadly as they came. He could let his gun bang with the best of them, and would do so at the drop of a dime. But he wasn't all brawn. He was exceptionally smart for a street dude, which was why he was the head of OTM. better known as ONLY THE MOES… The sworn enemies of 71st.

"Who was 'posed to be on security," he asked.

"Tae Moe. But they clapped him too," Ray Moe said, fear lacing his tone

Knock! Knock! Knock!

"Who da' fuck is it," he spat, pissed that someone was interrupting

"It's me, baby," Moni stated

"Didn't I tell you to wait in the car!"

"What da fuck I tell yo ass 'bout yellin' at me," she snapped, shaking her neck and rolling her eyes as if he could see her. "I got this cluck out here. He says he saw the whole thing."

A sinister smile spread across his hideous face as the thought of getting even crossed his mind. Lately they'd been beefing with so many hoods that it was impossible to pinpoint who was doing what. "Get da door," he told Raymoe.

The door swung open and in stepped Moni and a raggedy old man that they could smell the second he stepped through the door. Moni's 5'0" petite frame seemed out of place amongst the rugged men in the room. She was slim but had a little somethin'-somethin' in the right places. The high-heeled Red Bottoms and leather jacket with the pants to match made her seem like a movie star. Her hair was cut short with a bang that swooped over the left side of her face, giving her a Taraji. P. Henson look.

"Umm, I'ma head back to the car," she announced.

"Yeah, you do that," Trindog said giving her a pat on the ass. "So wassup," he asked as soon as Moni was gone.

"So it's like dis. Ole' Jim-Jim was tryna cop a bag fa da low, right? When dis nigga with long dreads and a big ass pitchfork on his neck jump out blastin'," he explained through rotten teeth.

"I thought it was two shooters?"

"It was but ole Jim-Jim was too busy having ass ya dig," he asked, grinning his last four rotten teeth.

"Like a muthafuckin' shovel," he said, leveling his gun with Jim-Jim's face.

Boca! The hydra shock bullet slammed into his forehead, spraying blood and brain matter everywhere. "Get this shit cleaned up and let errbody know it's up with them bitch ass Bricks on 71st," he growled.

"Man, that nigga crazy as hell. I thought we were next," Pewee confessed as soon as Trindog was gone.

"On Stone Ku. I thought it was curtains."

BACK ON 71ST

TT lounged on the steps of her apartment building with a freshly rolled Backwood dangling from her lips as she scrolled aimlessly down her Facebook timeline. It was her day off and she planned on enjoying every second of it. Secretly she was waiting on Star to show up. She figured since he didn't show up last night he stayed at his sister's house. She already had the whole day planned out for them and was anxious for him to pop up. First, she would take him shopping for a couple outfits and to get his haircut. Then she would take him out to dinner, and if he played his cards right… He would get his nuts out of the sand. As she continued to scroll aimlessly, Kierra's post from last night grabbed her attention. It Read: "The way this man is putting it down. He ain't never going nowhere," with the heart and lock emojis.

"Uh-uhn bitch," she mumbled, exhaling a cloud of smoke. "Spill the tea." she added dialing Kierra's number. After receiving the voicemail twice, she figured she was still asleep and decided to wake her. Plus, she still had her spare key. The closer she got to Kierra's apartment the louder the sounds of love making could be heard.

"Ah-ah-ahhhh! Sssshiiiit." Kierra moaned.

"Damn Ki. He got it like that," she whispered, placing her ear to the door being nosey.

"Tell me. You. Love. This. Dick." A familiar voice grunted.

She was positive she knew the voice, although she couldn't put a face to it.

"Uh-oooh, St-Star, I love it," she cried.

At the mention of Star's name TT's blood began to boil. She backed away from the door holding her chest as if she'd been shot. How could Kierra betray her like that after she told her how she felt about him? Her hurt and anger mixed together and instantly turned into rage and she wasn't leaving until she gave them both a proper "fuck you".

Boom! Boom! Boom! "Open this door, you snake muthafuckas," she yelled, kicking the door as hard as she could.

The sound of hushed whispers and sudden movements could be heard before the apartment went completely still.

"I know y'all fuckin' hear me!" She roared with spittle flying from her mouth. She was so enraged that she tossed her phone and the Backwood to the side like yesterday's trash.

The lock on the door twisted with a loud click before the door swung open. A half-naked Star came into view while Kierra played the background draped in a sheet. The smell of Kierra's perfume mixed with sex assaulted her nostrils, enraging her even further.

"Wassup, TT?" Star asked, clearly confused as to why TT was acting like they were a couple.

"Wassup, TT," she repeated before she cocked back and smacked him silly. "Nigga, that's wassup!" She roared trying to rush past him to get at Kierra, but he snatched her up. "Let me da fuck go!" She screamed, kicking and flailing her arms wildly, but her efforts to get loose were futile.

Star held firm; she kicked, screamed, and cried bloody murder but couldn't get loose. She was so loud that the entire first floor came out to watch the scene unfold.

"TT, look around you, shorty. You embarrassing yo' self."

TT looked around, shocked that half the building had come out to see her show her ass. She quickly pulled herself together and Star released his death grip on her.

"I'ma see yo lil' thot ass," she hissed before storming past her nosey neighbors.

"I told you that bitch was bat shit crazy," Kierra said as soon as Star closed the door.

"I see," he claimed, sliding off his boxers. "But in the meantime between time, bend that ass back over for daddy."

"I thought you'd never ask."

CHAPTER 4

SEVERAL DAYS LATER

Star overlooked himself in Kierra's full body length mirror and a smile spread across his face. He was dressed in a crisp pair of whitewashed Balmain jeans over a pair of all-white Air Force Ones. A tight fitting white tee hugged his torso, showing off his nicely sculpted biceps. His hair was freshly lined and tapered down to his full goatee which he trimmed into a five o'clock shadow. It had been so long since he looked this good, he hardly recognized himself.

"Damn, bae, I still can't get over how fine you look." Kierra cooed, wrapping her arms around his waist and kissing his neck.

"This all yo work," he claimed, turning to face her.

"Nah, boo, you had it in you all along," she said stealing a kiss. "You gone miss me while I'm at work?"

"C'mon now, you know that," he said palm-gripping her ass, and tonguing her down.

"Mmm-mmmmm. Don't start, I gotta go."

"I should be here when you get back."

"Nigga, ain't no should. You betta." She replied, giving him a wink heading out for work.

He waited a full ten minutes before marching up to TT's. For some reason he actually felt bad about how things went down last time they saw each other and wanted to clear things up. Plus, she still had the Glock Pap had given him and needed it so he could put the next phase of his plan in motion.

Before he could even knock on the door, TT snatched it open, mugging harder than Kanye West. "What? That thot ass bitch pussy done dried up already?"

"Damn girl why yo crazy ass always tweakin'?" He laughed, shaking his head.

She stood defiantly in the doorway with both of her arms crossed, causing the little shirt she was wearing to rise slightly. Revealing her silk panties and thick chocolate thighs.

"I'm not fuckin crazy! So don't call me that shit," she snapped. "Now, what do you want?"

"I wanted to apologize for all'at shit that went down the other day. I really ain't mean to hurt yo feelins. And I need what yo brother gave me."

"Hold up," she said, trying to slam the door in his face, but he caught it and forced his way inside. "Psst!" She smacked her lips and gave him her best eyeroll before storming off.

He couldn't help but watch her chocolate cheeks bounce with each step. "Damn," he mumbled biting his bottom lip.

She popped back up in almost ten seconds flat, shoving the gun into his hands. "Here. Now you can get up out my shit."

"Shorty, chill yo lil' mad ass out." He teased closing the door completely. "I need you to call up my brother and tell him I'm tryna link up."

Dayuum! Why this nigga got to come up in here all fine and shit? I'm supposed to be mad at him, she thought, trying her hardest not to smile. "Aight, but after that, I want you gone."

"TT, we both know if you ain't want me in here, yo crazy ass would have neva let me in." He pointed out flashing her his megawatt smile, soaking her panties in the process.

"Psst! Don't be smilin' at me." She huffed, dialing Pap's number. Even though he was banging Kierra and left her high and dry, she still wanted him in the worst way. She hated to admit it, but if he wanted her right there, she most definitely wouldn't refuse.

***

Kierra's apartment was packed from wall to wall with every Gangster Disciple in the area. Star knew if she was there to witness all the Air-Max, Jordan's and Timberlands standing on her white carpet she would blow a gasket. Once he linked up and shared his vision of bringing power back to the Gangster Disciples with Pap, the rest was history. Pap, Crazy G, and LayLow claimed to have the same vision as him and rallied the troops for him, knowing all he had to do was convince a bunch of broke, starving, and gang bagging grown men to follow his cause. Drinks flowed while Kush clouds filled the air, the men conversed amongst themselves. But not one man had a clue as to why they had been called out tonight. But like most black people, when they heard free liquor and free weed, they came running.

"Aye, let me have y'all ears right quick," Star said from the center of the living room.

Half of the room remembered Star from back in the day, while the other half was too young to remember, yet every man heard or knew the stories about him.

As soon as he had every man's attention, he continued. "Now, I know some of y'all know me and some of y'all don't, but I was raised, shot and arrested on this very block. I been bangin' GD before I was bangin' pussy." He paused to make sure he had every man's undivided attention. "The GDs used to be one of if not the most powerful mobs in the county. Now I'm not gone drag this out longer than I already have, but look around you. Not just at yo guys standin' next to you. I'm talkin' about everything. If you happy and content with livin' with the way you livin' then there is the door," he said pausing again to give anybody who wanted to leave a chance. "But if you know in your heart you was meant to be a boss. Meant to bleed blue like a real gangsta." He flagged the forks, the insignia for GD. Every man in the room returned the gesture. "Then stick with me. Pledge your loyalty to the nation and help me rebuild what the old man started. United we stand. Divided we fall."

"One love!" Pap yelled, throwing up the forks with both hands.

"Bos!" The room shouted back in unison.

"One love!"

"Bos!"

"Aight. Aight. Aight. I gotta get y'all the fuck up outta here for my girl come home snappin'. Look, we gone meet back here next Friday and put part 2 in motion. Now who gone say the prayer and close out this demonstration?" Star asked looking around.

"I a do it," Tito said, stepping in the middle of the circle.

"Aight, but before you start, you know the penalty of fuckin' up the prayer right?"

"Yeah, I know. But I got it. Stance," he yelled out.

Every man in the room responded by crossing their arms across their chest and sliding their heels together. The formal stance of the Gangster Disciples. Tito went on to say their creed without one mishap, bringing the meeting to an end.

"Aye, don't forget we meeting like this every Friday. If you don't show up next week, you not GD and you can't get down with us. Pap gone hit y'all with the details." He concluded, opening the door wide.

As the men filled out of the apartment, Tito and two other men stopped in front of Star.

"Big homie," Tito said. "This my nigga Tre, and Two, I'm Tito." He added reaching for his hand.

Star caught it and shook up with him. "Aight, cool," Star stated holding the door open a little wide, hoping they would catch the hint.

"Look, I was just tryna let you know whatever you need us to do, we riding a hundred grand. They call us Triple

Threats." He explained like he just said the coolest shit in the world.

"Say less. I'ma keep that shit right upstairs," he added before they scurried off. "Who da fuck was that?" Star asked, closing the door. It was just him, Pap, Crazy G, and LayLow.

"Some broke ass nigga my sister used to fuck with."

"Man, I hate that dick ridin' ass nigga." Crazy G huffed, flopping down on the couch and guzzling the leftover Remy. "I don't trust them niggas as far as I can throw 'em."

LayLow stood in front of the fish tank watching the fish swim back and forth. He was always so quiet people often forgot he was in the room, which is how he got the name LayLow.

"Good to know. But them niggas might be useful later on," he claimed, scratching his beard. "Look, this how we gone get this money. It's kinda fluky so pay attention."

TWO WEEKS LATER
7:45AM
MATTESON, IL

Gina slid from her Nissan Altima with her coffee in one hand and her keys in the other. She half-skipped to the Chase bank with the new Taylor Swift album pumping through her AirPods. As she stuck the key in the bank's door, her AirPods were snatched from her ears and something hard was jammed in her back.

"You scream or make one false move, I'ma send you to meet yo maker!" Star growled.

He was flanked by Crazy G and Pap. They were all dressed identical in all-black breakaway joggers with covid masks and baseball caps to cover their faces. LayLow was on standby in their stolen Charger to do what he did best, and to watch for any nosey-roseys. Star could've stayed back and let them handle the dirty work, but he wanted to let them see how he got down firsthand. He wanted to show them he wasn't afraid to get his hands dirty.

"Now open the door nice and easy. And make sure you disable the alarm." He coached.

Gina was barely able to open the door, her hands shook so violently. "P-Please don't hurt me." She stuttered, unlocking the door and hustling towards the alarm. She briefly thought about typing in the emergency code but the hard steel in her back persuaded her not to.

"You got the key to the vault, right?" Pap asked once inside.

"Y-Y-Yeah, b-but only one person can step inside at a t-time or the alarm w-will set off."

"Good girl. Now when we get to the safe, I want you to fill these up," Star said, pulling out there heavy-duty laundry bags. "And Gina?" He paused, waiting for her reply.

"Y-Yes," she whispered, shocked that he knew her name.

"No dye packs, or shit will get ugly fa you and yo family."

She quickly nodded her understanding and led the way to the vault, with Star and Pap in tow. Crazy G stayed back to watch the front door in case any unwanted guest showed up. She opened the heavy duty safe in record speed and began filling the bags. She was halfway through the second bag when gunfire erupted from the front of the bank.

Boc! Boc! Boc! Boom! Boc! Boc!

"What da fuck?" Pap hissed, slinging the first bag over his shoulder, trotting back to the front with his SEG aimed high.

"Please," Gina begged, tossing the bag at his feet. She had never been more scared in her life. "I don't know what's going on," she cried with tears spilling from her eyes.

"I know you don't," he said, cocking back and punching her in the mouth, knocking her out cold. He scooped up the bag and darted back to the front of the bank where he found a security on the floor bleeding with multiple holes in his face and chest.

Pap and Crazy G had the door open for him while LayLow had brought the Charger to a screeching halt in front of the bank. They all sprinted to the Charger, and LayLow pulled off as if they had done nothing wrong. The sirens and flashing lights could be seen and heard as they approached from the other side of the street.

"Fuck! What you want me to do?" LayLow asked locking eyes with Star in the rearview.

"Just be easy. If they make us, get ghosts." Star stated cooly, but on the inside his heart was pounding wildly and his stomach did backflips.

Time seemed to move in slow motion as the patrol cars flew past them and into the bank's parking lot. They were home free… for now.

***

Agent Fletcher jumped from the all-black Suburban, and with a flash of his credentials he was allowed inside the bank. The forensics team scurried about taking pictures, bagging, and scanning for prints. He stooped over the dead security guard and a shockwave of rage instantly flooded him. The only thing he despised more than a rapist was cop-killers. He examined the old man's body riddled with bullets, and his revolver still in hand. He had at least gone down fighting.

"Umm, I was told there was a witness. Do you know where she is," he asked one of the forensic techs to straighten back up to his 6'0" frame.

"She was taken to St. James," the tech said fumbling a bag full of bags.

"What's in the bags?"

"Some type of laundry bags. I guess they used them to fill up with money."

"Can I see that?"

"Sure," he replied.

Fletcher examined the laundry bags and a smile spread across his warm-like face. The words Pink Elephant screamed at him in bright pink letters. *Gotcha*, he thought, handing the bag back to the tech. He pulled his phone out and googled The Pink Elephant, and found only two of them in the whole city. To top it off, they both were on the southside.

ON 71ST
HOURS LATER

Pap, Star, Crazy G, and LayLow occupied Kierra's living room feeling like superstars. They had just finished counting over 150-thousand in dead presidents. Plus, they had another job lined up in a couple days, and if it went as well as the first, they would be able to put the next part of their takeover in motion.

"Aye, look," Star said, commanding the attention of his top lieutenants. "We got a lil' over 150 bucks. So, what I'm thinking is we each gone take 20 for ourselves which leaves 70 bucks. We take another 30 and get us all some slight legit wheels to move around in. With the last 40 we gone put 20 to the side to start a safe box in the event anybody gets locked up. And the last 20 we gone pass out to the guys for groceries, rent and shit like that." He explained pausing to let everything he just said digest. "Now, anybody disagree?"

"Fuck naw, boy. 20 thou' and a car sound good to me," Crazy G said first.

"C'mon now, bro. You know we in this shit 110%," Pap claimed.

"I'on know about you niggas, but my pussy rate finna go through da roof," LayLow said, tossing a handful of money in the air, making them all crack up laughing.

CHAPTER 5
THAT FRIDAY

"Wait. Wait. Wait. Go back," Agent Fletcher demanded leaning down to get a better view of the monitor. He was at the Pink Elephant on 69th and Ashland reviewing the security footage a couple days before the robbery. He stuck out at the one located on 89th, so he desperately needed this to work.

"Tell me when to stop." The potbellied security guard huffed.

"Riiighhht there," he said. "Can you zoom in for me?"

"Yea, but only a little."

As the guard zoomed in on the man, his face became almost unidentifiable, but the pitchforks tattooed in the middle of his forehead was clear as day. Fletcher didn't have enough to arrest the man, but it was a start. He was 99% sure he had an informant in the area that could ID the man. Once he brought this case to a close, he was sure to get a promotion, and get an easy desk job with a high salary. A sly smile spread across his face as he envisioned himself with his feet propped up on his desk. It was game time.

ACROSS TOWN

Star rolled over and a devilish grin stretched across his face. Kierra laid on her side in nothing but a black lace thong. Her ass slightly poked out from under the sheet, giving him an instant hard on. He wasted no time sliding her panties to the side and sliding deep into her abyss.

"What da fuu—" She gasped her eyes popping open

"I need some of this before I go," he claimed, grabbing a fist full of her hair. He started with a slow stroke to allow her juices to flow, then gradually picked up the pace. "Damn girl." He huffed.

"Fuck me!" She demanded, throwing her ass back.

He gladly obeyed her commands and began to pound her mercilessly.

"Ah-ah-ahhhhh! L-Like that." She moaned.

He yanked her head back and sunk his teeth into her neck, knowing she liked a little bit of pain with her pleasure.

"Fffuuuck," she cried, unable to hold back the floodgates.

Star knew she was coming and kept plowing into her relentlessly, her kitten making a squishy sound every time he slammed home. He could feel his own climax approaching and quickly pulled out. He wasn't ready to finish yet.

"Get on top. I wanna watch that ass bounce," he claimed, placing his back against the headboard for support.

She climbed on top of him, reverse cowgirl, and guided his rock-hard missile into her slippery lovebox. "Ssss! You so deep," she whispered.

She tried to keep a nice, slow pace, but Star wasn't having it. He reached up and yanked her back down into him over and over. *Clap! Clap! Clap!* Their skin sounded off every time he pulled her down.

"I-I'm c-cumin." She announced with her legs shaking violently.

"Me, too." He grunted, painting her walls with his seed.

Without warning she leaped off him and took him into her mouth. She slurped, licked, and dee- throated him until he was back at full length.

"Damn, bae." He grunted, biting on his bottom lip to keep from moaning out like a woman.

"Mmmm." She moaned in between slurps. Her head bobbed at the tip while her hand pumped nice and slow at the base.

"Ssshit, girl."

Knowing he was on the verge of exploding, she took his whole shaft into her mouth. Deep-throating him until tears welled up in her eyes.

"Aarrgghh! Fuck! Gotdamn!" he roared with his toes curling, and a death grip on the back of her head as he released his load into her throat.

"Uh-hh. Talk that shit now." She teased, crawling up to him and snuggling in.

"What, you tryna get a nigga to marry you or somethin'," he joked still tryin got recover.

"Nigga, you gone marry me. Fuck you thought?"

"Of course I am," he claimed through half open eyes.

"Yo betta not go to sleep. We 'posed to go car shoppin' before I go to work," she said, shaking him.

"I'm not. Go start the shower." He started giving her rear end a slap.

"Aight, don't turn me back up."

"We gone see."

HOURS LATER

I'm wit the gang with the mob. What was you thinkin'/Remember them days when that shit was hard a nigga been thinkin'/I put a 4 in a 20oz a nigga been drinkin'/if you wit' the squad I give you my heart lil' nigga I mean it. "Cal Boys Envy Me" blasted from the speakers as Star cruised through the streets in his all-black Kia Optima. The Optima was a 2010 with 3% tents on each side. It wasn't new or luxurious, but it was his and in great condition… but the main thing he loved was that it was inconspicuous. He made a right turn off Jeffery and on to 71st, and panic immediately consumed him. Police cars had on their red and blues, and had the entire block sewed up. From where he was he could see a white sheet covering what he knew was a body.

"What da fuck," he mumbled pulling the Optima into Kierra's apartment complex.

Vvrrmm! Vrrmm! Vrrrnnn! His iPhone vibrated in his pocket, scaring him half to death. Up until then he had forgotten that he'd bought the thing days ago.

"Yo," he said into the receiver.

Vrrrrm! The phone vibrated against his face, letting him know he forgot to press answer.

"Dumb ass phone," he mumbled swiping right like Kierra showed him. "Yo," he answered. It was Pap.

"Where you at G? Shit crazy out her on 71st. One of the lil' G's just got smoked." He explained.

"I'm in the parking lot in this all-black Kia."

"Aight, I see," he said, ending the call.

Thirty seconds later Pap slid into the passenger with LayLow and Crazy G sliding into the back seat all wearing the same puppy dog look on their face.

"What da fuck happened?" Star asked, putting the car in drive. He had to shake all the police activity. It was making him sick.

"I'on know fa' sho. We just got here too. They say lil' G was talkin' to his girl when a red Buick pulled up tossin' and killed folks," Pap explained.

"Damn. Ain't nobody clap back?" Star spat, mad that he had lost a soldier. "Who da fuck would be gunnin' for us already? We ain't did shit to nobody yet." He nodded, locking eyes with Crazy G in the rearview.

"OTM." Crazy G mumbled, but Star heard him loud and clear.

"OTM? What da fuck is OTM?"

"Only The Moes. They a group of bitch ass Stones that rotate on 79th and Dorchester," LayLow said.

"We been beefin' wit they ass fa as long as we can remember," Pap chimed in.

"And y'all just now sayin' somethin'? That shit could have been avoided!" Star roared, not afraid to let them know he was disappointed. "Tell everybody to meet us at the spot on Jeffery." He added as he turned on 71st. "Make arrangements so we can pay for lil' G's funeral. I'ma get at you niggas lata. I got some shit to handle real quick."

As soon as they exited the car, Star mashed the gas pedal, leaving a cloud of smoke.

"Fuck that nigga tweakin' on? Tal'm 'bout that shit could have been avoided like that's our fault folks got killed." LayLow spat.

"Aye, fuck that shit!" Pap snapped, catching both Crazy G and LayLow by surprise with his aggression. "Like it or not, he right. If we woulda told him earlier, shit probably woulda went way different. He 'posed to tell us when we fucked up. So quit bitchin' 'bout them lil' ass words and let's focus on the real opps."

LayLow was speechless. He couldn't believe Pap was siding with Star over him. In his mind, they should have been running everything. After all, they were the ones who put everything together.

***

Star pulled into the Diamond Wheels parking lot and killed the engine. A wave of mixed emotions washed over him. He wondered how his GD plug would react to seeing him after fifteen years. Even though when he left they were on good terms, he knew popping up out of the blue asking to buy a boatload of work might cause suspicion. He jumped from his car and bopped to the entrance. Before he could reach for the door, it swung open and a pitch-black man with long dreads appeared in the doorway.

"Can mi help ya," he asked in his thick Haitian accent.

"Zoe?" Star asked, locking eyes with his old plug.

"Who dat?"

"Star, my nigga."

"Wat kinda black magic is dis? Wassup, friend," he yelled, embracing Star bear hug style.

"Glad to know I was missed."

"Mi heard ya was out. But mi ain't believe da pussy clots."

"Hell yeah, I been out almost two months. But fuck all'at. You know why I'm here." Star said, getting straight to it.

"Mi knew da second ya said ya name, rude boy. What ya need?"

LATER THAT NIGHT
JEFFERY TRAP HOUSE

The inside of the trap house that served as their new meeting spot was filled to the hilt. Unlike Kierra's small living room, they had a little more room to operate. Especially since there was not one piece of furniture inside the house, except the folding table that sat in the middle of the floor littered with stacks of money.

"Aye, y'all niggas listen up," Star said as he paced around the table. The way the MOB crowded into the living room looked like a deformed circle with Star in the middle. "This was supposed to be a celebration," he said, nodding at the money on the table. "But I'm sure everybody heard 'bout lil' G. So instead of celebratin' we gone put shit in order so somethin' like this never happens again." He paused to let his words sink in. "Now, how many blocks do we really have control of, or can really say that they're ours," he asked no one in particular.

"4." Tito answered. "Jeffery, Wabash, Western, and 71st."

"Aight. As of right now our count is 26. That's more than enough for us to secure all our blocks. Before we start making any money, we gotta have shit on smash and operate as a unit… Tito?"

"Wassup, big homie?"

"I want you to pick 5 members and hold down Wabush. Everything goes through you before it comes to me. With that being said, you responsible for any fuck ups."

"I got it, big bro," he claimed, cheesing like the first day of school.

"Me, Pap, LayLow, and Crazy G gone take 71st while Buddah and whoever he picks gone take this spot right here. The rest of y'all got Western. Any problems with what I just said?" He inquired, scanning the crowd for any foul body language. Once he was certain he saw none, he continued. "Now, before everybody leaves, come see me and grab a stack on your way out. It ain't much but it a hold you over until the plug sends the shipment. Pap, take us out."

"Stance," He yelled.

CHAPTER 6

The last two months breezed right on by Star and the MOB, bringing up November. As promised, Star made sure every man was eating. He had Buddah on Jeffery with the Heroine, and Tito on Wabash with the crack. He left the youngins on Western with the pills and weed. Even though Tito, Buddah and Fey Fey ran those blocks, he made Pap, LayLow and Crazy G in charge of collecting the money and settling any disputes. Being that they used 71st for headquarters and meetings amongst the top lieutenants, he decided to keep it clean.

After receiving his lawsuit settlement of $375,000, he bought him and Kierra a house out in Richton Park— a suburb on the outskirts of the city. The only person who had the address was Pap. Since Tito started making money hand over fist, he and TT were back together and going strong. Crazy G and LayLow got a spot on 57th and Shields and were bringing in many recruits that they started a new branch on 57th. Their numbers swelled to just under 80 men and were growing by the day. Their beef with OTM was still going, but Star called a temporary standstill while everybody got their coins up. He wanted them to think they'd forgotten about lil' G, then when they were relaxed, they would crush them totally.

"C'mon, baby, get my picture. You know you gone wanna remember this fineness for foreva'." Star bragged, pulling at his tie. He was dressed to impress in an all-black Armani suit with a smoke grey shirt and black tie to match. A pair of

Gucci loafers graced his feet, and he traded in his afro for a low fade with waves.

"Boy, please. You ain't all'at." Kierra joked, snapping pic after pic. She was killing it, also rocking a smoke grey Versace tube dress that hugged her figure perfectly. Her hair was slightly curled and hung loosely around her neck. The Red Bottom pumps she wore raised her 5'10" frame just enough to see eye to eye with Star.

It was two days before Thanksgiving, and Star wanted to do something nice for the community. So, he organized a free turkey pass out on 71st out of Kierra's old apartment. Though she no longer stayed there, Star still used the space for headquarters for the nation.

"C'mon, we gotta go. I'on wanna be late," he claimed.

"You the one wanna take all these pictures for Facebook." She teased him, following him out of their house.

AN HOUR LATER

The November wind swirled lightly as tiny snowflakes drizzled from the sky and covered the ground, giving this year's Thanksgiving the perfect setting. Temperatures hovered just above 30 degrees and yet people from all over the city collected a free turkey. The line stretched from the headquarters down to the middle of the block. Star made sure to shut down all the traps for the day and had thirty Gangster Disciples on security ready for whatever. Today was about the community, and he wanted it to stay that way.

"Happy Turkey Day!" He repeated as he passed out turkey after turkey.

"Happy holidays," Kierra sang as she did the same with the apple pies.

"God bless your soul, young man," an elderly black woman said, patting Star's face lovingly.

Star nodded and couldn't stop the smile that tugged at the corners of his mouth until the next person in line stepped forward. "What da fuck you doin'? That nigga got all'at ice on and he got you beggin' fa free turkeys," he whispered harshly.

Christina couldn't even look Star in the eyes. She just snatched the turkey out of his hands and bolted before he embarrassed them both.

Star Stood there dumbfounded. He couldn't believe Christina was really treating him like the enemy. He was starting to see exactly what TT was saying. Gotti truly had control over Christina.

"Aye, Pap, I need you to take over for me," Star said, passing him a turkey. "Aye, LayLow," he yelled, waving him inside the apartment.

LayLow half-jogged up the block and climbed the stairs to the complex, curious as to why he had been summoned. "Wassup G," he asked once inside the apartment.

"I need you to help me handle something. So, get a fast car and meet me on Wabash."

"Sayless," he said before scurrying off to stand on the business.

"Is everything okay?" Kierra asked, popping out of nowhere. The look on her face told him that she was worried.

"Naw, but it's gone be," he assured me, pulling her in for a quick kiss.

It was time to punch Gotti's and anybody claiming OTM's clock. The nice guy was officially gone and being replaced by the demon. He was about to remind the streets exactly who he was.

"Aye, you seen Crazy G?" Pap asked, still passing out turkeys.

"Now that you mention it, hell naw. Did you hit his line? That nigga know its mandatory for him to be here, right?" Star asked, searching the sea of people for Crazy G, but he was nowhere in sight.

"I been lighting his shit up. I sent out a memo lettin' everybody know it's mandatory."

"Say less… Look, I got some shit to handle. Y'all straight holdin' down the fort right," he asked sounding more like a statement than a question.

"I got you, G."

"Where you runnin' off to now? We was supposed to have dinner." Kierra whined… something she had been doing a lot of lately.

"We still are, I just gotta make a move real quick." He explained over his shoulder without breaking stride. He was on a mission and had his mind set on one thing and one thing only… Crushing his enemies totally.

AN HOUR LATER

"Aww shit!" LayLow yawned from the driver's seat of their stolen Nissan Rogue. He had his seat leaned back as far as it would go and his hoodie pulled tightly over his head. His Glock 30s with a 21-shot clip laid in his lap cocked and loaded. "Why we sittin' here again?" he asked, rubbing his tired eyes.

"Why you think?" Star replied, sliding on his black leather gloves. Like LayLow, he had his seat leaned back and his hoodie tied over his face. But instead of a Glock, he had an 8-inch Bowie hunting knife.

"You sure you don't want this?" he asked lifting the Glock.

"Nah. I want this nigga to feel it," Star claimed, tossing the knife from hand to hand. It was a masterpiece of a knife that had a long curve just for this occasion. Sure, he could gun him down and keep it moving, but he wanted to lock eyes with him when his soul left his body. "Here that nigga comes," Star said ducking low in his seat.

Gotti zoomed in his normal parking spot, completely oblivious to the imminent danger— known as Star --lurking in the shadows. He flung his car door open and wobbled out. "Daammn! I'm fucked up!" he slurred, closing the door and storming towards his house.

Star crept from the Nissan, crouching like a lioness stalking its prey. “Wassup, fat boy?” he taunted as soon as he was behind Gotti.

Gotti spun around and locked eyes with Star and immediately reached for his gun. But the liquor coursing through his veins made him slow, and Star was already on top of him. His hand moved in a blur, and before Gotti knew what was happening, the Bowie was five inches deep inside of his chest. His eyes stretched so wide they looked as if they would pop out of his skull. He tried to scream for help, but the knife in his chest made it impossible. Star twisted the knife a few times before pulling it out and jamming back into his stomach.

“P-Please. D—” He tried to say as he slumped to the ground.

“What happened to all’at GDK shit?” Star taunted, swinging the knife in a high arching motion. It landed in Gotti’s forehead with a loud *thunk!* As promised Star stared into Gotti’s eyes until he was sure the fat man was dead. He reached out and snatched Gotti’s chain. He straightened back up and peaked around for any prying eyes. Sure that the coast was clear, he casually strolled back to the Nissan cackling like a Hyena. “Take me through 79th,” he said climbing back in the Nissan.

“You can’t go through there wit’ no knife,” LayLow said, looking at Star like he had two heads. After seeing the way Star carved Gotti up, he was sure the nigga was bat-shit-crazy.

“I know,” Star said grabbing LayLow’s Glock 30s. “That’s why I’ma bounce out with this,” he added waving the gun back and forth, cheesing from ear to ear. Killing Gotti made him feel like his old self, and he couldn’t deny how good it felt.

They rode in complete silence until they turned on 79th. The block was nearly vacant except for three dudes who occupied the middle of the block. They sat on a parked car with music blasting, drinking and smoking as if they didn't have a care in the world.

"Them niggas OTM?" Star asked as the dudes carried on, oblivious to the Nissan idling at the end of the block.

"Yeah, them two is but I don't know the other dude."

"Don't even matter. He picked the wrong niggas to hang with tonight." Star smiled, jumping out the Nissan and limping towards the trio.

"Aye, who da fuck is you?" One of the men yelled, putting the rest of the group on alert.

"C'mon, baby! It's ya uncle Red. I'm tryna cop one for ten!" Star yelled, scratching his arms and chest. "You know I'm good peoples. I'm just tryna get that monkey off my back."

"Man, it's a fuckin' hype." One of the men pointed out.

"Aye, we closed fa the night. Ain't shit shakin' right now," another claimed.

Star ignored them and continued to inch closer. Thankful that the hoodie covered his face completely.

"What da fuck? You deaf? I said we closed. Now turn yo cluck ass around before we beat yo ass," the last man warned.

Fuck it, Star thought. He felt he was close enough already anyway. He pulled out the Glock and let it speak. *Blocka! Blocka! Blocka! Blocka!* The first four shots found home in the first two merks' neck, chest, and face, killing them instantly while the last man took off like he played for the Chicago Bears. Star chased after him stride for stride until he was in arms' reach.

"Please! I got kids!" the man yelled, still trying to get away.

Blocka! A well-placed shot hit the man in the back, sending him skidding across the pavement, begging for his life. Yet his pleas would fall on deaf ears. Star stood over the man smiling wickedly and dumped three hot ones in his chest. The impact from each shot lifting him off the ground.

LayLow zoomed the vehicle to Star's position and they eased off, making another smooth getaway.

BLACK FRIDAY
DAYS LATER

The informant's leg bounced rapidly as he chewed on his fingernail ferociously. It was clear he was uncomfortable with what agent Fletcher was asking him to do. The Gangster Disciple nation was becoming more and more powerful overnight, and he wasn't sure the FEDS could protect him the way he claimed. But the AR-15 and half of brick of coke he was caught with was enough to send him away for life.

"Look, I can't ID this man for you. But if you want my help IDing the GDs I got you," he said truthfully.

Agent Fletcher looked at the man and smiled. The way his leg bounced, how hard he chewed his nails every ten seconds, told Fletcher everything he needed to know. He couldn't wait to bring down the Disciples and retire. He was ready to leave all this field shit to some young buck trying to make a name for himself. "Look," he said, taking his feet from the top of his desk. "I'm letting you know you lie about one name, you lie about one event, you're done," he added giving the informant his good old fashioned bad cop stare.

"I know, damn. What exactly you wanna know?"

LATER ON 71ST

Headquarters wasn't as packed as usual. Instead of calling every member out to meet, he only called his top lieutenants… Better known as regionals. In the Disciples nation regionals were responsible for the block, hood, or area they reigned over. Which was how the name regional came about. Pap, LayLow, Buddha and Tito lounged around smoking weed and sipping Hennessy as they listened to Star.

"Aight, now that we got the money talk out the way," he said pouring himself a full cup of the brown liquor. "It's Black Friday so I wanna make it real black with all the

Stones blood. Them niggas think we fell back or forgot about lil' G." He paused to puff on the blunt that was passed to him and take a hefty swig of his cup. "Now rumor has it that them bitch ass niggas having a candlelight for them niggas I put in the dirt. I want Pap, LayLow and Tito to handle that. The rest of y'all need to be on high alert in case them niggas get froggy."

"You know that," Tito said smiling and throwing up GD as hard as he could.

The entire room returned the gesture twice as hard.

"Aye, any one of y'all heard form that nigga Crazy G?" Star asked.

"Not since last night." Pap replied.

"Shiiit it's been a couple days since I seen that nigga." Buddah huffed. He was a bear of a man at 6'3", 240 pounds. He wasn't all fat nor was he all muscle. He reminded you of an offensive lineman… fat but solid.

Star was bubbling on the inside. Since he gave him the spot on 57th, Crazy G had either been showing up late or not at all. *I got somethin' for this nigga*, Star thought.

Knock! Knock! Knock! At the sound of someone banging on the door every man drew his gun.

"Hold up," Tito said creeping to the door and peeking through the peephole. "It's yo sister, G-ball," he stated nodding at Star.

"Thousand parts. After we say prayer we gone get outta here," he said snatching open the door.

As soon as it opened, Christina's puffy red eyes locked on to the five-point Star chain that hung from Star's neck. Star had only wore it during meetings as an ultimate sign of disrespect. "You bastard," she yelled, swinging on him wildly.

He quickly wrapped her up in a bear hug and snatched her into the apartment.

"Let me go! I hate you! I fuckin' hate you!" She roared, still kicking and swinging wildly. One of her knees managed to catch Star in the stomach, forcing him to drop her and double over in pain.

"Arrgh! Grab that bitch." He groaned.

Pap and Tito sprang into action, both grabbing one of her arms.

"Get yo muthafuckin' hands off me!" She screamed trying to shake loose, but Tito and Pap held fast.

"Aye, chill da fuck out before somebody think we tryna do somethin' to you." Star snapped.

"Fuck you!" She hollered before hawking up a loogie and spitting it directly in the center of his face. "You killed my baby daddy! I fuckin' hate you. I'ma make sure they take yo bitch ass back to jail!"

Star wiped the loogie from his face with the back of his hand and disappeared into the back then returned with his Bowie.

"You want us to slide?" Buddha asked.

"Naw, I want all you niggas to see what happens to traitors," he said through clenched teeth.

"So-So you finna kill me," she asked, suddenly shedding her tough girl rant.

"Nobody's sending me back! Hold that bitch tight." He instructed.

Tito and Pap did as they were told, but they both turned their heads, unable to watch what was about to take place.

"W-Wait, Star! Please! What 'bout my kids," she cried, trying to break free, but her efforts were futile.

They held her in a vice grip lock. The first stab landed in the middle of her chest with a loud squishy sound, but he didn't stop there. He stabbed and slashed her repeatedly, twisting the knife like a dirt bike every time it landed home. Christina's head tilted to the side as her lifeless body slumped to the floor. Star finally stopped and they finally let her body slump to the ground. The way his chest heaved, mixed with the blood covering his body, made him look like a maniac. But he could care less; he was sending a message.

And from the looks on their faces they heard him loud and clear.

"I'ma say prayer and get us outta here. Buddha, I need you to help me clean up this mess. Call Twan and tell him to hold Jeffery down until we finish. The rest of y'all know what it is… Stance!"

CHAPTER 7

HOURS LATER

79th was littered with people of all ages. Everybody that was a somebody was out tonight to pay their respects to the fallen. The temperature was a chilling 48 degrees, but the way everybody partied and mingled one would have thought it was mid-June. Almost the entire block had on black t-shirts with the letters "OTM" plastered across in big red letters. On the back were pictures of their fallen comrades living their best life. A mini memorial was stationed in the middle of the block, exactly where they had lost their lives. Balloons, candles, and more pictures covered the ground, and life-sized cardboard pictures of the dead were everywhere. It was clear they spared no expense, for they were truly loved.

"Maann, where da rest of that Hennessy at?" Trindog slurred from his seat on the porch. Since Star came home and unified the GDs, it made it almost impossible to hustle, plus he was losing soldier after soldier… and it was hitting him hard.

"Baby, you don't need no more. You know I don't like drivin' that big ass truck," she claimed plopping down on his lap. It was hard for her to see him like his. He was normally so gangster and cold-blooded.

"I'm Gucci. I barely even feel that shit." He slurred.

"Bae, noooo. We 'bout to light the candles in like five minutes. Then you can drink all you want at the crib." She whined. She really didn't want to have to drive him home in his oversized Escalade truck. She hated that truck with a passion and could barely see over the wheel.

"Aight, whateva," he mumbled closing his eyes in a futile attempt to sober up.

TWO BLOCKS OVER

"Man, I'm tellin' you niggas, any nigga that can stab a muthafucka to death, let alone his own sis' is fuckin' crazy." LayLow pointed out. "You shoulda seen that nigga when he stabbed Gotti. Then when he chased them OTM niggas down, I swear he was smilin' the whole time."

Him, Pap and Tito were parked in their hijacked Dodge Avenger, waiting for the candlelight to start so they could make it rain hot shells on anybody out.

Tito simply stared out the window and chose not to comment, while Pap continued to watch his ex Ashley's live, who just so happened to be at the candlelight. "Man, if you ask me, he did what needed to be done," Tito finally spoke up.

"Of course you would say that. You ain't see the way he did them niggas."

"Man, he carved that nigga Gotti up so bad. Dude not to be fucked with," Lawlow said.

"That's exactly why he chief." Pap chimed in.

"Maaan, it's like I was sayin' the otha day. He only chief cuz we let him be. If niggas in the hood ain't see how we respected him or ain't get that memo from us, them niggas would have been smoked his ass; tryin' all'at structure shit!" LayLow snapped.

Both Tito's and Pap's heads turned so fast they could've snapped their necks, clearly letting LayLow know he was out of line and where their loyalty lied.

"It's go time," Pap said powering off his phone and scooping up the AR-15 that was at his feet. "And LayLow," he asked pulling back the slide, chambering a .556 into the barrel.

"Sup?"

"Don't eva let me hear you talkin' like that again." He stated, staring him directly in the eyes.

Tito was strapped with twin Glock 17s, both equipped with 33-shot clips. Star had made it very clear he wanted the streets to bleed with the MOES blood. Even LayLow was strapped with a Smith and Wesson .40 and was ready to hop out and shoot. As soon as LayLow pulled to the end of 79th, all there men leaped from the Avenger, guns blazing.

Paka-Paka-Paka-Paka! Boc! Boc! Boc! Boc! Boc! As usual, once shots started ringing, civilians scattered like project roaches looking for cover. Hearing the gunfire seemed to wake Trindog up. He slung to the floor, pulled out his XD-9 and returned fire. *Pac! Pac! Pac!* Trindog's aggression caught the trio off guard and sent them scrambling. Like the shark he was, Trindog could smell blood in the water and continued to squeeze on his trigger. *Pac! Pac! Pac! Pac! Pac!*

"Arrghh! Fuck! I'm hit! I'm hit!" Laylow cried as he spilled to the ground.

Hearing LayLow scream sent Pap into overdrive. He aimed the AR at Trindog's flash and let it rip. *Paka-Paka-Paka-Paka-Paka!* With one sweeping motion of the monster, he forced Trindog to duck for cover. But not before one of the .556 slammed into his stomach and exploded through his back. Pap's pressure gave Tito enough time to grab LayLow and toss him into the back seat while he jumped into the passenger seat, still aiming the AR. Tito burned rubber as soon as Pap closed his door.

"Arrrghh. Sshiit! That muthafucka shot me." LayLow groaned, using both hands to clutch the right side of his chest.

"Just hold on, you straight. We gone be at the hospital in no time." Pap assured.

"That's what my d-dumb ass gets. Y-You know I-I just drive." He laughed before slumping to the side motionless.

"LayLow! LayLow!" Pap yelled on the verge of tears. He turned in his seat and shook him a couple of items, but LayLow didn't budge.

They pulled up to St. Bernard's emergency room entrance and carried him through the front doors.

"Aye, we need some help!" Tito yelled.

"My brother's been shot!" Pap added, drawing the attention of every single person in the emergency room.

Before you knew it, they had LayLow on a gurney, wheeling him to the back. Security tried to question Pap and Tito, but they were already halfway out the door, leaving the man with a half-assed story about a drive by.

MEANWHILE
ON 57TH AND SHIELDS

Crazy G leaned on the banister overlooking the four blocks he controlled and nodded his approval. Everything was running like a well-oiled machine. From his apartment balcony he could see from Racine to Shields. It was one of the main reasons he picked the place for him and LayLow. Even though Star controlled and had the last say in everything, being on 57th gave him a sense of control… A sense of being his own boss. He put the finishing touches on the Backwood filled with Gelato and sparked it to life.

"Mighty fine system you got going on," Star said.

Crazy G damn near jumped out of his skin. He spun around with his MP9 aimed high. "Nigga, what da fuck," he yelled, relaxing after he saw it was only Star. "Damn, nigga, you don't know how to knock?"

"I got keys, nigga. Da fuck I'm knockin' for?" He taunted, jingling the keys so Crazy G could see.

"Right. But wassup? I know this ain't no social call," Crazy G claimed, puffing on the Backwood.

"Nah, it ain't. What's the count for the week," he asked, joining him at the banister. Star had to admit the way Crazy G had Racine and Shields running was impressive. The blocks came together and formed the letter H. On all four corners he had look-outs equipped with walkie-talkies that connected to the two snipers on the roofs in the middle of each block. No transactions were made out in the open. They were made from the alleys which led into the trap houses where six armed guards stood with heavy artillery.

"C'mon, nigga, cut the small talk. I know you ain't here for no count, so wassup? And the count is 48."

"I got a proposition for you," he claimed, accepting the Backwood and taking a heavy pull.

"Awe, yeah? Like what?"

"I like you. You remind me a lot of me when I was younger, but just cuz I like you odn't mean I won't fuck you up," Star said locking eyes with him to let him know he was serious. "Now I know you wanna be your own boss and all. But every great leader was once a great follower. I say that to say this. You get to run Shields how you see fit, as long as I agree. And you show up to meetings on Friday." He concluded, passing him the Backwood back.

"We got a deal," Crazy G said smiling.

"And G," he asked, turning to leave.

"What's the word?"

"Don't make me have to come back out here."

Before he could give a proper response, both their phones jingled, snatching their attention. They gave each other a knowing look before answering.

"Yo!"

"Run ya mouth."

45 MINUTES LATER

St. Bernard's emergency room was packed to capacity with family members and members of the OTM. During the candlelight, 7 were shot, 2 killed, and one in critical, which was Trindog. He was clinging on to life like a crackhead holding on to his sobriety. The entire waiting room grew dead quiet as Crazy G and Star stepped through the doors.

Suddenly the already crowded waiting room seemed as if it was going to explode any second from the heavy tension.

"I'm lookin' for La- I mean Rayquan Norwood," Crazy G said as he walked to the desk.

The overweight hippo of a receptionist glanced up from her phone call for a brief second before pointing to the sign behind her. It READ: *All visitors and family members must fill out visitor forms. NO EXCEPTIONS!*

It took every ounce of restraint Crazy G had left not to jump over the desk and strangle Ms. Piggy. "Look," he said, pinching the bridge of his nose in frustration. "My brother just got shot. His name is Rayquan Norwood. If you would be so kind to take the phone from yo *fat funky ass ear* it would be greatly appreciated."

The woman put the phone down, ready to go all Wendy Williams, until she peeped the menacing scowls on both Star and Crazy G's faces. "Psst! Hold on." She sucked her teeth as she typed on the keyboard. "He in room 107. But you ca—"

Before she could finish they were halfway down the hallway and standing in front of LayLow's room. But to their surprise, LayLow was nowhere in sight, and a tech was inside the room preparing it for the next patient.

"The man that was in this room. Where did they take him?" Star asked the Jim Carry look-alike.

"Down to the morgue," he replied nonchalantly. "Is there somehtin' I can do for you fellas?"

Hot tears welled up in Crazy G's eyes, but he refused to let them fall. If they had taken LayLow's body to the morgue, then that could only mean one thing… His best friend was gone. "Muthafuckas!" He roared, punching a basketball-sized hole in the wall.

Jim Carry backed into the corner of the room, scared to death with a white-knuckle grip on the mop. "N-Now I'm going to have to ask you folks to leave."

"Don't worry, we were doin' just that," Star claimed, grabbing Crazy G's shoulder and steering him towards the exit.

"You bastards!" an older woman said blocking their path. She was flanked by a mob of angry women.

"I know you had somethin' to do wit' this," another snapped before slapping the taste out of Crazy G's mouth.

Instinctively Crazy G cocked back and gave the woman a left hook that put her to bed. Before she hit the ground, three dudes jumped up and rushed them, but they were met by Star's Glock 30s. Loud gasps could be heard before the waiting room grew eerily quiet.

"I know y'all upset. But if you people don't mind, I'll be takin' my brother and we'll be on our merry way," he said, sweeping the Glock back and forth.

The crowd parted like the Red Sea as they made their exit. Crazy G went to grab Star's Optimum while Star held the people at bay with the Glock.

Sccuuurrrtt! "Let's go!" Crazy G yelled from the driver's seat.

"That's all folks." He smiled, jumping in the car.

HOURS LATER
HEADQUARTERS

The ambient glow from the fish tank gave the smoke-filled room a mysterious setting. Star and Crazy G smoked blunt after blunt filled with the most exotic weed they could find. An almost empty fifth of Remy Martin was glued to Crazy G's fingertips as he lounged on the couch, reminiscing on the past. He was taking LayLow's death hard and so was Star. He felt he was responsible for sending LayLow to do something he normally didn't do. As their leader it was his job to protect and guide them into the future… and he felt like he failed.

"You know that nigga the one named me Crazy G?" He slurred before guzzling the last of the bottle as if it was water.

"We was in the 8th grade and them high school niggas used to always try to bitch us and chase us home. But I never ran. They used to beat my ass everyday. Until one day I found my granny's .25 Ruger. Them niggas thought they was finna beat my ass that day. I upped and shot all three of them bitch niggas," he said, smiling to himself

"Hell naw. That's funny as hell." Star laughed, texting Pap.

He knew Crazy G was gone out of his mind and wanted Pap to make sure he got home safe.

"Even after all'at, them bitch ass niggas had the nerve to call the police on me."

"Get da fuck outta here."

"Yup. Cost me two years in the lil' joint," he replied tossing the empty bottle aside and sparking a pre-rolled blunt to life.

Knock! Knock! Knock!

"Who dat?" He slurred, reaching for his gun, but Star quickly stopped him.

"Be easy. It's just folks." He assured, opening the door. "Wassup, G?"

"Not shit fa real." Pap shot back.

Star could tell LayLow's death was hitting Pap just as hard from his blood shot eyes and the blood-stained clothes he still had on. His normally amped up demeanor was drier than the Sahara Desert.

"Aye, uh. Look," he said, scratching his head, trying to find the right words to say. "I know shit fucked up right now for us. I know y'all was a lot closer to bro than I was. But I want you to know I feel behind this shit too," he added, pulling Pap in for a brotherly embrace. "I promise we gone murda everything movin'. Anything claiming OTM. We putin' em in the blender."

"You know that. Now help me get this drunk ass nigga in the car." Pap smiled half.

MEANWHILE

Agent Fletcher watched Pap and Star carry Crazy G from the comfort of his state-issued Chevy Impala. He had his HD Sony pixel camera out snapping away. So far, his informant's intel had been spot on. Except not being able to not identify the man with the pitchfork when Fletcher was staring directly at him. He snapped a few more still shots of Star standing alone. He put the car in gear, ready to follow Pap. He was sure he could find out where Crazy G laid his head if he followed.

"Hellooo, sexy chocolate," he mumbled, snapping more shots of TT and Pap entering his apartment. He couldn't stop himself from smiling. He knew this would definitely be the case that concluded his career and stamped his legacy forever. Now all he had to do was continue to watch the Disciples. Sooner or later they would slip, and he would be there to *catch* them.

***

"You sure you okay? I know that look. It's the same one my brother has when he's up to no good," TT claimed, positioning herself next to Star on the couch.

Star could barely hear a word that she was saying. He was completely lost in his own thoughts. All the Henny and Exotic he smoked had him in la-la land. All he could think about was murdering anybody claiming OTM. *Man, I shoulda made that nigga stay behind the wheel, then none of this shit woulda happen*, he thought.

"Star? Did you hear me," she asked shattering his thoughts.

"Naw. What you say," he asked looking her way the first time since they entered the apartment, and she was killing it.

Her hair was freshly straightened making her beautiful face pop. Her pouty lips were glossed to perfection and screamed kiss me. She sat Indian style making her stretch pants cling to her voluptuous thighs, outlining the fat kitty between her legs. He didn't know if the weed and liquor clouded his judgement, but he wanted her in the worst way.

"I said are you okay?"

"I don't even really know. Shit so crazy right now." He laughed, scratching his beard.

"I know. I can only imagine how my lil' brother feels," she whispered.

"We gone fix them niggas though. On the G. We gone fix they ass." He slurred.

"I hope so," she claimed, jumping to her feet. "I'ma be upstairs. If you hungry, let me know. Tito should be on his way back by now."

"TT?" He called out, standing up behind her.

"Yeah?" She turned around.

Instead of wasting any more time talking, he covered her lips with his. To his surprise her lips parted like the Grand Canyon, allowing him full access. Their tongues performed a slippery slow dance as his hands found her plump cheeks. He hoisted her off the ground and she wrapped her thick thighs around his waist, still ferociously sucking his face. Her back found the wall while Star expertly used one hand to remove her legging.

"Fuuuck me." She moaned into his mouth.

He quickly freed himself and she reached down and guided him into her soaking love box.

"Oooohh!"

"Fuck!"

They groaned in unison. Her walls gripped him like a pair of needle nose pliers while his length and girth filled her to the hilt. He threw one leg over his shoulder and gave her long, slow, deliberate strokes. Her pussy was wetter than anything he'd ever fucked before. He could feel her juices dripping on his balls and down to his thighs.

"D-D-Don't stop," she cried digging her nails into his back.

"Damn, TT!"

"Ooo-ohh-uuhhh-aaahhn!" She moaned, squirting all over him and the floor.

Star pumped into her with everything he had until he was no longer able to hold back. "Arrrghh! SSSShiiit," he whispered as he released in big globs. "What da fuck did we just do," he asked, staring deeply into her brown eyes.

"I-I don't know," she said, returning his stare. "But it was like nothing I ever felt before." She added sticking her tongue back down his throat.

Even though he hated to admit it, she was right. He had never groaned, moaned, or came so hard in his life. He just hoped like hell things didn't change for the worst.

BACK ACROSS TOWN

Fletcher watched in awe through his camera lense at the hustle and bustle of Shields. The security was airtight so he was forced to park three blocks away. He still didn't have an address on Crazy G, but he narrowed it down. Besides, he was way too excited about his new discovery to let that dampen his mood. He knew their operation was big, but he had no idea it was on this level. He smiled again as he snapped pic after pic… It was definitely retiring time.

CHAPTER 8
TWO DAYS LATER

Star rolled out of bed, wiped the cold from his eyes, and slipped in a much-needed stretch. He glanced over at Kierra to ensure she was still sound asleep before heading for the bathroom. He opened the door, and Christina jumped from out of nowhere, wrapping her bloody hands around his neck.

"You murderer!" She screamed with blood pouring from her mouth. He tried to fight her off, but she had the strength of ten grown men. "Die muthafucka. Die," she growled before snapping his neck.

"Fuck!" Star yelled, shooting straight up like a rocket.

"What's wrong baby? Another nightmare?" Kierra asked, sitting up to.

His chest heaved and sweat beads peppered his forehead. The look in his eye told her he was shook. even though he tried to play it off. "Y-Yeah, I'm straight."

"If you ever need to talk about it, I'm here," she whispered gently, taking his hand and placing it in hers.

Star remained silent, still trying to wrap his head around the situation. He had killed more times than he could count and never felt anything. So, what was with the nightmares? Was he regretting killing Christina? Or was his conscious eating at him? He gave Kierra a peck on the lips and climbed out of bed to start his day.

Thirty minutes later he was in his all-black Optima, gliding through the streets in deep thought. He figured he was seeing Christina so much because he failed to give her a proper burial. In his mind, once that was taken care of, his conscience would let him rest. On his way out the door he phoned Pap and let him know to set up a meeting with the regions. He wanted to set a plan in motion to exterminate OTM once and for all.

Whoop! Whoop! The flashing red and blues in his rearview stole his attention.

"Fuck," he mumbled looking at the speedometer. He was doing 50 in a 35. For a brief second, pulling over crossed his mind. But the $60,000 in cash and the Glock 30s sitting on the passenger seat said different. "Aight, let's play, bitch," he said mashing the gas pedal.

The Optima took off like a rocket, but the supercharged Ford Fusion the officer drove held its own. Every which way Star turned, the Ford turned right behind him. He glanced in the rearview mirror and saw two more cars joined the chase.

"Let's see if you bitches ready to die." He laughed, jumping in the wrong lane. He expertly weaved in and out of oncoming traffic, narrowly missing cars. Most of the cars stayed in the right lane and pursued the best as they could, but the Ford was still on him.

The way the Ford chased after Star, one would have thought his job was on the line. He weaved in and out of traffic as flawlessly if not better than Star. He was blood thirsty and wouldn't stop until he placed his icy bracelets around Star's wrist.

"Damn!" Star growled, punching the steering wheel.

He knew if he didn't shake the thirsty-cop soon he would have to shoot it out… jail was not an option no matter how big or how small the charge was. He swerved back into the right lane, then made a quick left. Without a doubt or contradiction, Sir Thirsty was right behind him. It was clear Star wasn't going to lose him in a high speed, so he was taking his chances on foot.

He quickly shouldered the bookbag and grabbed the Glock before mashing the brake with two feet. *Sccc Uuuu Rrrr Tttt!* The Optima fishtailed before jumping the curb and coming to a stop. Star wasted no time flinging his door open and hauling ass. Sir Thirsty was caught off guard by Star's sudden stop and had to yank the wheel to avoid a head-on collision, but as expected, he recovered and jumped from the Ford in hot pursuit.

"Stop! I don't want to shoot," he yelled.

MEANWHILE AT HEADQUARTERS

"I swear to God!" Crazy G yelled, punching a hole in the wall. "On the G, if that wasn't his mama, I a ice that bitch!" His fist landed with a loud thud, spraying dust and drywall everywhere.

"Aye, my boy, I know you mad. Shit we all is. But this ain't our shit fa you to be punchin' holes in the wall." Pap checked him.

He, Tito, Buddha, and Crazy G were waiting for Star to show up when Crazy G dropped the bomb on them. Bernice, LayLow's mother, informed him that LayLow's funeral would be held in Atlanta, their hometown, and under no circumstances were they allowed to attend. She blamed Crazy G and the Gangster Disciples for his death and wanted nothing to do with them, then slammed the door in his face and threatened to call the police.

"I know you mad, folks, but believe me when I say we all feel the same. We might not have known folks as long as you or been as close, but in this short time we been united, shit I look at you niggas like my brothers," Buddan claimed, draping a meaty arm around Crazy G's shoulder.

"Man, why don't we celebrate Broksi in our own lil' way?" Tito said, stealing the attention of every man in the room. "I wasn't that close to folks either. Shit, I don't even think we seen eye to eye. But one thing I know we all can agree on is he wouldn't want us standin' 'round all depressed. He was way too cool for that shit. He would want us turnin' up, fuckin' bitches and killin' Moes in his name." He added, his words ringing true in every man's ear.

Pap was the first to break the silence. He scooped up Crazy G's fifth of Dusse. "For LayLow," he yelled, taking a heavy swig from the bottle. Tito and Buddah repeated the process, passing the bottle to Crazy G.

"For you, my nigga," he whispered before he downed the rest of the Dusse.

FIVE BLOCKS AWAY

Star effortlessly leaped over the 8-foot gate with his gun still in hand.

Sir Thirsty was giving him a run for his money, but Star had gained a slight advantage. "Stop! Muthafucka!" He huffed as he slowly climbed the gate.

Star was already across the small yard and over the next gate. He glanced back to see where Sir Thirsty was and a grin crept on his face. The man was running out of gas. He turned back around just in time to see the massive Rottweiler charging his way.

Guuurr! Woof! Woof! Woof! The dog barked, snapping at him viciously. He hoped over the next gate; the dog just barely missing his leg. He was so busy trying to avoid the dog that the Glock slipped from his hand and landed right in front of the Rottweiler.

Fuck it! he thought, debating on going back for the gun. He got his answer when the squawk of Sir Thirsty's radio grew louder. Fuck it. He booked it up the street. A full minute later he was in front of headquarters banging on the door. He left his keys inside the Optima so he hoped like hell the others were there.

The door was snatched open and he was greeted by four pistols inches away from his face.

"It's me! It's me!" He yelped, bolting inside and closing the door. He double locked it and went to peek out the blinds, leaving the entire room puzzled by his paranoid antics. His chest still heaved from the marathon he just ran, and his normally crisp Air Force Ones were seized and covered in mud.

"Everything good G?" Tito asked what he knew everybody else was thinking.

"Fuck naw! I just got chased by twelve. I shook most of them bitches but one of their ass was ova on me. I ain't neva seen twelve so thirsty," he explained, still peeking out the blinds.

"DJango!" he repeated, turning to face them. "Fuck? Y'all know that thirsty muthafucka?"

"Everybody from 69th to 79th know that bitch." Crazy G spat.

"That bitch ass nigga be chasin' niggas like a run-a-way slave." Pap added.

"That's why we call that bitch Django," Buddah claimed.

"I like the way you die boy," Tito said, doing his best impression of Jamie Foxx in the movie *Django*.

The entire room fell out laughing, including Star.

"What da fuck?" Star snapped, noticing the softball sized hole in the wall.

The room fell dead quiet as every man watched Star in anticipation.

"Crazy G, yo ass payin' for my wall," he stated, shooting him a knowing glance. "Now let's get down to business."

"Actually, if you don't mind, boss man. We had somethin' different in mind," Tito said, stepping to the middle of the floor.

"What's the throught?" Star replied, gazing at the rest of the gang to try to gauge what was in the aim.

"LayLow OG don't want us a part of his funeral. And she takin' his body to Atlanta to be buried."

"What da fuck you mean she don't want us part of the funeral?"

"It's true, G-ball. She told me she was gone cause a scene and call them people if we showed up." Crazy G whispered through clenched teeth.

"Damn. So what y'all have in mind?"

"Since we all know that nigga was a pervert, we figure we should tear the King of Diamond down. See some ass and titties, get fucked up in his name, then purge the city of every MOE in his name later." Pap stated passionately.

"I'm wit it for bro. Buddha, take us out. Pap, call my girl and tell her to report that Optima stolen."

"Stance."

MEANWHILE ACROSS TOWN

Kierra posed in front of her full body length mirror stark naked as she tried to imagine herself pregnant. Her cycle was two months late and the two positive pregnancy tests confirmed her suspicions. She smiled at herself as she extended her stomach, making herself look pregnant. "I'm 'bout to be a mommy." She cheered gleefully

She just hoped Star would be as happy as she was and would finally leave the streets for good, now that he was about to be a father.

CHAPTER 9

LATER THAT NIGHT

"Say lil' bitch you can't fuck with me if you wanted to/These expensive/These is Red Bottoms/These is bloody shoes." Cardi B's *Bodak Yellow* pumped from the speakers and had every stripper in the club shaking their money makers. The King of Diamonds was jam packed and rocking as usual. Naked bodies gyrated on any dude who was willing to throw a couple of dollars while topless waiters in G-strings hustled about filling orders. Cheap perfume mixed with the smell of stale cigarettes and weed but still wasn't enough to mask the smell of sweat and used pussy.

"Damn, I feel good!" Tito yelled, throwing a stack of ones on the chocolate goddess who twerked inches from his face. Him, Star, Pap, and Buddah were tucked away in their own V.I.P. section enjoying the fruits of their labor.

LayLow visited the club so much that the bouncer immediately recognized Pap and laid out the red carpet for them. Especially after hearing that LayLow had passed away. Crazy G declined to join them tonight. He claimed that he would much rather try to catch a Moe by his toe than throw away his hard-earned money on funky pussy.

"I ain't gone lie, me too," Pap claimed drinking straight from the bottle of Ace of Spades. He was the only one in their section without a butt-naked freak twerking in his lap. Instead, he sat off to the side, smoking and throwing money.

Tonight, they made sure no expense was spared. Naked freaks danced all over their section while bottles of Hennessy, Dusse and Ace of Spades littered the table. A quarter pound of Gelato accompanied the liquor along with a few X-pills. They even went as far as to match in blue and black everything— rocking the Disciples signature colors.

"I think we all needed this lil' break. It's been so much shit going on. We never really got to enjoy this money." Star concluded as the voluptuous Jalo galloped in his lap. He had both arms scratched out on the couch with a Backwood the size of his thumb in his mouth. He was never a heavy smoker, but since Christina had been terrorizing his dreams, that's all he did.

"Aye, where da fuck is Buddah?" Pap asked, suddenly alert.

"He said he was going to the bathroom," Tito said palm-gripping Ms. Chocolate's ass.

"Yeah, that was like five minutes ago."

"Well, let's go find the nigga." Star started tossing Jalo to the side like yesterday's trash.

"Aye, don't go nowhere. Matter of fact, get yo shit and meet us at the front." Tito instructed before shoving all the ones he had left in the front of Ms. Chocolates G-string.

"Okay, daddy," she squealed, scurrying off to collect her things.

As the trio marched down the steps of V.I.P., they could see Buddah arguing with four men who Star and company could tell were Vice Lords. A deadly gang that plagued the west side of the city and some of the south. Vice Lords were like the Black P. Stones and considered themselves people, which meant they represented the five-point star. While the GDs and BD's claimed to be folks and rode under the six-point star. Known as the Star of David, the founder of Folks.

"Nigga, you heard what da fuck I said!" Buddah yelled, mugging the quartet.

"Man, Lord, fuck that nigga. He flodgin'. He really ain't crazy, shorty," a fat, dark skin dude with dreads claimed.

"Hell nah, Lord. Shorty actin' like he crazy," another spat.

"Whoa! Whoa! Whoa! What seems to be the problem?" Star asked, walking directly in between the Vice Lords and Buddah. He was flanked by Tito and Pap.

"We were just waitin' on shorty to apologize. Then we was on our way." The brown skin dude in the middle replied. He had a full goatee with a low fade and the VL sign tattooed on his cheek. The way he spoke for the entire group let Star know he was in charge.

"What? I ain't apologizing to no hooks!" Buddha spat, using the disrespectful name for Vice Lords.

That was all it took to get the royal rumble started. Before Star knew what hit him, the fat dude rocked him with a two piece that staggered him. Buddha instantly returned fist with a right hook that landed with a sickening catch, turning the man's lights out. Without a shadow of doubt his jaw was broken. Tito and Pap exchanged punches with the other three lords until Star and Buddah jumped in. Within seconds, tables, bottles and blood was everywhere. It seemed as if the entire club gathered around to watch the brawl.

"Fuck that nigga yo!" Ms. Chocolate yelled as Tito smacked one of the Lords with a bottle.

Security was finally able to rush the scene but only succeeded in escalating the flight. What started out as Lords versus GDs quickly turned into them versus security.

"C'mon y'all! Break that shit up! The police on they way!" The DJ's voice boomed over the P.A. system.

Only then did the fight seem to stop. Both crews gathered their injured and raced to the parking lot to avoid the boys in blue. They all piled in Buddah's Durango and burned rubber, leaving behind Pap and Tito's cars. Being that his car was "stolen", Star rode with Buddah.

"Damn! That bitch ass nigga stabbed me with somethin!" Pap hissed, pulling down the sun visor to examine the damage. Crimson poured from the side of his head and ran down the side of his face.

"I know G. That's why I put that bottle on that nigga. That muthafucka wouldn't break for shit. I felt like I was whoopin' Kunta-Kinty or some shit." Tito joked sending the entire car into a laughing fit.

"I'm glad we doin' all the he-he and ha-ha-ing cuz yo ass paying for my seats to get clean." Buddah half joked.

"Bullshit. Nigga, you the reason I'm leakin'."

"If I was you, I'd pay his big ass. He see how he laid dude ass out." Ms. Chocolate snickered.

At the sound of her voice, everybody's head snapped in her direction. Amidst all the chaos and commotion, nobody seemed to notice her climbing into the truck with them.

"Lil baby, who told you could ride with us?" Star joked.

"Big daddy." She cooed, licking the side of Tito's face.

"Boy, you betta watch her lil' ass. TT might kill both y'all asses." Pap laughed.

"Shiiit. I gotta mean left hook too, boo," she claimed throwing air jabs.

"Trust me short stuff, you don't wanna see TT, so kill all'at noise." Star stated.

The rest of the ride they laughed and joked about the brawl. Tito and Ms. Chocolate, known as Bree, crashed at the new Budget motel on 89th while Star went to headquarters. Buddha and Pap crashed on Shields with two of Pap's freak hoes. Their night was ending, but others were just getting started.

SEVERAL BLOCKS AWAY

"Say you my nigga I'm be yo killa nobody gone play witcho when I'm witcha/go against any nigga like fuck this glitter skeet burn nigga/I'll put it in for you I'll spin for you wahteva you wit I'm wit it/How you gone cross a nigga that's rockin' witcha I got lit in the city." Kodak Black's "Super Gremlin" lightly hummed from the speakers of Crazy G's Charger. He silently rapped along to the lyrics before he sniffed the crushed up Percocet off the back of his ID. He

rinsed it down with the last of his Apple Crown Royal and tossed the empty bottle on the passenger floor where six other empty bottles sat.

"C'mon bitch. Where you at," he mumbled gripping his 1911 Colt .45. He was high out of his mind and beyond drunk but refused to return home without a kill. Somebody had to pay and that somebody was Moni. He was so desperate and so high that he found himself posted outside of St. Bernard's Hospital.

Initially he was set on finding Trindog's room and emptying the clip in his face… Then Moni came out and jumped into Trindog's Escalade truck. So engrossed in her phone she never noticed him following her all the way home. She left the Escalade started and jetted inside the house almost ten minutes ago. As soon as she came back out, he was on top of her like flies on shit. A sinister smile spread across his face as he pictured her begging for her life, right before he blew her brains out.

"Yeah, I got somethin' fa that ass." He laughed, wiping his runny nose with the back of his hand… He was on cloud nine.

Whoop! The flashing blue and red in his rearview seemed to sober him up instantly. He quickly tucked the 1911 under his leg, plotting his next move. The second the cop stepped to the window and smelled the alcohol on his breath he would be asked to step out, and that would be all she wrote. *Fuck that!* he thought. Somebody had to pay, and since he was saving that somebody, the cop was next in line.

The door swung open and out stepped a Steven Segal look alike.

"Good, this muthafucka white," he hissed as the officer approached.

Then out of nowhere the Segal look alike stopped in his tracks and strained to hear his radio. He yelled something inaudible into his radio then sprinted back to his cruiser. He turned on his sirens and shot past Crazy G like a rocket. It was definitely both of their lucky day.

"I'll see you lata bitch." He huffed before putting the car in drive. His night was officially over.

THE NEXT MORNING AT HEADQUARTERS

Boom! Boom! Boom!

"Staaarr!" TT groaned from under the silk sheets of Star's king sized bed.

"Hmmm!" He groaned back.

Last night's fuck session lasted until early this morning and left them both exhausted. They literally just closed their eyes an hour ago.

"Get the door, please." She huffed rolling on her side and pulling the sheets over her head.

"Aight. Aight," he snapped, flinging the sheets off him. He slid into his boxers and stomped to the door.

Whoever was at the door better have a good reason for banging on his door at 8:30 in the morning. He snatched the door open and damn near had a heart attack at the sight of Tito.

"Sup G?" He greeted me trying to enter but Star placed a firm hand on his chest stopping him.

"Wassup? I got company right now," Star claimed nodding towards the back.

"Damn, my bad, play-playa." He smiled for a brief second before a menace replaced his smile. His eyes had locked on to something behind Star.

"The fuck wrong witchu?" Star asked, glancing back to see what grabbed his attention.

TT's work uniform and shoes lay sprawled out directly in the middle of the floor in a crumpled mess. To make matters worse, her car keys, ID card and name tag were only a couple feet away, making it impossible to deny what was taking place.

"TT here," he asked, his voice raising a few octaves.

"What da fuck? Why would she be here, nigga?" Star snapped feigning irritation. Even though they were caught red handed, Star would lie to the bitter end.

"Nigga, you heard what da fuck I said! Is Tacarra here!" He reiterated clenching his jaw and balling his fist up.

"First off, watch who da fuck you talkin' to. And take all'at aggression out yo' body language. Two, nigga, I just fuckin' told you she ain't fuckin' here. You at my door at 8:30 in the mornin', tweakin' and shit." Star knew he was dead wrong, but that didn't stop his blood from boiling. Right or wrong he wasn't accepting any disrespect.

"Aight. Whateva you say, Big Homie." Tito replied through clenched teeth. He was beyond hot and it took every ounce of restraint he had not to punch Star in his lying face. He knew he had to get out of dodge before he did something he would later regret.

"Yeah, aight," Star shot back before slamming the door in his face. The way Tito handled him had him seeing red, but he knew he was a foul and deserved it, but knowing that still didn't help him feel any better.

"What was all'at about?" TT asked as soon as he stepped into the room.

"Tito," he mumbled, crawling back in bed.

"Who," she asked, sitting up suddenly alert.

"Tito."

"What da fuck did he want?"

"I neva got to find out… I think that nigga saw yo uniform on the floor."

"Oh my gawd, fa real," she whispered. She loved Tito and didn't want to hurt him, but she wanted Star more.

"Yup. He asked me was you here. I swear that nigga was ready to go ten rounds."

Vrrrnnn! Vrrrmm! Vrrrmm! On cue, her phone vibrated on the nightstand with Tito's name shining brightly. She let the voicemail pick up, but he was calling again.

"What we gone do now," she asked.

"Shit, what we been doin'. He know now." Star replied nonchalantly.

TT had to hide the smile that crept onto her face. Secretly she hoped this would set them both free so they could finally be together. But what she failed to realize is that Star loved Kierra whole heartedly and wasn't leaving her anytime soon. "Fa' real," she asked.

"Yeah, fa' real. You don't sound too worried."

"Cuz I ain't. I'm a boss bitch! And I need a boss nigga."

"Is that right," he asked pulling her to him by her ankles.

"You know it is, daddy." She cooed spreading her legs wider than the Mississippi river.

Star couldn't identify what it was about her that made him weak for her. Whatever it was, he knew he had to figure it out fast before it was too late… or was it already?

ST. BERNARD HOSPITAL

Trindog's eyes fluttered then popped open. He looked at the hospital room in a daze. Flowers, cards and balloons cluttered the window seal, letting him know he had been there for a while. His head pounded like a bass drum, and his throat was begging for a glass of water. Memories from the shooting came back to him slowly but were a little fuzzy. He tried to sit up and pain espoused throughout his entire midsection.

"Arrrghhh!" He winced, glancing down at his stomach.

His eyes all but popped out of his head at the sight of the colostomy bag attached to his stomach, filled with fresh feces. A single angry tear slid down the right side of his face as thoughts of a life with a colostomy bag flooded his mental. He was about to unleash hell on earth on the GDs and paint the city red with their blood. The gloves were officially off. His eyes roamed around until he spotted the nurse call button.

Somebody betta tell me somethn', he thought, pressing the button repeatedly.

***

Clap! Clap! Clap!

"Oo-ooohh, I-I love you." TT moaned, gripping the sheets as if her life depended upon it.

Star had her on all fours at the edge of the bed while he pounded her out mercilessly.

"I love you too." He huffed yanking her hair so his lips were centimeters away from her ear. "You ready to have my baby?"

"Y-Yesss." She squealed, flatling out in an attempt to run from the pounding, but he was all over her.

He gripped the small of her back and pinned her down with his weight. "I can't hear you!"

"I-I wanna have yo' baby! I wanna have yo' baby," she cried drenching the sheets with her juices.

"Arrghh! Fuck, I'm cumin'," he whispered stabbing as deep as possible before erupting inside of her. "Damn!" He huffed giving her cheeks a nice smack.

"Aight, nigga, don't hink I'm havin' no abortions." She half-joked.

"Shut up," he said rolling off of her. "You know a nigga couldn't pull out if he wanted to." His heart almost did a backflip as he locked eyes with Kierra.

She was holding his gun, shaking with raindrop-sized tears pouring from her eyes. He opened his mouth to speak, but no words came out.

"You know I got that slip and slide." TT bragged totally unaware of Kierra's voice. Her eyes inflated to the size of tennis balls then they locked on to the Glock. "Now KI, hol—"

"Shut da fuck up, you grimmy ass bitch!" She roared, swinging the Glock TT's way." I knew somethin' was off the second yo' thot ass tried to be my friend again. Never thought it was to fuck my man!"

"I swear to God it ain't like that, Ki, please." TT cried cowering under the sheets.

"It ain't like that? It ain't like that? Bitch, it's definitely like that!" She screamed. She was irate, and Star saw his window of opportunity with her focus on TT.

He leaped off the bed and lunged for the gun.

Boc!

ON 57TH

Pap looked down on the block from Crazy G's balcony watching the early morning rush hour. His head throbbed from last night's events, and it definitely wasn't from the alcohol. As he surveyed the block, he couldn't help but reflect on the last couple of months and how drastically his life changed. Three months ago he was flat broke, robbing anybody and everybody, and riding in stolen cars for the hell of it. Now he was closing in on a hundred thousand in cash, had his own set of wheels, and if he wanted, his own house or apartment. Yet he still felt like something was missing. He already told himself once he had 250 thousand, he would walk away from the streets permanently. But strangely he felt like that time was now. The streets had been nothing but cruel to him. It helped him gain his financial independence, but it snatched both of his best friends. One to the gun, and the other to the bottle.

Since the death of LayLow, all Crazy G did was drink and snort Percocet's. Last night he stumbled in, rambling about killing some woman. Now not even six hours later he was already high out of his mind and drinking. Pap couldn't stand to see him that way. *That* was the main reason he was on the balcony to begin with.

"You okay, boo?" Lay-Lay, one of Pap's fuck buddies, asked, wrapping her arms around his stomach and hugging his back.

"Yeah, just thinkin'," he claimed, caressing her arms lightly.

"'Bout Crazy G."

Pap spun around puzzled. She always seemed to read him like a book. Aside from her juicy lips, red skin, and slim but thick figure that was one of the main reasons he rocked with her so hard. He didn't have to spell everything out for her. She just knew as if they were connected mentally. "How you know," he asked with a raised eyebrow.

"C'mon now. Boo, you know we connected." She sang, tapping a manicured nail against her temple.

"Connected, huh? How you figure?" He smiled, pulling her 5'2" frame into his.

"Really nigga," she asked, shaking her neck and rolling her eyes playfully. "Your favorite color is blue. You hate repeating yo' self and shit being repeated to you. Your sister is your heart. You love yo' mama but can't stand being in her presence. Yo' favorite gun is a seg or sig. We both know I know how you liked to be fucked. Anything else?" She smirked.

Pap couldn't help but cheese from ear to ear. He was definitely impressed. He hadn't told her any of these things, yet she knew them all. It was crystal clear that she was paying attention to his needs and was rocking with him the long way. "How you know all'at?" He teased.

"Cuz I pay attention to what I want."

"And whatchu want?"

"Stop playin' wit' me. You know I been supposed to be wifey," she snapped, punching him in the arm, playfully.

"Wife? So you tryna be exclusively mine?"

"Nigga, I been exclusively yours. Don't no other nigga get to smell this pussy. I'm not that type'a bitch. The fuck," she snapped.

"Aight. Well, I need you to take me to get my car wife," he said covering her lips with his, but she pulled away.

"Don't be playin' wit' me. Gasin' my head up and shit. Cuz you and whateva bitch gone get fucked up. And I'm not even playin'."

"C'mon now. Ain't we 'posed to be connected?" He teased tapping his temple. "You wifey. I wouldn't even play like that."

Lay-Lay grabbed the sides of his face and pulled him in for a big, juicy kiss. She licked and sucked his face for a full two minutes.

"C'mon now. You keep that shit up it's gone be trouble."

"I like trouble."

"Girl, let's go before them people tow my shit."

BACK AT HEADQUARTERS

The room was eerily quiet. Star and Kierra stood frozen in shock as they stared at a motionless TT. She laid flat on her back with blood pouring from somewhere on her body—staining the silk sheets.

"I-I didn't mean to. I ain't mean to kill her. It just went off. The gun just went off!" Kierra cried.

"That's what happens when you play with guns," he snapped snatching the gun out of her hands. "Tal'm 'bout you ain't mean to." He was beyond pissed. Not only did he have to cover up a murder, but he would have to explain to Pap how his sister died behind his bullshit.

"Nigga, if you ain't fuck this bitch none of this woulda happened!" She shot back.

He knew her words held the absolute truth, but they didn't help their current situation. So, he let her have her say while he thought of a solution.

Then as if possessed TT sat up. "Owwww! She shot me! That bitch shot me," she cried holding her shoulder in a frivolous attempt to stop the bleeding.

"Bitch you lucky I didn't kill yo' ass!" Kierra hissed.

"Both of y'all shut da fuck up!" Star roared, starling both women. "The fuckin' police could be on they way and y'all sittin' here arguing like it's chicken ass or sum shit."

"But she s—"

"What da fuck did I say! Now I'ma go pull yo' car around front while you help her get dressed so we can go to the hospital."

"I'm not helpin' that slut do shit. And she definitely not 'bout to be bleedin' all up in my shit," she snapped, folding her arms defiantly.

"Okay, sure. Let's wait for the police to show up and you can explain to them why you shot her," he said popping a squat on the bed as if he had all the time in the world.

The sight of Star and TT naked in the bed enraged her even further, but she checked it, storing away in her memory bank for later. Right now, Star was 100% correct, no matter how bad she wanted him not to be. "Pssst! Okay, damn. Where her shit at?"

"I-In the livin' room." TT winced, clearly in an immense amount of pain.

Kierra stomped off to find TT's belongings while Star quickly got dressed.

"I know that shit hurt, T. But you gotta keep pressure on it," he said, tossing her one of his shirts, then bolting out the front.

She caught the shirt with her good hand and placed it on her shoulder like she'd seen in the movies. Kierra hustled back to the room with TT's belongings and had to force herself not to jump her right then and there. Every time she saw her black ass butt naked in her old bed, it made her blood boil. Mainly because her body looked so good. She helped her slide into her pants first, then came her shirt.

"Ahh! Shit!" TT yelped when Kierra pulled the shirt down over her arm.

"Aww, I'm sawwy." She taunted, smiling from ear to ear.

"Bitch! Wait 'til my shit heal up, I'ma—"

Beep! Beep! Beep! Their little showdown was interrupted by Star honking the horn like a mad man. He wanted to get as far away from the apartment as possible. The last thing he needed and wanted was the police showing up.

"C'mon," she snapped, pulling TT to her feet.

"Bitch you don't gotta be so rough. You already shot me." TT dissed, snatching her good arm away from her. She definitely couldn't wait for her arm to heal.

"Bitch you ain't seen rough," she claimed sashaying out the door.

TT walked behind her and was extremely thankful that it was still early and no nosey roseys were out. Because she was sure somebody would have called the police. Kierra climbed in the back seat while TT played the front. They rode to St. Bernards in complete silence with both women's angry eyes glued to his face… He was officially fucked.

THE KING OF DIAMONDS

Pap was glad to see his car was still parked exactly where he left it, completely unscathed. Lay-Lay navigated her Honda Civic through the deserted lot until she was directly across from Pap's G6. Before he could even put two feet on the ground, two enormous bouncers stormed from the club in their direction. Pap immediately recognized them from last night's brawl.

"Aye, gone head, pull off. I'ma catch up with you lata," he said before slamming her car door shut.

"Boy," she said rolling down the window. "If they wanna tweak, let's tweak." Her hand dipped in her purse and came back out with a can of bear mace.

"I'm not playin'. Stay yo lil' ass in the car." He barked. He liked that she was on go mode, but didn't want her in the way if he had to shoot.

Lay-Lay reluctantly stayed in the car pouting, but told herself if shit hit the fan she was jumping out blinding niggas.

"Wassup?" Pap asked as soon as they were face to face.

"Nigga, you know wassup! All'at tweakin' you and yo' homies did last night. I couldn't wait 'til you brought yo' bitch ass back up here so I could stomp a mudhole in yo' ass!" The Bobby Lashly look-alike growled, balling his fist up. He was the biggest of the two, and clearly thought he was in charge.

"Well, you gone stand there running yo big bitch ass lips or you gone do somethin'?" Pap taunted.

They both advanced on him, but Pap pulled his SIG out with the speed and grace of a trained professional. Freezing them both in their tracks instantly. The smaller one even threw his hands up as if he was under arrest.

"Don't stop now. Let's see if all them muscles protect you from these hallows." He laughed, leveling the SIG with the big one's face.

"Just like a fuck nigga. Can't fight so you gotta pop a nigga," the big one said, unfazed by the cannon in his face.

"Yo' big bitch ass can't fight either. That's why y'all tried to jump me. I'ma jump in my car and be on my merry fuckin' way. One of you niggas play crazy I'ma pop the skin off y'all ass," he said, opening his car door. Neither muscle head moved a muscle as Pap jumped in his whip and cranked the engine. They knew their muscles didn't stand a chance against the cannon Pap held. As he pulled out the parking lot, he made sure to give the muscle heads a proper fuck you before burning rubber.

"Ah-ha! Y'all some big bitchesss!" Lay-Lay yelled as they pulled off.

"I got sum fa dat ass," he mumbled, pulling out his phone.

"Whatchu finna do, bro?" The small one asked.

"9-1-1, what's your emergency?" The operator asked.

"Somebody just pulled a gun on me and my brother," he screeched as if he was scared for his life.

"Are they still there now? Is anyone shot?"

"No, they left. And I can tell you what he's driving," he said, smiling slyly at his brother.

CHAPTER 10

ST. BERNARD'S HOSPITAL

The Price Is Right with Bob Barker hummed from the old box TV that was mounted on the wall. The smell of disinfectant mixed with plastic filled the air of the partially vacant emergency room, making Star sick to his stomach. He hated hospitals with a passion because they reminded him of his mother's death. As they waited for the status of TT's arm, he couldn't help but pace the shiny floors.

Kierra sat across the room as if she didn't even know Star. She couldn't stand to be around him right now. He'd just got caught cheating on her and here he was pacing the floors worried about the next bitch. She made sure to give him the stare of death every time they locked eyes. As Star paced the floors, the only thing he could think about was Kierra. He knew he fucked up big time, and hoped she forgave him. Yet strangely another part of him hoped TT was okay and would forgive him too. He was literally torn between the two. He loved Kierra but wanted TT at the same time. Kierra was his comfort and his peace, while TT was his wild side and would pop off at the drop of a dime.... She was his gangster bitch. They both gave him exactly what he needed on different levels. His stomach rumbled, reminding him that he hadn't eaten since last night.

"Aye, I'ma run to the vending machine real quick. You want somethin'," he asked a mean mugging Kierra.

"Do I want anything? Hmmm, let me think. A faithful boyfriend would do."

Star bit the inside of his jaw to restrain himself. He knew he deserved everything she was sending his way, but it didn't make him feel any better. He loved Kierra. To see her hurt and displaying this type of aggression towards him was unsettling. He nodded before turning on his heels. He strolled to the cafe and started to open the double doors when a couple emerged mugging.

"Star, right?" The man asked.

"Who wanna know?" Star shot back even though he knew exactly who the man was. It was his job to know the enemy.

"Trindog!"

"Aww, yeaaah… Neva heard of you." Star laughed.

"All'at. You know wassup Ku. It's all well," he said addressing Star as if he was one of the Moes purposely.

"Ku?" Star repeatedly scrunching his face up as if something stunk. "Aight, I hear you G. I see you and yo' niggas like the hospitals these days." He added before walking pass the two.

"Bitch ass brick." Trindog spat.

"You know I'ma die 5!" Star yelled over his shoulder, never breaking stride. He didn't have time to argue, plus he didn't need the extra attention being drawn to him. Just days ago he was in the lobby waving a gun.

"C'mon, bae, fuck that nigga. They know wassup with you," Moni claimed, grabbing his hand.

"Them bitch ass niggas just don't know how ugly it's finna get." He huffed through clenched teeth. Had it not been for his current condition, he would have went Boosie Bad Azz and SET IT OFF. Instead, he took it on the chin and kept it moving. The GDs were about to be in for a rude awakening.

BACK ACROSS TOWN

Pap zig-zagged in and out of traffic like a Nascar race car driver. To his surprise Lay-Lay was able to keep up in her Honda Civic. *Vrrmmm! Vrrrnn!* His iPhone rattled in the cup holder stealing his attention. He scooped it up and answered it. It was Lay-Lay. "Lemme guess, you can't keep up and you want me to slow down?" He laughed into the receiver.

"No nigga, the Sherriff been following us since we jumped on the highway."

"You sure," he asked, glancing in the rearview.

"Yes, I'm sure. Slow down so I can pull up on the side of you."

Against his better judgement, he slowed down to a medium speed. As promised, Lay-Lay and a Cook County Sheriff pulled up next to him.

"Be cool, he probably just ridin'," Pap said not believing his own words.

Then like magic the Sheriff swerved behind Pap and turned on his red and blues. *Woop! Woop!*

"Fuck! Just go ahead. He probably on us for speeding," he said tucking the SIG under his seat.

"Hell no," she snapped. "I'm not leavin' you wit' some racist ass police. They be killin' people."

"Aight. Don't say shit and let me handle this."

"Ooh, you know I like it when you talk to me like that." She purred, making him cheese from ear to ear.

He navigated the G6 to the shoulder of the road with Lay-Lay not on the Sheriff's heels. The door opened up and a black officer stepped out making Pap tense up immediately. Most people would have been happy to see a brother step out, but not Pap. He knew all too well that the black officers did way more than the whites. You would let your guard down thinking you caught a break, then would end up in the back of the squad car with a zillion charges.

"Can I ask you why you stopped me," he asked as soon the officer approached his window.

He was a tall, brown skin with a bald head and a medium build. Huge sunglasses covered his face making him impossible to read. His hand rested on the butt of his gun letting Pap know he wasn't friendly. "Turn off the vehicle and step out with your hands where I can see them." He demanded.

"For what? I ain't did shit," Pap claimed.

"Step out the car now," he reiterated, unlatching his Glock from its holster. "I ain't asking again."

"Get yo' supervisor out here. I know my rights," Pap said, rolling his window up.

No sooner than the words left his mouth, six more pulled up with their lights flashing. Two of them went as far as pulling their cars directly in front of his. Boxing him in completely. The rest of them jumped out of their cars with their guns out, surrounding his car quickly.

What da fuck? Pap thought, throwing his hands in the air. He knew now that this wasn't an ordinary traffic stop… This was a hit.

"Get the fuck outta the car now!" The first officer repeated, his gun drawn too.

"Oh my Gawd! What da fuck is going—" LayLay cried.

Pap totally forgot she was on the phone until then.

"I'on know but we finna found out."

"Nooo, bae, please don't get out that car. Just pull off."

"I can't, I'm boxed in." He informed.

"This is your last warning: roll your window down and step out of the car or we will use force." Another officer yelled.

Pap reluctantly did exactly as they instructed him to do. The second he was out of the car he was slung to the ground and cuffed instantly. "I ain't even resisting," Pap said in his usual calm demeanor. He knew they were trying to get a reaction out of him so they could beat him, but he wouldn't give them the satisfaction.

"Stand up!" The officer yelled yanking Pap up by the handcuffs, so they dug into his wrist.

Pap smiled slyly and secretly zoned in on the officer's name tag. *Omerey. Good, you shouldn't be too hard to find*, he thought as they escorted him to the back of a squad car.

He knew for sure he was going to jail once they found the SIG tucked under his seat.

As soon as he was placed in the car two officers began to search his car. Not even a full two minutes later they came out holding two guns in the air as if they were trophies. At first he thought they planted the other gun, until the light bulb went off in his head. He'd totally forgotten about the other gun he drove to the club with last night. Whatever the case, he was definitely fucked. A female officer walked back to where Lay-Lay was, panicked, and said something that Pap couldn't make out. The next thing he knew she was out of her car and headed straight for him.

The female officer opened the door and walked away. "You got two minutes honey," she said over her shoulder.

"Thank you," Lay-Lay said before turning to Pap. "They takin' you to jail for intimidation with a gun and possession of two illegal firearms by a felon," she whispered sadly.

As soon as she said the charges, he immediately put two and two together. "That bitch ass nigga," he growled. He would definitely see those muscle heads again.

"Damn this a crazy ass first day," she said as a huge semi-truck roared past them.

"Times up." The officer informed walking back up.

"Look, I need you to call Star and tell him what's going on and don't give my pussy away. I'll be back shortly." He winked.

"Okay, bae," she said before leaning in and planting a juicy one on his lips.

"Damn," he mumbled as the door was shut on him. He knew it would be a minute before he saw the streets again. He was already on probation for an unlawful use of a weapon, now he was on his way back for two more. He knew the chances of getting a bond would be slim to none, and if he did get one it would be impossible to reach without drawing attention. And the last thing he wanted was the feds to come knocking… Little did he know they already were.

45 MINUTES LATER

"The family of Taccara Riggins?" A slender white woman wearing a doctor's jacket over scrubs yelled.

"Right here," Star said, strutting over and meeting the woman in the middle of the waiting room.

Kierra reluctantly followed Star. She definitely wanted to know the status of TT.

"Hi, I'm Dr. Page." She chirped, extending her hand. She was mid-thirties with blue eyes that seemed to glow.

"Star," he replied, shaking her hand

At first, she looked as if she wanted to press for his real name, but the looks on both their faces quickly changed her mind.

"Well, I have good news. The bullet went straight through without breaking any bones or doing too much damage to muscles and tissue… But the bad news is she's lost a lot of blood and will have to be kept overnight… Just as a precaution as we give her blood. Any questions for me?"

"Is she awake?" Star asked.

"I'm afraid not. She's lost a lot of blood and is heavily sedated. She probably won't be awake for a couple hours. But you're more than welcome to stay until visiting hours are over." She sang.

"Oh no. That's okay. Tell her we will be back tomorrow to get her." Kierra stated giving Star the *I wish you would try me* look.

"Okay, and you are?"

"Her sister and this is her brother-in-law." She shot back putting extra emphasis on *in law*.

"Oookay," Dr. Page said looking back and forth from the two. "You guys have a nice day." She added before scurrying off.

Thirty minutes later Star pulled Kierra's Nissan Rogue into their driveway and killed the engine. Neither party made a move to get out the car, they just sat there in thick silence, lost in thought.

"So we not gone talk? We just gone act like this never happened," she asked. Her voice was full of emotion as she turned to face him.

Star turned in his seat and locked eyes with her. It was a hard task with the hurt expression she wore. It was as if he could see how bad she was hurting. How bad she wanted him to make things right, but somehow he knew he never could. "I-I know I fucked up, Ki." He started using her nickname to lighten the mood. "I could sit around and make a bunch of bullshit excuses for what I did but I ain't gone even play with you like that. All I can say is I was a weak ass man, and I fucked up. And if you accept my apology and willing to forgive me, I will never fuck up again," he claimed, reaching for her hand, but she snatched it back.

"Out of all the bitches out there," she whispered with tears streaking down her face. She tried to swipe them away but the floodgate was open.

"I don't know, Ki. Shit, maybe cuz she was available," he lied knowing it was much deeper than that, but fear of losing her kept him from admitting it.

"You told that bitch you love her!" She screamed while opening her car door, but he immediately clamped her arm.

"Just hear me out, Ki, damn! I know I fucked up. But I love you, not her. People say whateva during sex. I wanna do whateva I can to make this shit right." He pleaded. "Just give me another chance."

She climbed back into the car and sat silently, pondering his proposal. "First thing tomorrow you tell that bitch when we pick her up it's over."

"Done," he replied without hesitation.

"Nigga, it ain't that easy. You gone bring yo' ass home every night. I don't care what time you leave the hood. And I need Sundays reserved for me." She stated.

"You got that."

"Finally, you gone sleep on the couch until I'm ready to share a bed with yo' lyin' ass." She concluded, staring at him with a cocked brow, waiting for his response.

"Aight, damn. Anything else?"

"Sure the fuck is. If you ever cheat on me again, yo' bitch won't be the only one gettin' shot." She mugged, staring him directly in the eye.

He could feel his dick jump in his pants. He loved when his woman got gangster. He smiled at her and nodded his agreement.

"Don't be smilin' at me. We ain't cool. And tell yo' boy Tito I said thanks for the tip."

"What," he snapped.

"C'mon, boo. You had to know. Since when do I pop ups with yo' guns?" She pointed out "Oh, and congrats," she said digging in her purse

"Congrats? Congrats for what," he asked, completely thrown off. She was all over the place, and it was confusing him.

"You're 'bout to be a father," she hissed, throwing the pregnancy test at him and getting out of the car, making sure to slam the door.

Star was dumbfounded as a wave of mixed emotions washed over him. Bomb after bomb had been dropped on him today, leaving him with a monster headache. Today was definitely one for the record books. Just when he thought he had enough for the day, his phone jingled in his pocket.

"Who dis," he answered not knowing the number.

"This Lay-Lay. Pap girl."

"Who eva da fuck this is, stop playin' on my fuckin' phone. Pap don't have a girl."

"Yess da fuck he do! But that's not what this call 'bout. I got a message from him for you." She informed in a sassy hood-rat tone.

"What's the message?"

"He just got locked up and told me to give you the details."

"Locked up," he repeated, sitting straight up in his seat, suddenly alert. "And shorty, if you playin' on my phone right now, with the way I'm feelin', I'ma find you and smoke yo' whole family."

"Boyyy, whateva. So, this what happened."

CHAPTER 11

TWO DAYS LATER

Clang! Clang!

"Get up! You got a visitor." The red-faced guard yelled, kicking the bars, jolting Pap awake.

"Yo coulda just called my name like a normal fuckin' human being." Pap snapped. He hated being scared awake.

"Did I scare ya, pussycat? You got two minutes then I'm comin' to getcha," he claimed before slinking his hefty frame out of view.

Pap rose from the thin twin sized mattress and stretched until he heard multiple bones crack. "Aaawww, shit." He groaned looking around the filthy 6 by 8 in disgust.

Had he not been awake for twenty-eight hours, he probably would have never even sat on the stale mat. Scratching his beard, he wondered who his visitor could be. Mr. Teddeso, the lawyer Star sent for him, already came promising to have him out in a month or two. Lay-Lay tried to come visit multiple times, but they shot her down every time. So, he was racking his brain trying to guess who the mystery person was. As promised, a minute and a half later the guard came back and escorted him to an interview room.

"Someone will be in to talk to you in a minute," the guard said then left.

Almost five minutes later a tall, slender white man entered with a thick manilla envelope tucked under his arm. "Good morning, sir. I'm agent Fletcher with the FBI," he said flashing his credentials and taking a seat. "How are you? Can I get you anything?"

"Naw, I'm decent. What does the Feds have to do wit' my case?" he asked, getting straight to it.

"Well, since you put it like that. It has nothin' to do with your case. For now anyway. This has to do with your runnin' buddies or G's as you like to call them," he snickered.

"Da fuck is you talkin' 'bout. I'on know shit 'bout no G's, big dog."

"No. You sure you don't know about Gangster Disciple or Growth and Development?"

"I'on know shit 'bout none of that." Pap reiterated with a scowl on his face.

"You're funny," he said pulling out the contents in the manilla envelope and spreading them across the table. New glossy 4 by 6 photos of almost the entire nation. But the one that stood out the most was of him, Star and Crazy G at headquarters days ago.

"Now, I know you wanna maintain your tough guy persona, but this is the big leagues. The first one to snitch gets the deal. And trust me, with all this evidence somebody will be singin'. So, you might as well be the first." He smiled as if he was saying something slick.

Pap had to admit the evidence on them being a gang was undisputable, but that seemed to be all he had. Besides, he wasn't a rat and would never convert to one.

"Still don't feel like talking… Mr. Regional?"

"I already told you, Mr. Swine. Lawyer!"

"Your funeral," he said gathering up his photos and papers in one big swoop. "When you're down at the MCC facing kingpin charges with Mr. Cross AKA Star, you'll be begging to talk to me. Believe me you," he claimed, storming out of the room.

Pap leaned back in the chair and reflected on his conversation with Fletcher. He had almost every active member on 79th pegged down to their status, but he had little to nothing on 57th. Letting him know that whoever was snitching was close to him, and it made him sick. He had to warn Star A.S.A.P. *These niggas foul*, he thought.

MEANWHILE AT HEADQUARTERS

"So, you say this a ghost Glock? And this button on the back makes it shoot fully auto?" Star asked as he toyed with the Glock 23 in his hand.

"Abso-muthafuckin'-lutely," Taydoe, Buddah's gun connect, claimed. He was short with long dreads that stopped at the middle of his back, and had enough guns to supply a small terrorist group.

"I told you this nigga had some shit." Buddah cheesed, holding the AR pistol as if he was in the middle of a shootout. "I like this muthafucka."

"Sooo how much for the Glocks, beans, bullets, and 300 Blackouts?" Star asked.

"How many Glocks and how many Blackouts you want?"

"Four and four," he replied. The Glocks were for him, and he'd put a Blackout in each trap for extra security. The last two days had been shootout after shootout, and three of the GDs ended up shot. Trindog was clearly making good on his threats.

"For you, just because Buddah stamped you, $9,500. And I'ma throw in the beams and extendos for free."

"Bet it up. I need a crate of throw-aways too for some of the homies. How much that's gone run me," he asked as he counted out the change on the living room sofa.

"Another G and we even."

"Here ya go, my nigga," Star said handing over the $10,500.

"It's been a pleasure. Anytime you need anything, just hit the line."

"Aight, what 'bout this ARP? I'm feelin' this muthafucka," Buddah claimed sweeping the cannon back and forth like he'd seen in the movies.

"I was just finna say. Just throw me a P of that gas you smoked with me and it's yours. That shit got me high as a muthafucka." He smiled through chinky eyes, drawing laughs from both men.

"Just meet me at my spot and I'ma situate you," Buddha said, shaking hands with him.

"Say less."

"Good lookin' out." Star stated, rising from the sofa to shake his hand also.

"Anytime. Anytime. I'ma have some new shit in a couple weeks. I'ma make sure I hit y'all first." He announced on his way out the door with Buddah in tow.

"Aye, what kind of shells these muthafuckas take?" Buddah asked.

"Fuck I look like, Smith and Wesson? I just sell the shit," Taydoe cracked sending them all into a laughing fit.

Ten minutes later Star found himself alone. He liked being solo lately. A Backwood filled with Purple Runtz while he played with his new Glocks, he swiped his lighter from the table and sparked the wood to life. Sucking in a huge cloud of smoke, he watched the fish swim back and forth in the ten-gallon tank for a couple minutes lost in thought. The last two days had been wild, and he couldn't shake the nagging feeling that things were about to get worse. It felt as if everything was coming together but falling apart at the same time. He had to make some major changes now that Pap was gone, but he truly didn't trust anybody as much as he trusted Pap. He was cut from the same cloth as his deceased right hand Buckwild, and was loyal to the core. He was Buckwild without all the wild.

Knock! Knock! Knock! Three quick taps on the front door shattered his thoughts immediately. He definitely wasn't expecting anybody, so his antennas shot up on high alert. He slid from the couch with two of the brand-new Glocks in each hand and crept to the door. A wave of relief washed over him at the sight of TT standing on the other side of the door.

She was dressed in all-white yoga pants with the matching jacket halfway on because of the sling that cradled her left arm. Her hair was freshly straightened but slightly crinkled at the end the way he liked it. Minus the sling, she was looking good enough to eat.

Knock! Knock! Knock!

"I know you see me standin' out here, cold ass fuck," she snapped, shivering from the December wind.

It was already a chilling 17 out, and with the east side of Chicago being so close to the lake, all it took was one wind gust to make it feel like the North Pole. Against his better judgement he opened the door and allowed her to enter.

"What took you so long? Shit, a bitch almost froze to death." She huffed, strutting past him as if she owned the place, and he couldn't help but watch her ass jiggle every step of the way.

"Wassup, TT? I thought I explained to you at the hospital that we couldn't do this no more," he said, taking a seat directly across from her deliberately. He needed to keep her at bay in order to resist the urge of taking her right then and there. She was killing it.

"Can't do what," she asked as if she was confused, picking up the half smoked Backwood and relighting it. "I'm just here to talk 'bout my lil' brotha and what you plan on doing to that fuck nigga Tito." Her mouth was saying one thing, but her eyes and body language told a different story.

"I sent your lil' brotha the best lawyer I could find. He should be out in a month or two. As for dat nigga Tito, I called a meeting tonight. I'ma have that nigga violated then I'm dropping that nigga to a solider." He explained taking the wood back.

For about two minutes they just smoked in an awkward silence until the Backwood was gone.

"Star?" TT said breaking the silence.

"Wassup?"

"Why you actin' like you don't want me," she asked, joining him on the other couch. "I know you want me as bad as I want you. I can feel it and see it in your eyes. So, let's stop playin' and be together. Fuck what everybody else think and want and let's do us." She added, taking his hand in hers.

Star was dumbfounded. This was one of the main reasons he was attracted to her. She read him like a book and wasn't afraid to say what was on her mind. She was literally this female version of him but still loved Kierra. He just wished there was a way he could mix them together or have them both like the show Sister Wives.

"I-I feel the exact same way but I—"

"Then that's all there is to it." She interrupted straddling him cowgirl style. "I know you love us both. I promise you Kierra won't be that hard to convince. We used to mess around all the time," she whispered.

Before he could respond she covered his mouth with hers, and his mouth parted instantly, inviting her tongue to dance with his.

"Fuck me." She moaned, raising up just enough so he could remove her pants, which he did with ease.

He freed his rock-hard missile and guided it into her already soaking abyss. Her sugar walls gripped his pole like a condom and she was hotter than a sauna.

"Fuck, TT," he growled as he palm-gripped her ass and guided her up and down his pole slowly.

"Uhhh. Faster!" She moaned.

He gladly obeyed her commands and thrust into her like he was trying to break her.

"Uhh-ahh-ahh-ahhh." She cried wrapping her good arm around his back. "D-Don't stop!" She rolled her hips in rhythm with his stroke.

"Fuck, you so wet," he growled watching her creamy juices coat his pole.

"I love you, Star!" She screamed.

"Cum for me bae. Cum on yo' dick." He grunted feeling his own orgasm rearing his head.

"I-I'm c-cumin' for you," she whispered, slumping on his chest.

"Arrgh! Me too," he hissed, releasing inside her abyss.

"Star," she whispered.

"Yeah," he replied, still palming her ass cheeks.

"I really love you like fa' real fa' real. I don't think I can live without you," she claimed rocking back and forth on his semi erect penis.

"I know. I feel the exact same way," he said as his pole rocked back up.

ACROSS TOWN

"And I know you're not no good for me. But you look so good to me/I don't need another broken heart or a sleepless night/God please guide me right/She looks like the girl of my dreams"

Rod Waves "Girl Of My Dreams" pumped from the speakers as Crazy G watched Moni from the comfort of his Charger. The 5% tent on his windows had him invisible, and the three Adderall he snorted had him geeked. Moni, completely oblivious to his presence, loaded bag after bag into Trindog's Escalade.

"Damn, where you going, lil' bitch," he mumbled, letting his perverse eyes roam over her fat ass as she bent over in the back seat.

He peeked around to make sure the block was clear of any onlookers. Once he was sure it was clear, he rolled his shiesty mask down and cocked his 1911. The second he slid from the Charger, Trindog came strolling out of the house, Glock in hand. Time seemed to slow down as they locked eyes.

"Muthafucka!" Trindog growled, letting his tool bang. *Bapa! Bapa! Bapa! Bapa!*

Caught off guard, Crazy G was forced to retreat. He leaped over the hood of the Charger firing blindly. His 1911 woke the block up. *Blocka! Blocka! Blocka!*

"Get da fuck in the truck," he yelled at Moni who was frozen in place.

Crazy G peeked from behind the Charger just in time to see them trying to escape. He aimed his cannon and let it rip. *Blocka! Blocka! ... Blocka! Blocka! Blocka!* Two of the shots found home in Moni's neck and chest, killing her almost instantly, while the other three narrowly missed Trindog and slammed into the house behind him.

"You bitch ass nigga!" Trindog roared, squeezing on his trigger relentlessly. *Bapa! Bapa! Bapa! Bapa!*

Crazy G ducked behind his Charger as the bullets slammed into the hood and the windshield, spidering it instantly. Sirens wailed in the distance, forcing both men to jump in their cars and burn rubber, leaving a dead Moni on the cold ground.

"Damn! This bitch ass nigga got nine lives!" Crazy G huffed, punching the steering wheel as he snatched off into traffic.

CHAPTER 12

HEADQUARTERS
HOURS LATER

Every regional was in attendance with the exception of Pap. Two young soldiers from Shields named LJ and Tay-Tay were selected for security purposes and stood at the door on high alert. The two delinquents were huge in stature and looked like they should have been playing football in college instead of gangbanging. Tay-Tay, at 19 years old, stood a hulking 6'3" and weighed in at 240 pounds of solid muscle. An unruly afro sat on top of his head and a permanent scowl was plastered on his face. LJ, although not as big as Tay-Tay, wasn't too far off at 6'1", 215. Long dreadlocks that twisted into frenali braids with the sides shaved bald was his style of choice. The duo looked like security guards at a nightclub.

Star, Buddha, Crazy G and Tito occupied the kitchen, going over small but necessary adjustments to the organization. Since Trindog's release their war had picked up intensely.

"So, everybody cool then, right?" Star asked from his seat at the kitchen table.

Buddha sat next to him while Tito and Crazy G posted across from them.

"Hell, yeah I'm straight." Buddah yawned.

"Aside from that shit earlier, I'm cool." Crazy G added.

"What 'bout you Tito?" Star questioned, ice grilling him.

"I'm Gucci," he replied, returning his mug.

"Aight," Star said, nodding his head. "Before we close out, though, me you and them two big youngin's ova there got some business to handle." He added standing up.

Crazy G and Buddah followed Star's que and stood up as well, and began to move the furniture in the living room.

"What business is that?" Tito asked, standing to his feet as well.

"That business is you's a snake ass nigga and don't belong with the status I blessed you with," he snapped, pointing his finger inches away from Tito's face.

"Fuck you mean, nigga?" Tito hissed, scrunching his face up. "I been nothin' but loyal to you and the nation. So, stop all'at cap!" He roared, not backing down.

Buddha and Crazy G watched the drama unfold in front of them with sly smirks on their faces.

"Loyal to who? Yo' dick?" Star cracked drawing snickers from the room. "This nigga right here got mad that me and my old flame started back fuckin' 'round. Instead of tellin' me to fall back and he had feelings for her, he runs back to my bitch and tells her where to find us."

Every head in the room instantly swung in Tito's direction, waiting on him to deny the allegations. But he never did. He stood there defiantly with his head held high. In his eyes Star was the snake for messing with TT in the first place.

"Naw, you ain't do no shit like that." Buddah stated trying to hide the smile that crept on his face.

"I did, nigga. But that don't make me no snake. This muthafucka the snake for fuckin' my girl behind my back then smiling in my face, preachin' all'at loyalty shit," he snapped, advancing on Star with his fist balled up.

"Hol' up, bro," Crazy G said, placing a firm hand on his chest. "That's still our leader, my nigga. Just take what you got comin and move on."

"Just give us the word and we a smash this tender dick ass nigga." Tay-Tay growled, slamming one hefty fist into the palm of his hand.

"Naw, y'all be easy. I got this," Star claimed waving off the goon squad. "So you wanna bear arms against me? The nigga that put you in this shit. For pussy. For a woman that wanted nothing to do with you long before I showed up," Star said, an angry smile spreading across his face as he pulled his shirt over his head, exposing his ripped chest, washboard abs, and sculpted arms. Even though he didn't work out as much when he was on lock, he still did calisthenics almost every morning.

"You forgot to add the nigga that stabbed me ina back."

"I knew TT had some good ass pussy." Crazy G whispered to Buddah, causing them to laugh uncontrollably.

"Let's make a deal. If I beat yo' ass, you no longer my regional and you owe the nation 20 bands." Star smiled pacing back and forth with both hands clasped behind his back.

"And if I win." He challenged confidently, removing his hoodie and passing his gun to Buddah.

"You get to stay regional and I owe you 20 bucks."

"Well you betta get my money ready cuz I'm 'bout to show yo' pretty ass how I'm comin," he claimed, bouncing around like Floyd Mayweather.

"Aye y'all don't break this shit up unless I say so." He informed assuming his fighter stance.

As soon as he was set, Tito rushed him with a two piece combo that he was barely able to slip. Tito was way faster than he looked. Before he could regroup, Tito was back at it. This time he faked with two up high, then caught Star in the ribs with a left hook that knocked the wind out of him. Star stumbled and tried to return a combo of his own, but Tito quickly stepped out of his range.

"C'mon now, Chief, you gotta do better than that," he spat sarcastically.

Without warning Star rushed in, feigning a jab, and Tito took the bait, giving Star time to land a vicious straight left-right cross combo, that snapped Tito's head back. He tried to return fire, but Star ducked and landed two haymakers to the mid-section that doubled him over. He grabbed the back of his neck with both hands and thrust it down until it connected with his knee. Busting his nose and sitting him on his back pockets. Sealing the deal for him. Star had to admit Tito had heart, but Star had spent the last 15 years in Gladiator school becoming a warrior.

"I can still fight." Tito mumbled trying to shake the Tweety birds that flew around his head.

"That shit over with. You done," Star said, towering over him. "I like yo' heart though. So, this is what I'ma do. You owe the nation 20 bucks. And you can keep yo' status," Star said, reaching out his hand to pull Tito up.

Tito reluctantly accepted his hand and stood to his feet.

"Shake up G."

"It's all love," Tito claimed shaking up with him.

"Aight, now let's get da fuck outta stance!"

LATER THAT NIGHT
COOK COUNTY CORRECTIONAL

Pap looked around the crowded bullpen, amazed and disgusted at the same time. He'd never been past the courthouse, now he was crammed in a holding tank with sixty other grown men who haven't showered in days. The smell was bad enough to make a garbage truck jealous. Almost every other dude wore a mean mug on his face as if he was auditioning for Chicago's toughest gangster. Four fights had already broken out while several dope fiends lay scattered on the floor, dope sick from withdrawal. Then to cap it all off he was starving. They'd only given him a quarter juice and a bologna sandwich with three pieces of bread. If not for the tan jumpsuits with the letters DOC plastered across them, he would have sworn he was in the circus. All the stories he heard about "Savage Life" had his mind running wild. He wasn't scared, but he would most definitely be cautious.

Savage Life was a group of individuals from all over the city that terrorized the county. The group of renegades robbed, stabbed and jumped anybody who opposed them. But they were infamous for what they called "G'tting' that Butt." After they knocked you out, they pulled your pants and spit in the crack of your ass. Not only did they humiliate you throughout the entire county, but in the streets as well. Once the officer reported this incident, the counselor automatically could call your next of kin, reporting that you've been sexually assaulted. Imagine trying to explain that to your people. *I wasn't reaped, they just spit in my ass…* disgusting.

Pap wasn't going at gunpoint. He knew if anything remotely close to that happened to him, he would never go home. He would surely beat or stab the culprits to death. His name along with several others were called. As they exited the bullpen they were given a bedroll containing hygiene, sheets, and blankets.

"What division I'm goin' into?" A Mexican inmate standing next to Pap asked. He was short and stocky and had tattoos covering his entire face.

"Division 9." The officer replied with a smirk.

"Hell yeah!" The dude yelled like he'd just won the lottery.

"You wanna go to max and deal with all that monkey ball shit?" The officer asked, confused. He was extremely tall with a head full of salt and pepper.

"I'm a gang member so it's only right I be with otha members," he claimed.

"Yeah. You sound just like them clowns. That's where you belong." The officer replied motioning for them to follow him.

They followed him down a series of tunnels that twisted and turned like an underground maze. They walked for what seemed like hours until they reached a big yellow gate. The words "Division 9" were painted on the top in big white letters. 9 was the worst division the county had to offer. It was the home of wolves, lions, and savages. Home of the knife talk and soap socks. It was where if you weren't going you didn't eat or use the phone… But worst of all it was the home of Savage Life.

Fuck, Pap thought as he stepped through the gates of hell.

THE NEXT DAY

Star cruised down the Dan Ryan in Kierra's Nissan Rogue without a care in the world. He wasn't riding dirty, so he let his foot abuse the gas pedal and opened up the V8 to a quick 75 miles per hour. He was almost to his exit when flashing blue and reds caught his attention. He navigated the truck to the shoulder of the road and slammed the gear in park.

"Driver, turn the car off now!" A familiar voice demanded.

What da fuck? Star thought as he turned the car off. "I gotta be trippin'," he mumbled as the officer stepped from the car and sashayed to his door.

A bloody Christina stood at his window with her hand wrapped tightly around her holstered Glock. It was mind boggling. She looked exactly like she did the night he stabbed her.

"Don't be scared, lil' bro, I bring good news." She smiled, pulling out her Glock. "Your world is going to burn to the ground. The flames will engulf you, and your mouth will taste of ash," she said in a demonic voice before levelling the gun with his face and firing. *Boc!*

"Ahhh! Shit!" Star yelled, jumping up from the couch, holding his face. He looked around in a daze until he remembered he was at home on the couch. Lately Christina was haunting him every night. He thought by setting her kids straight for life with their auntie she would let him be. But that only seemed to make matters worse. "Damn!" He huffed, wiping the cold from his eyes.

Vrrrmmm! Vrrrnnn! Vrrrmm! His phone vibrated in his pocket. He pulled it out and answered it without even looking.

"Yo."

"This is a collect call from an inmate at the Cook County jail. To accept charges, press 5 to—"

That was all Star needed to hear. He instantly pressed 5, silencing the monotoned operator, or so he thought.

"Thank you for using Securus. You may start the conversation now."

"Yoooo!" Star yelled loud enough to wake a sleeping Kierra.

"Yooo!" Pep yelled back. "What the fuck is up, nigga? Did shorty give you my message? Everything kosher out there? That nigga Crazy G good?" He rattled off.

"Slow down, jailbird. You been gone three days, not three years." Star teased.

"Fuck you, nigga."

"But to answer yo' questions. Shit been crazy fa' real. Like everybody tweaking. But ain't shit I can't handle. What's up with you, though. The lawyer talkin' good so you should be out soon," he said switching the phone to speaker. His stomach was rumbling, so he slipped into the kitchen to find something quick to eat.

"True. True. But look, this a free call so we only got 10 minutes. So, I need you to listen real quick." He stated seriously.

"Aight. Wassup?" Star said, tossing the phone on the marble countertop while he rummaged through the refrigerator.

"Look, shit ain't what it seems. Watch the company you keepin'. Niggas ain't right. Them big boys came askin' 'bout us. They even had a whole drawin' of the company with you as the owner," he said in code to let Star know the Feds were watching.

"Yeahh?" Star said, standing straight up. "I got some shit in play. I'm just waitin' on you."

"You have one minute left." The operator interrupted.

"Aight, say no more."

"Bet. I'ma send you a stack as soon as the phone hang up. Find a couple niggas to go to commissary for you. I know that county food bogus as hell."

"Thank you for using Securus. Goodbye!" The operator sung before hanging up.

"Dayum!" Pap hissed slamming the phone down.

He spun around and found all eyes on him. Division 9 pods were split into top deck and bottom deck. 12 cells were up top and 12 at the bottom. They alternate day room times every day. The top deck got three hours, then the bottom got three. Pap was housed on the top deck with a dude named Gutta. He was a gorilla of a man, but surprisingly he was as laid back as they came. They had a lot in common except they were in different gangs, but nowadays with the exception of a few areas, it didn't matter what you were, it only mattered where you were from.

"Aye, boy! We all gotta use them phones. So don't be slammin' them." A dark skin dude with dreads snapped. He was seated at one of the back tables by the showers and stalls, playing cards.

"Boy?" Pap said, looking around as if he'd lost something. "Ain't no boys this way; not period." he shot back

Though this was his first time being locked up, he was a stranger to the rules of the jungle. He peeped the play from a mile away. He was the new man on location and all eyes were on him, and he knew how he handled this situation would make or break him.

"You heard what I said, fam. Don't be slammin no phones."

"Or what, nigga? Fuck is you, the phone police or somethin'?" Pap challenged.

The deck was so quiet you could hear a roach fart. Every man stopped in his tracks to watch the dilemma unfold.

"Nigga, what?" The dude snapped, throwing his cards on the table and jumping to his feet. "Check it out, we finna bump shorty," he said waving Pap to the stalls, which they called the alley.

The alley was about the same size as a cell with three toilets and three sinks, making it impossible to fight. Most of the time it turned into a swinging contest and whoever hit the hardest won.

"Aight, it's whateva," Pap claimed following the dude but was cut off by Gutta.

"Aye, Trello, this my celly. We gone leave all'at shit where it's at. You said whachu said and he said what he said." Gutta stated calmly.

"Hell naw. Dat nigga just called me 12." Trello scoffed, shedding his DOC top like yesterday's trash, exposing his fat but muscular build.

"Nigga, didn't bro just say that shit was dead? That means that shit ova with." Another man spoke, smiling as if he had just told a joke. He was at least two inches taller than Gutta and had to have at least twenty extra pounds of muscle. He was caramel skinned with shoulder length dreads that were dyed red at the tips.

"Man, DT. You and Gutta always tryna run some shit, but it's cool. If that nigga woulda called one of y'all 12, the deck woulda flew." Trello huffed, snatching up his top and ice grilling Pap who returned his mug. It was clear Trello didn't want any smoke with either of the giants.

"Y'all ain't even have to do that. I woulda shot one with him," Pap claimed.

"Except it wouldn't be no one on one. Them scary ass niggas woulda tried to get you in the alley and jumped you," Gutta said.

"That's all they do is jump niggas." DT spat loud enough for Trello and his comrades to hear.

"Damn, that's a good lookin' out."

"This is my man's DT, or Ox. Whichever one is cool."

"Pap," he said, shaking hands with him.

"Aight, bet. Look, this really my shit right here. These niggas gone do whateva I say. Gutta told me you were on your way back home. So just sit back and enjoy the ride."

"Say less."

CHAPTER 13

THREE WEEKS LATER

Agent Fletcher's office was quiet church mouse, as he sat behind his cluttered desk glaring at his informant. "So," he said taking off his prescription Cartier frames and twirling them in his left hand. "You're trying to tell me that you had no knowledge of this second branch of lunatics on 57th," he asked searching the informant's face for any signs of deceit.

"No, not fa' real. It must be new," the informant claimed.

"Not fa' real? Which is it? You knew or you didn't? There is no in between."

"No, I didn't know. I've been out of the loop for a minute, remember?"

"Alrighty. I didn't want to do this," Fletcher claimed standing up and pulling out his cuffs. "Stand up! You're under arrest."

"Whoa! Whoa! Whoa! Aight! I knew about it. I just didn't wanna tell you cuz it was my area and I was tryna protect my right hand," Laylow said defeated.

"Tell me everything from the beginning and don't leave anything out."

"Aight."

"And Derrick?"

"Wassup?"

"Don't ever fucking lie to me again. Or I'll have your ass in jail so fast you'll make it in time for lunch." Fletcher warned.

"Man, I just told you about 5 bodies this nigga did right in front of me. Ain't that enough? I don't wanna snitch on my boy." He was suddenly regretting his decision to snitch in the first place.

"It's enough when I say it is! I don't see what the problem is anyway. Everybody thinks you're dead anyway."

Had it not been for dumb luck and Fletcher's fast thinking, everybody would have known Laylow was living. And probably would have killed him for his betrayal. The secretary at the hospital gave Crazy G the wrong room number purposely just to piss him off and it ended up playing right into Fletcher's hands. Once they discovered everybody assumed LayLow was dead, he immediately hatched a plan to deceive the GDs. He even came up with the script for LayLow's mother who hated the GDs and everything they stood for. So, convincing her was easy. After all, what mother wouldn't help her child in danger?

WABASH
HOURS LATER

The ranch style trap house was jumping as usual. Fiends constantly knocked on the back door in search of a high, while Tito, Tre, and Twan got their party on with Ms. Chocolate and friends. Even though Tito's status had yet to be restored, he was still able to be in the mix due to the fact Star gave his status to Tre who just so happened to be Tito's right-hand man. The seven of them turned the small, scarcely furnished living room into a party zone. Music blasted from the 42-inch flat screen that was stationed on the floor directly in front of a PS4. An old, tattered couch took up the middle of the floor surrounded by old take out trays and cigarette butts. Twan, Tre and Tito occupied the couch, while their companions gyrated to the beat in their laps.

"One of y'all niggas get da door," Tito said as he scooped up Ms. Chocolate and disappeared down the hall.

"You heard him, nigga, get the door." Tre stated tossing a handful of ones on Ms. Piggy who grinded on him as if her life depended on it.

"Maanm last time I checked I ain't the fuckin' corner boy." Twan huffed, tossing his dancer to the side and stomping to the door. Completely frustrated from the demands of Tre, he swung the door open without even peeking through the peephole, and was met by the business end of Trindog's Glock 23.

"Scream, you die, fuck boy," he hissed, grabbing Twan by the collar of his shirt and dragging him towards the living room.

Pewee and Raymoe immediately rushed the trap behind him and scurried off to secure the rest of the trap.

"Let's go, bitch," he growled, pushing him towards the living room.

Pewee and Raymoe already had Tito, Twan, and their mistresses on their knees in the middle of the floor at gunpoint.

"Bricks and Brickettes. Y'all know how this shit go. Tell me where that shit at and we good to go. But if y'all make me look for it, shit gone get ugly," he said putting his Glock to the back of Twan's head and pulled the trigger.

Boca! Twan's head snapped back violently, spraying blood and brain matter everywhere.

"Oh my gawd!" Ms. Piggy screamed.

A head nod from Trindog made Raymoe's twelve-gauge shotty roar to life and open up her chest wider than the Grand Canyon, sending her skidding across the floor. If he hadn't made his point earlier, he damn sure made it now. With the exception of the music blasting from the TV the living room was silent.

"Now let's try this shit again. Where that shit at?"

"Under the couch," Tito said without hesitation.

"Everything?"

"Yeah, everything," he whispered.

Trindog casually stolled over to the couch and kicked it over, and as promised two duffle bags stared back at him.

"Good boy, but unfortunately, you niggas picked the wrong day to be GD." He laughed, spinning around and letting his tool bang. *Boca! Boca! Boca! Boca!* When the dust settled, all that remained breathing was Trindog, Pewee, Raymoe, and Tito.

"Damn, you wasn't fuckin' 'round," Tito said standing to his feet, and admiring Trindog's handy work.

"I never do. Let's hurry up and split this shit. That music might not have drowned out all the noise," Trindog claimed, scooping up one of the duffle bags.

"Aye, don't forget," Tito said, tapping him on the shoulder.

"Forget what," he asked, spinning around.

Boca! Boca! Two shots from Tito's .40 cal caught Trindog in the chest and stomach, folding him instantly.

"Don't nothin' beat a cross but a double cross." He smiled standing over Trindog. He looked for Raymoe and Pewee's assistance, but the smiles on their faces told him everything he needed to know. He had been slimed out by his own men.

"These boys feel like OTM needs a new leader who is better than you," he claimed squeezing the trigger silencing Trindog forever.

Raymoe and Pewee grabbed the duffles and they quickly made their exit, $45,000 richer and with almost $100,000 worth of crack cocaine.

MEANWHILE
AT THE COUNTY JAIL

Gutta, Pap and DT sat at the very last table playing dominoes for pushups and conversing amongst themselves. Since his encounter with Trello, the trio had basically become inseparable. They worked out, ate, and played dominoes on a regular basis. They were from different parts of the city but were so much alike it was crazy. The more they hung out the more Pap learned from and about them.

Gutta was locked up for an armed robbery and attempted murder that one of his best friends told on to save himself. DT, on the other hand, was the devil himself. It was rumored that he single handedly took down the Mexican mob and got into a shootout with police that left an officer in critical. He was locked up for an attempted murder on the police and a slew of other charges. Before all the murder and mayhem, he had a promising career as a boxer, before the mob killed his father and woke his inner demon up.

"Domino, nigga!" Pap yelled, slamming down his last bone on the table aggressively.

"Maaan. This muthafucka gotta be hiding bones in his pocket or sum," Gutta said.

This was their fourth game, and Pap had won them all.

"This nigga had the domino since we started playing." DT added.

"C'mon now. You two big muthafuckas just mad cuz I ain't did not one pushup. Lemme get that 100." He teased.

"Aye, Gutta. Boy, the Heights on the news," someone yelled out.

Gutta immediately rose from the table and jogged over to the TV area where everybody gathered to watch the breaking news.

"I'm Golden Davis with Fox 32 and I'm standing in front of the very spot where officers engaged in a shootout less than four hours ago with Kiante Newman and three other unknown assailants. Though it is unclear how many fatalities there actually were, the Chicago Heights Police Department has confirmed all gunmen are deceased… Jill, back to you."

A single tear slid down the side of Gutta's face. It was clear that one of or all of the men in the shootout were close to him. He stormed over to the phone and the crowd parted like the Red Sea for the angry giant. He snatched the phone off the hook and began punching in numbers.

"C'mon now, Gutta. We know you mad but we all gotta use them phones," Trella said from his usual seat at the Spades table.

Before he could fully process what was going on, Gutta bolted over and hit him with a two piece that knocked him out of his seat. He followed up with a swift kick to the ribs that folded him into fetal position. One of Trello's homies jumped up from the card table and blindsided Gutta with a hook that sent him stumbling to the wall. DT and Pap wasted no time swarming the card table, and came to Gutta's aid. DT put a straight left upper cut combo on the dude who snuck Gutta and instantly pressed his snooze button while Pap chased the other around the deck, raining down blows on the back of his head. By now Gutta had recovered and pulled the phone out of the wall. He had the cord wrapped around his hand while the receiver dangled freely.

"Bitch ass niggas," he growled, swinging the phone.

It landed on top of Trello's head with a loud *crack!*, instantly opening him up, but Gutta didn't stop there. He hit him two more solid times, breaking Trello's jaw and nose in the process. Back up finally came, and the police rushed the deck, spraying mace everywhere. The entire deck was coughing up their lungs.

"Get da fuck down!"

***

"I know that I'm beneficial. I can't show no feelings/bently windows tinted. Now days ain't no time for me to kick it/business to attend to/They gone say that I been actin' different. I'm beyond they mental/I moved on from slinging drugs and robbin can't be thinkin' simple." Star sang along to Lil' Baby's "Real Spill" as he glided through the streets in his royal blue Aston Martin. He just dropped $100 thousand flat on the beauty and was feeling himself. The futuristic dashboard looked like a video game, while the

Italian leather seats seemed to caress his body. On top of that, Kierra was finally letting him back in their bedroom, plus he and TT were still getting their freak on every chance they got. So far, the moment everything seemed just right.

Vrrrnnn! Vrrrmmm! Vrrnn! His phone rattled in the cup holder stealing his attention… It was Kierra. "Wassup, bae," he answered.

"Baby, I-I need you to come home. I fucked up," she cried hysterically.

"Wait, slow down and tell me what's wrong," he replied making a wild U-Turn in the middle of the road.

"I don't wanna say it over the phone. I just need you to come home."

Star could feel his heart sink to the pit of his stomach. The tone in her voice let him know that whatever was wrong it was serious. He'd never heard her this shook, not even when she shot TT. He mashed the pedal and the V12 engine roared to life. It was time to see what the 100-thousand-dollar beauty could do.

He put the pedal to the metal all the way home and made it there in twenty minutes flat. His eyes almost popped out of his head at the sight of TT's coupe in the driveway. "Lord, please don't tell me she done killed this girl," he said out loud as he jumped from the Aston Martin and trotted to the door.

He grabbed the handle and the door swung open on its own.

What da fuck? he thought, pulling out his Glock and switching it to fully auto. He smelled a trap and refused to go out like dark skin Jermaine. As he stepped through the door with his Glock aimed high, the sight of a butt naked Kierra on all fours confused him. Her wrist was tied behind her back along with her ankles.

"What da fuck is going on," he asked.

"Don't move, muthafucka!" A familiar voice hissed, pressing something hard into his back.

CHAPTER 14

"I know that I'm beneficial/I can't show no feelings Bentley windows tinted/ Nowadays ain't no time for me to kick it/Business to attend to/ They gon' say that I been actin' different I'm beyond they mental/I moved on from slingin' guns and robbin' can't be thinkin' simple."

Star sang along to Lil Baby's *Real Spill* as he glided through the streets in his royal blue Aston Martin.

He just dropped a hundred thousand flat on the beauty and was feeling himself. The futuristic dashboard looked like a video game, while the Italian leather seats caressed his body. On top of all that, Kierra was finally letting him back into their bedroom. He and TT were still getting their freak on every chance they got. So, for the moment, everything seemed just right.

Vrrrmm! Vrrrmm! Vrrrmm! His phone rattled the cupholder, stealing his attention… It was Kierra.

"Wassup, bae?" he answered.

"Baby, I—I need you to come home. I fucked up!" she sobbed hysterically.

"Wait, slow down and tell me what's going on," he replied, making a wild U-turn in the middle of the road.

"I don't want to say it over the phone. I just need you to come home."

Instantly, he could feel his heart sink to the pit of his stomach. The tone in her voice let him know that whatever was wrong, it was serious. He'd never heard her shook, not even when she shot TT. He mashed the pedal, and the V12 roared to life. It was time to see what the hundred-thousand-dollar beauty could do. He put the pedal to the metal all the way home and made it there in twenty minutes flat. His eyes almost popped out of his head at the sight of TT's coupe in the driveway.

"Lord, please don't tell me she done killed this girl," he said out loud as he jumped out the car and trotted to the door.

He grabbed the handle, and the door swung open on its own.

"What the fuck!" he thought, pulling out his Glock and switching it to fully auto.

He smelled a trap and refused to go out like dark-skin Jermaine. He stepped through the door with his Glock aimed high, and the sight of Kierra face down, ass up, with her hands tied behind her back stumped him.

"Da'fuck is going on?" he asked.

"Don't move, muthafucka!" a familiar voice hissed as they jammed something hard into his back. "Drop that gun."

Reluctantly, Star did as he was told and raised his hands in the air.

"Now turn around."

Star turned around and locked eyes with a water-gun-wielding TT. She had nothing on except a pair of red bottom heels. Her mocha skin was oiled to perfection, with her hair down and slightly crinkled the way he liked it.

"Hey, daddy," she giggled, pumping the water gun.

He looked Kierra's way, and she shot him a wink, then licked her lips seductively. Instantly, his dick stiffened in his pants as thoughts of fucking both their brains out flooded his mental. He tried to pull TT into him, but she stepped out of his reach.

"Uh-uhn." She pushed him down onto the couch across from Kierra. "I'm running the show."

She joined Kierra on the couch and sprayed her entire body with the oil-filled water gun. Satisfied with the amount, she ditched the water gun and slowly started rubbing it in, making sure to show Kierra's ass extra attention.

"You like that, daddy?" She bit her bottom lip and stared directly into his eyes.

Star felt like his dick was going to burst through his pants, he was so hard. He tried to join them, but both ladies shook their heads.

"Damn, what y'all on wit' me?" he mumbled, flopping onto the couch.

"I told you… Ima let you know when you can join in, comprende?" TT smiled.

He nodded his head and bit down on his jaw. He was on fire and ready to pound them out. TT continued her massage, then dipped her hand into Kierra's wetness. She darted in and out of her a couple of times, then sucked the juices off both fingers. Palm gripping Kierra's plump cheeks, she spread them, then stuck her face into her honey pot.

"SSSS-um-oooohhh," Kierra moaned, arching her back.

TT rolled her tongue perfectly while her thumb made its way to Kierra's clit.

"Y-Yeah. U-uuh-Uuuhhn. Ah." Kierra grinded into her face.

TT slurped and licked Kierra's walls like her life depended on it. Before she knew what hit her, Kierra's legs started to shake violently, then she was covering TT's face in her juices.

"Ooohn! Unh-ooooo. T-TT," she whispered, squeezing her eyes shut.

To hell with waiting—Star had seen all he needed to see. He pulled his shirt over his head, kicked off his shoes, and ripped down his pants and boxers in one swift motion. Knowing what time it was, TT dropped to her knees and guided his throbbing pole into her mouth.

"Fuck me, bae," Kierra whined, but TT was on a mission.

She bopped her head hard while her hands slowly twisted at the base of his dick. Then, without warning, she swallowed him until his balls were on her chin and she was gagging. Star's toes instantly curled. He had to snatch his pole out of her mouth or cum right then and there.

"Fuck, TT," he whispered harshly.

He climbed behind Kierra and slid into her searing box. TT slid under Kierra and licked her clit while Star pounded her out.

"AAAhhn! Y-yaaa'll! W-ooooo! Ooo my fuckin' God," Kierra cried out.

Star smacked her oily ass as he dug inside of her. Pregnant pussy was definitely the best pussy. She was as slippery as a bottle of baby oil and clung to him like a crackhead holding his last rock.

"I—I. S-Star! Ahh!" Kierra moaned as she was rocked by another breathtaking orgasm.

After untying her arms, Star pulled her down on his face. Taking the opportunity, TT mounted his dick and arched her back just right, steadying herself on his abs. She started galloping faster than a pony.

"Star," they moaned in unison.

Hearing them both moan his name at the same time was driving him crazy. He couldn't believe Kierra was getting down like this. When TT claimed she'd handle her, never in his wildest dreams did he imagine this.

"Ahh-Ahh-oooo-Aah," TT moaned as she bounced on his pole.

Star's tongue darted in and out of Kierra while she humped into his face. Then he did the unthinkable and stuck his tongue in her ass.

"Ooooo! Eat that ass, baby," she cried.

"I'm finna cum!" TT announced, galloping faster before squirting all over him and the couch.

Though he tried to fight it, he was ready to explode.

"Arrggh! I'm 'bout to…" he groaned.

Later that night at Headquarters

"You might as well stop tryna call that fuck nigga," Star clenched his jaw. "This shit got his name all over it. I shoulda smoked his bitch ass when he told Kierra that fuck shit."

Buddah and Crazy G listened from their seats on the living room couch as they all tried to come up with a logical explanation as to why Tito was missing in action. Star already knew what was up the second Buddah explained the scenario. He was just making sure he had all his ducks in a row before he put Tito on blast and marked him for death.

"You really think Tito grimy enough to do some shit like that?" Crazy G asked.

"Why not? He can get back at me and come up in one swoop," Star replied.

"Yeah, I see that part… I just don't see him being cutthroat enough to clap both his day-one homies. Them niggas was like real brothers," Buddah claimed, pulling out an ounce of purple Runtz and a pack of Backwood Stout.

"And you said that nigga Trindog was slumped with them. That's what's throwing me off," Crazy G added.

Star listened to both his regionals and had to admit they both had valid points, but he couldn't shake the nagging feeling in his gut. He knew Tito was responsible. For one, the money and dope was gone from the stash spots, and for two, he seemed to be the only survivor and was M.I.A.

"All that shit sound valid." He reached into the ounce and pulled out a couple nuggets. "But everything in me say this his work. Ain't no way OTM kidnapped him, and they know how that shit go. You give the merch up, you give yo life up."

"Yeah, makes sense," Buddah claimed, putting the finishing touches on his Backwood.

"So how you wanna play it?" Crazy G looked his way.

"The only way to play it… shoot on sight when we find his bitch ass. He's an enemy to the people."

"You know we gon' have to switch everything up? That nigga know way too much," Buddah pointed out.

"His stupid ass coulda over-hit us if he woulda been thinkin'." Star shook his head.

"He don't know shit 'bout 57th," Crazy G sparked his Backwood to life.

"Which is why that's gon' be the new headquarters until we exterminate that bitch ass nigga," Star locked eyes with Crazy G.

"I shoulda kept my shit closed," he spat, clearly annoyed.

He didn't want Star all over his shoulder telling him what to do and when to do it. He loved 57th because it was his, and he got to do what he wanted when he wanted.

"Don't worry, G. I ain't gon' cramp yo shit. We just gon' meet there. Then after that we gone. That's still yo shit." Star smiled.

"I hope so," Crazy G claimed, exhaling a cloud of smoke. "We gotta change phones too. I'm tellin' you, muthafuckas was followin' me."

"Right. But how you wanna go 'bout switchin' traps?" Buddah questioned.

"Simple." Star flamed his wood and took a long pull. "It's like this…"

ON 79TH & KINGSTON

The trap house was filled with about twenty Black Stones, and every one was either known for their gunplay or held some type of status for the mob. Tito made his way to the middle of the crowd, flanked by RayMoe and Pewee. He opened the duffels filled with money and coke, and immediately the house fell silent. He started pacing the circle like he'd seen Star do numerous times and instantly became drunk with power.

"Aye, I ain't here to change shit y'all got going on. Or try to send y'all off to do some shit I wouldn't do." He paused to make sure he still had their attention. "Shit, we all want the same shit… to ice all them bitch ass GDs."

"Ain't you GD?" one of the Black Stones blurted out.

"Yeah, I am. But that don't mean we don't share the same hate for them niggas. All y'all know I was just on the front line for them niggas, and they backdoored me. So I say all that to say, any nigga who lock in wit' me gon' get fed. Any nigga who put they trust in me gon' get rich."

"Man, where da fuck Trindog?" another Stone yelled.

"When me, him, and Pewee set this play up, he got hit in a bang out and ain't make it." He shared a brief glance with Pewee and RayMoe. "That's why it's time to slide. I know everything 'bout bitch ass niggas. Just to show y'all brothers I ain't cappin', everybody leavin' this bitch wit' a stack." He started digging in the bag.

Chatter instantly filled the living room. Some men wanted to lock in with Tito, while others saw him for exactly what he was.

"You expect us to believe that shit?" a tall darkskin dude named 50 said, scrunching up his face.

"Aye, check it out." Pewee stepped to the center of the circle. "That shit 'bout Trindog facts. Me and RayMoe was right there. I saw Tito out two of his day-one niggas down behind that shit… so I know ku fuckin' wit' us. But ain't you niggas tired of starvin'? I'm tired of bro nem dyin' for nothin' at all. You niggas ain't blind. I know y'all see we losin'. Ion know 'bout you niggas, but I'm tired of playin' backseat to them niggas. This our chance."

If Tito didn't have them convinced, he definitely did now. He could literally see the change in their faces once Pewee was done. Unbeknownst to Tito, Pewee was like their honorary leader. When Trindog was away, it was he and RayMoe who held things together. The Black Stones had real love and respect for Pewee, versus with Trindog they feared him.

"I ain't gon' lie. I wasn't fuckin' wit' you at first. But if Pewee vouchin' for you, then I'm bangin' this OTM shit 'til I die," 50 claimed, holding up his Glock.

Everybody in the house followed suit. There was enough guns in the air to start a mini gun shop.

"OTM!" RayMoe yelled.

"OTM!" they shouted back.

DAYS LATER ON 57TH

"You lyin', nigga. Ain't no way Kierra gave you a 3-sum. Especially wit' the bitch she shot for fuckin' you. Nah, I ain't buyin' that. You frontin' yo shit." Crazy G shook his head as he rubber banded another stack of money.

He and Star were in his living room preparing for their re-up. Since Tito skated with fifty thousand in cash and forty in product, they agreed to put the money back out of their personal stashes.

"Nigga, on the G, I ain't frontin' shit. They probably still in bed together right now with sore pussy and sore throats. I been fuckin' the shit out they ass off that Blue Chew," Star bragged.

"Damn, was it fluky at first or y'all got right to it?"

"Nah. We was in sync the whole time… They think I can't tell they did that shit before. You shoulda seen TT eatin' her pussy from the back." Star smiled as the image popped in his brain.

"Damn! That shit sound ova good. So who got the best pussy?"

"Both my bitches gotta bomb. Fuck you talkin' 'bout."

"C'mon now, nigga." Crazy G raised an eyebrow in disbelief. "You tryna tell me that both they shit feel exactly the same?"

***

"Nah, I'm tryna tell you they feel good in different ways, nigga." He smirked, tossing a stack into the bag.

Crazy G laughed. "Good fuckin' answer. Good answer, my nigga."

"Man, where da fuck is Buddah and Tae-Tae? It don't neva take that long to clear an already empty trap." Star huffed, pulling out his phone.

He'd sent Buddah and Tae-Tae to clean out their old traps almost an hour ago.

"They should be on they way back. You know Buddah fat ass lazy as hell. He probably got Tae-Tae big swole ass doin' all the liftin'." Crazy G smiled.

"On everything." Star dialed Buddah.

***

"C'mon, nigga. You takin' all damn day." Buddah half-joked as he leaned on his truck.

"We coulda been done if yo fat ass woulda helped me... I mean, you da one who got all this extra shit in da trap anyway." Tae-Tae held up the box filled with video game accessories for emphasis.

"You got all them muscles for what? Them lil' ass boxes can't be givin' you all that trouble. Don't tell me that shit for show." He laughed.

Poca! Poca! Blah! Blah! Poc! Poc! Poc! Blah!

Shots rang out and slammed into Tae-Tae, knocking him off his feet. Buddah ducked behind his truck, pulled out his Glock, and let it speak.

Boc! Boc! Boc!

He fired at the car as it crawled past. Tito and RayMoe hung out the window, letting their tools bang.

Poc! Poc! Poc! Blah!

Bullets zipped past or slammed into the side of his truck, rocking it.

"I'm hit! I'm hit! Arrggh!" Tae-Tae yelled, pulling out his Ruger.

Boca! Boca! Boca!

He fired blindly at their car.

Scuuurrrt!

Pewee stomped on the gas, leaving a cloud of smoke, but not before Tito and Buddah locked eyes. Buddah chased after their car, squeezing his trigger until his gun de-cocked, signaling it was empty.

"Damn!" He huffed, running back for Tae-Tae.

The second he popped from behind the truck, Tae-Tae swung his Ruger Buddah's way with murder in his eyes.

"Whoa! Nigga, it's me!" Buddah yelled, covering his face. "Can you move?"

"I-I think so," Tae-Tae wheezed.

Buddah quickly helped him to his feet, then into the truck's back seat. From what he could see, Tae-Tae was hit in the stomach and thigh and bleeding profusely. Buddah let the V-8 growl as he zipped through the streets.

"Hold on, nigga. We gon' get you straightened out. Just stay wit' me."

DIVISION 9, COOK COUNTY JAIL

Pap half-walked, limping through the tunnels on his way to court. The shackles bit into his ankles while the waist chain connected to a blue box restricted his breathing. Two members of the Emergency Response Team, known as ERT, escorted him in their full riot gear, ready to pounce at any sign of resistance.

The fight with Trello landed him and Gutta three months in the hole on elevated security, which was on IF. IF was the worst hole/segregation in the county. It was specifically for staff assaulters and weapon violators.

ERT worked the wing instead of regular C.O.s, making everything ten times worse. ERT followed the rules by the book, and if you stepped out of line, they physically put you in your place.

Then to make matters worse, his lawyer got him an emergency bond hearing without his knowledge. Now he had to go in front of a judge that didn't like him, looking like a mass murderer. He just prayed that the judge understood.

HOURS LATER

"On the G, as soon as I'm back, I'ma smoke every one of them faggot ass niggas. On Folks nem grave." Tae-Tae promised, slamming his fist into his palm.

He was laid in his bed fresh out of surgery with pure rage in his eyes. The bullet to his stomach was a through-and-through and would heal quickly, but the one he caught to the thigh chipped his femur and would take 4–6 weeks to heal.

Aside from the zipper down his stomach and his leg being wrapped in a cast, he felt fine—or in the doctor's words, one of the lucky ones.

"C'mon now, G. You know what's understood ain't even gotta be explained. Right now, all you gotta do is rest up. By the time you healed up, the Moes gon' be extinct." Star claimed, sitting at the foot of the bed.

Buddah sat in the chair while Crazy G stood guard at the door. After Buddah delivered the news, Crazy G and Star rushed over and waited until he was awake.

"I can't believe that snake ass nigga… Tito. You sure it was him?" Crazy G asked.

"Ona G, we locked eyes as they slid past. He was wit' that big goofy ass nigga RayMoe," Buddah explained.

"RayMoe!" Crazy G spat. "I been tryin' to clap that fake tough ass nigga for a long time.""You shoulda let me choke that pussy nigga lights out when he first violated," Tae-Tae growled, his voice full of emotion.

"I wish I did. But we gon' catch his ass. I'ma make sure you the one to put that snake ass nigga lights out. So rest easy. We gon' be back in the a.m." Star stood to his feet. "You a good lil' nigga, Tae-Tae. Stay solid and you gon' make it to the top," he added, nodding at Buddah and Crazy G.

THE NEXT MORNING
DIVISION 9

Pap paced his tiny cell with a vengeance. Yesterday his judge uplifted his probation hold, and he was set to have a bond hearing in the next 30 days. He was beyond anxious and couldn't wait to finally receive a bond hearing. That's all he could think about.

He couldn't wait to beat down Lay Lay's walls, secure his money, then step away from the streets for good. That was, of course, after he personally disposed of OTM.

By him being in the hole, he still hadn't received the news about switching sides or Tae-Tae being shot. Once he did… he would be seeing red. He never liked Tito from the jump. Since the very first day TT brought him around. He saw right through his mask and knew he was putting a ten on a two. He was corny and always wanted the spotlight.

Tap! Tap! Tap!

Three quick raps on his vent shattered his daydreams.

"Wassup!" He yelled, stepping on his toilet so he could be right at the vent.

"What you on over there?" DT asked.

"Shit, pacin' the fuck out this floor thinkin' 'bout this bond hearing… What you on?"

"Shit, waitin' on them to tell me where I'm goin'. If I ain't goin' back to 9, I'm refusing."

"Damn, you do get out today. That 30 days flew," Pap claimed.

DT only received 30 days because he didn't use a weapon. The only reason he was on elevated security and high-risk movement was because of his disciplinary history. He was a known knockout artist and didn't discriminate with inmates or officers.

"On foe nem grave it feel like we got here last week." He laughed. "You told Gutta?"

"I think his ass sleep. I been callin' his ass all mornin'."

"He gon' be up at trays."

"True… But on some real shit, gang, if I don't land on a deck wit' you before you slide, go out there and stay out the way. The streets is dead, my nigga. This shit right here for goofies. Even if you gotta do a couple years in the joint. That's lil' shit. A lot of these niggas gon' die behind these walls. And a lot of them that's around you don't wanna see you winnin'… Ion mean to preach, my nigga, but you already ran it up. Got a shorty who rockin' wit' you. Snatch her up and get da fuck out the Raq before it's too late. The only shit that come behind this is a life sentence or early grave."

CHAPTER 15

DAYS LATER

"TT!" Kierra yelled, shaking her awake.

"MMM," she groaned, covering her head with a pillow.

"Get up. We need to talk."

"Can't it wait 'til I get up?" She peeked up at her.

Kierra hovered over with a mug plastered on her face and her arms crossed. Right then and there TT knew drama was around the corner. She knew Kierra like the back of her hand.

"Wassup, Ki?" she huffed, sitting up and rubbing her eyes. She was dog tired.

Last night it was as if Star was possessed by some type of demon. He fucked and licked them every which way. The X pills and liquor he consumed had him seeing red. Their freak-off lasted until the wee hours of the morning. It was amazing that Kierra was out of bed fully dressed.

"You know exactly wassup, T," Kierra said sarcastically.

"No, I don't. So let me know. I'm tired as hell," TT replied nervously.

Kierra was a loose screw that was liable to snap at any moment. She'd already shot TT in the shoulder when she caught her in bed with Star months ago. Plus, the angry look in her eyes made TT extremely uncomfortable.

"I bet you tired." She forced a fake smile. "Now what the fuck you tryna pull?"

"Whatchu mean what I'm tryin' to pull?" TT scrunched her face up, instantly irritated. "I ain't tryin' to pull shit. So don't start this emotional shit, please." She pulled the sheets over her head, but Kierra snatched them back off.

"Bitch! Don't play wit' me because I will get on ya ass, pregnant and all!"

"Kierra!" TT jumped out of bed. "I ain't tryin' to pull shit. I love Star. Just like I love yo crazy ass. I'm not tryin' to take yo spot. I'm cool wit' the way we are. I'm chillin'. You can calm down."

TT wrapped her arms around her, but she didn't return her hug, nor was she convinced.

"That's what you said last time. So I ain't tryna hear that shit."

TT claimed, pinching the bridge of her nose in frustration. "This is nowhere near the same."

"The fuck it ain't."

"We were six-fuckin'-teen dealin' wit' a creep ass grown man who didn't give a fuck about neither one of us as long as he was runnin' dick in us wheneva, whereva."

TT rolled her eyes and snaked her neck. "That's how."

"So, if it's not the same… You ain't gone care if I lay down some rules then?" she raised her brow.

"Oh my Gooood! Whateva, Ki. If that's gone make you believe me, then be my guest."

"You can't fuck Star unless I'm present."

"Aight."

"Saturday is my day with him alone."

"Done."

"And one more thing… You can't get pregnant."

"Uhh, I-um… I'm already P."

"I fuckin' knew it!"

MEANWHILE

Crazy G made a left on Kingston, and a light smirk crept on his face. A couple of the Moes were outside doing what he liked to call "dangling," which meant they were so engulfed in what they were doing, they were oblivious to the sharks circling them.

"Spin back through, then we gone chase they bitch ass down," Star instructed, switching his 50-shot Glock to fully auto.

He had it filled to capacity with hydra shocks, ready to body anything in his path. Crazy G did as Star instructed, and as soon as they made it halfway up the block, he slammed the gear in park, and they jumped out with their guns aimed high.

"On that car!" Pewee yelled, ducking behind a parked car and pulling out his XD.

Star aimed his Glock at the crowd, but before he could shoot—

Boca! Boca! Boca!

Pewee let his tool bang, grazing Star in the neck.

"Fuck!" he yelled, scrambling for cover.

Crazy G swung his 1911 Pewee's way.

Blocka! Blocka! Blocka! Blocka!

His .45 woke up the block, but his aim was off, so his bullets sailed harmlessly over Pewee's head. Star aimed where he thought Pewee was and squeezed—

FFFaaaattt!

The Glock jerked violently in his hands as over 20 hydra shocks chewed up the car. One of the slugs ripped through and found a home in Pewee's calf.

"Arrggh!" he cried as he spilled to the ground.

Just as they were advancing on Pewee, Ray Moe appeared out of nowhere clutching an AK-47 with a banana clip.

Doc! Doc! Doc! Doc! Doc!

He let the street sweeper roar, waving it back and forth. The .223s ate through everything in their path, forcing Crazy G and Star back into their car.

Quickly, Star slammed the gear in reverse and stomped on the pedal.

Scccuuuurrt!

Their Honda screeched up the block and turned the corner as RayMoe chased after them.

BACK AT THE HOSPITAL

"Damn folks," TaeTae said with a mouth full of food. "I'm happy as hell you came. This hospital food ain't shit." He was sitting up in bed munching on a double quarter pounder with cheese.

"I'm already knowin', G," Buddah replied in between bites of his own burger. "I had that goofy ass COVID shit. Put a nigga in the hospital for two weeks. The highlight of my day was when baby girl came through the door wit' food."

"Baby girl?" TaeTae repeated. "What, yo girlfriend?"

"My BM, nigga."

"You got a baby mama?" TaeTae looked at Buddah like he had two heads.

"Duh, nigga. Who don't got a baby mama, nigga? You actin' all shocked and shit."

"Yeah, I know allat. It's just you don't eva talk about it. Shit, I ain't neva seen you wit' a girl."

"That's 'cause I don't bring my house to the trenches, and I don't bring the trenches to my house. The less these niggas know 'bout you, the harder it is to set up. Or what the shorties say—back door. The streets grimy, G ball. Niggas get it fucked up tryna make a career out this shit, when you supposed to get in and out. Growth and Development… At least that was Larry Hoover's message and goals."

"Damn. You went all Malcolm X on a nigga. I was just sayin'. I ain't know you had a BM."

"It's a lot you don't know 'bout me." He smiled, stuffing a handful of fries into his mouth.

"I see… But what about that other shit I asked you 'bout?"

"I'ma have it before you get released tomorrow."

"Bet." TaeTae smiled wickedly. "But you can't tell big bro. Ion wan' him tryna talk me out this shit… Aight?"

"Aight."

"Naw nigga, slap it."

"Slap it?" Buddah's face wrinkled in confusion.

"Like merch it." He laughed. "I be forgetting how old you are."

"Maan, you lil niggas got a new sayin' every day." Buddah shook his head. "Ona G, I ain't gone say shit."

A COUPLE HOURS LATER

"Ion know what you want me to say, Kierra. You act like I did that shit on purpose," Star said, switching his phone to his left ear.

He was held up at TT's apartment, pacing the floors with his Glock dangling at his side. He was already sizzling that Pewee and RayMoe had almost killed him. His neck still throbbed and burned from where Pewee grazed him, and Crazy G was trying to spin through Kingston again. He was on 100 and not in the mood to hear Kierra cry over spilled milk. What did she think was going to happen? They were throwing a freak show every other night. Plus, TT and him had already had unprotected sex numerous times.

"Nigga, you know exactly what I want you to say. Tell the hoe to get an abortion," Kierra hissed, venom dripping from every word.

"What da fuck I look like, Kierra? You know I ain't doin' no shit like that. I don't support no goofy shit like that, period… Like why you so mad anyway?"

"Because neither one of y'all seem to give a fuck 'bout how I feel. I already let her share a bed wit' us to make you happy. I ain't sharin' my baby's father wit' her. Hell no. The hoe ain't takin' my spot. Hell no! Fix this shit or I will!" she yelled, then hung up.

"Goofy ass shit," he growled, sitting his phone on the table as he took a seat.

All he could think about was killing Tito and OTM. It was obvious that Tito had put the Moes on point. Star had been down 79th and Kingston many times, and never had they ever responded guns blazing. The money and bricks he took from them seemed to put some life in them. Even though he promised TaeTae he was going to let him kill Tito, he knew he was going to be the one to end the serpent's life. Unlike most of his victims, he wouldn't do it with a gun. It would be with his 8-inch bowie knife.

Vrrrmm! Vrrrmm! His phone buzzed, hopping across the table. He reached over and pressed the volume button, silencing the call. He didn't feel like tweaking with Kierra. He'd talk to her when he got home.

Vrrmm! Vrrmm! His phone rang again.

"Wassup, Ki?" he answered.

"Umm… is this Star?" a feminine voice asked.

"Who this?" He replied, looking at the screen. It read *unknown caller.*

"LayLay."

"LayLay?... Aw, Pap shorty. My bad, gotta lot of shit on my mind. What's the word?"

"Dang! That's crazy you don't even remember me," she said in her usual high-pitched tone.

"Naw it ain't like that, ona G. I got a new phone. Shit just been crazy today."

"You ain't answer my FaceTime or shit. Ima remember that shit," she half-joked. "But I got a message from Pap."

"Aight, what he need? Everything everything?" he questioned, his playful demeanor evaporating.

"He been in the hole, that's why he ain't been callin'. But he wrote a letter and don't want me to say it over the phone."

"You want me to drop the lo right now?"

"Yeah."

"Don't try no funny shit. Cuz my Glizzy don't discriminate," he warned, his voice low and intimidating.

"Boy, just drop yo location. You ova east niggas be killin' me." She laughed.

"As long as you know. And I need you to grab me some Backwoods and somethin' to eat. Ima CashApp you the money."

"Nah, you gone pay me for my services too, nigga."

"And you got the nerve to get down on ova east niggas. Yo lil ass somethin' else."

"You don't know the half."

"Aight, hurry up. I got shit to do."

MEANWHILE

"Is there something you want to tell me?" Agent Fletcher questioned.

He was seated behind his desk with one leg folded over the other, his brow cocked like a pistol, and his lips tight. A blind man could see he was pissed.

"Uh… No, I told you everything I know. I swear I don't know shit else." Laylow squirmed in his seat.

Fletcher's stare was making him uncomfortable.

"Sooo you don't know who these guys are?" he said, sliding a packet across the desk.

Laylow's heart instantly leaped in his chest as he flipped through Buddah, RayMoe, Tito, and Pewee's mugshots. He was starting to realize how deep shit was and wanted out but knew that would cost him his freedom, and he was nowhere near ready to spend the rest of his life behind bars.

"I know them. But I don't know who this is." Laylow slid TaeTae's mugshot back.

"Don't you fuckin' bullshit me!" Fletcher jabbed a finger in his direction. "You know exactly who that is! I told you to lie to me again and we're through."

"Maan, I swear to God I don't know who dude is. Why would I lie? I can tell you anything 'bout any one of these niggas. Especially him." He slid Pewee's picture back to him.

"Oh yeah? Like what?" Fletcher snatched up the mugshot.

"He be wit' OTM. And he the one who shot me."

"OTM? What the fuck is an OTM?"

"Only the Moes. They Black P Stones that be into it wit' us and some otha G.D.'s."

"So who the fuck is this again? I thought he was the GDs." Fletcher held up Tito's mugshot.

"That's Tito. He is GD." Laylow nodded.

"Well, why is my surveillance team telling me he's with these two almost every day?" He tapped Pewee and RayMoe's picture. "Even shot at these two with them," he added, nudging Buddah and TaeTae's photo.

"You sure?" Laylow asked, standing up.

"Positive."

Fletcher could practically see the wheels turning in Laylow's head and had to restrain himself. He wanted to smile, jump, and click his heels together. This case was huge. Not only did he have the Gangster Disciples caught red-handed on a slew of crimes—now he would be able to indict the Black P Stones as well. If he pulled this off successfully, his name would definitely go in the history books as one of the best agents in history. Plus, he was in the process of bringing down two brothers who were contract killers for the Santos Cartel. Once he tied a bow around everything, he would be set.

CHAPTER 16

LATER THAT NIGHT

"Damn, I wish I woulda known you was this cool a long time ago." LayLay smiled as she lounged on the couch.

"Why?" Star challenged.

He was seated at the kitchen table rolling another Backwood. They had been posted at TT's spot for almost three hours, smoking and conversing about all their problems… Well, really *his* problems, but with her occasionally giving her opinion or advice.

"Because we coulda been hangin' out, kickin' it. Stop actin' like I ain't cool as hell. I was just yo therapist for the last two hours," she looked his way.

"You wasn't my therapist." He laughed, joining her on the couch. "You a shorty. You too young to be my therapist," he added, sparking the Backwood to life.

"Too young? Boy, how old are you?" She snatched the blunt from him. "I'm grown as hell and been doin' grown people things." She licked her lips and looked him up and down.

Right then and there Star knew what she was hinting at, and he knew he should have checked her or at least removed himself from the situation, but he couldn't bring himself to do it. The lust shining in her eye had him. Plus, the skin-tight Kapri pants and half-top with her back out made his dick jump in his pants the second he opened the door. Her juicy lips and glowing skin sealed the deal. Pap had been nothing but loyal to Star since he'd been released from prison and was the main person who helped Star reunite the Gangster

Disciples—so fucking LayLay should have been the furthest thing from his mind. Except he wasn't thinking with his big head. His little head took control the second she licked her juicy lips. Then his eyes landed on her fat pussy print—it was really a wrap.

He rubbed up and down her thigh, and just like he thought, she spread her legs wider and laid back, giving him full access. With the quickness, he unbuttoned, then pulled her pants down.

"Damn, shorty," he mumbled, staring at her fatty.

She was hairless and smelled like mangos. He had to taste that. He kneeled down and sucked her lips into his mouth, then devoured her.

"Oooouu yeah," she moaned.

Star swirled his tongue viciously while his fingers dipped in and out of her wetness.

"AAhh—Ooooo—Aahh." She tossed the Backwood aside and gripped his hair with two hands.

LayLay tasted the way she smelled, and it was driving Star crazy. He swirled his tongue in figure eights and X's, making sure to show her lips some attention every now and then. Unable to hold back any longer, LayLay was covering Star's face in a milky mess.

"Ooooh—Ahhh." She cried out, barely above a whisper.

"Turn ova. I wanna see that fat ass bounce," he demanded, pulling out his rock-hard monster without hesitation.

She rolled onto her stomach just as Star slid a pillow under her to give her back the perfect arch.

"Damn."

"Ooohhh."

They moaned in unison. He filled her to capacity, and she was tighter than anything he'd ever slid in. He long-stroked her, giving her every inch.

"Oooohh. Aaaah. Oooooohhh," she moaned into the couch cushion.

Instantly, she was creaming, covering Star's log in her juices. He wrapped an arm around her neck, stuck his tongue in her ear, and pounded her with all his might.

"Oooohhh—Ahhh—Ahh! Oooooh—oooooo. My God!" she screamed.

Star was giving LayLay grown-man dick, turning her out, and she was instantly hooked.

"Mmmhm. Talk. That. Grown. Shit. Now!" he huffed.

"Oooooo—ooooo—oooooo! Oh my—my." She cried out, trying to wiggle free, but he held her in place.

Slish! Slish! Slish! Her wetness sounded off with every stroke.

"Fuck, this pussy wet," he groaned, pulling out.

He was almost about to finish early. She was super-soaker wet and tight as mosquito pussy. Young snapper was definitely giving pregnant pussy a run for its money.

"Roll over. I wanna look at that sexy ass face when you cum on this dick," he claimed, rubbing her ass.

LayLay rolled over, and Star tossed both legs over his shoulders, then slammed into her mercilessly.

"Ahh! Wait!" she screeched, placing both hands onto his stomach.

He smacked them away and continued his assault, diving so deep his tip poked her cervix.

"Ooooooohh-oooooooh! Star!" she hollered, digging her nails into his back.

Her mouth hung wide open while she squeezed her eyes shut as a breathtaking orgasm rocked her world.

"Open your eyes! Look at me!" he demanded, swirling his hips.

She stared into his eyes while he pounded her out.

"Ssss! I'm finna cum!" he groaned, picking up the pace. "I'm finna cum in yo pussy."

"D-D-Do it. Oooooh! C-Cum in my pussy." She gripped his back and pulled him all the way in.

"Arrggghh. Mmmmmm." He groaned as he released in big globs. "Damn shorty," he added, then went limp on top of her.

"Oh my God… I ain't neva been fucked like that," she whispered, still tingling all over.

Star was thinking the exact same thing but refused to say it. He didn't want to let her know she had him hooked.

"You ain't gotta say it. I know my shit the bomb, boy," she said as if she was reading his mind.

"Yeah, you good," he said nonchalantly.

"Good?" She rolled her eyes. "Nigga, did you see your face when you came? Yo back got stiff and all. Don't play."

Star just shook his head with a sly smirk on his face, then laughed, then frowned. Instantly, thoughts of Pap flooded his mind. He was dead wrong and knew it. He tried to find a way to justify his actions but came up empty every time.

"Nah, that's Lil Bro. He ain't tripping off no thotty… He ain't like that bitch-ass nigga Tito," he thought.

"Why you lookin' like that?" she asked, shattering his thoughts.

"Ain't shit. Some street shit from earlier," he lied.

"You okay?" She rubbed his back.

"Yeah, I'm Gucci."

"You sure?"

"Yeah, shawty." He winked.

"Good, 'cause I'm ready to go again." She rolled her hips and sucked his neck.

Instantly, he rocked back up, and just like earlier… he couldn't resist.

THE NEXT MORNING
F.B.I. HEADQUARTERS

Fletcher shuffled down the hallway with a smile on his face and an envelope tucked under his arm. Today he was going to petition for arrest warrants for Star and whoever was a known Gangster Disciple from 71st. He was chasing a

RICO act for all the foot soldiers and underbosses. Being that the RICO act fell under conspiracy, it would be easy to convict. But for Star, Buddah, and Crazy G, he had plans on charging them with kingpin crimes that involved racketeering, murder, running a criminal enterprise, and conspiracy to commit murder. He was ready to wrap things up and retire for good.

Knock! Knock!

"Who is it?"

"Fletcher, sir. May I come in?"

"You may."

Fletcher entered to find his boss, Agent Waller, sitting behind his desk reading files."What is it?" He glanced Fletcher's way, then went back to his computer screen.

Waller was a no-nonsense hard-ass who recently got promoted to director for Illinois after he chased down a vicious murderer named Darius "Slay" Jones halfway across the country. He and Fletcher came up in the academy together and had extreme dislike for each other, so his attitude didn't bother Fletcher one bit.

"Uh. I'm here to get an approval for a warrant," he said, placing the envelope on his desk.

"Is this about the Wells brothers?" Waller asked, pulling out the files.

"No… This is much bigger than that. This is about a gang war that has been going on for more than twenty years. A war between the Black P. Stones and the Gangster Disciples." Fletcher smiled like a proud father.

"Ok. I'll read over this and get back to you tomorrow morning," he said dismissively, instantly killing Fletcher's joy.

"Sure thing." Fletcher turned to leave.

"And Fletcher?"

"Sir?" He turned to face him.

"Don't ever start an investigation without my knowledge again."

BACK AT TT'S

Star's eyes snapped open the second he felt someone touch him. LayLay was snuggled up to him on the couch still butt-naked, rubbing the fresh scar on his neck.

"This look like it needs stitches," she whispered.

"What time is it?" he asked, sitting straight up.

She hit the lock button on her phone. "Almost eleven."

"Oh shit!" He jumped up. "You serious?"

"Yeah. Why?" she asked, standing up.

"'Cuz I'm supposed to meet my BM at the doctor this mornin'," he blurted, sliding into his jeans.

"Yikes. You shoulda told me. I woulda woke you up," she claimed, getting dressed as well.

"Nah, you good. It ain't shit… Ima figure it out."

"Just tell her you got shot and had to lay low or some shit. That way she can't be mad. Even if she is mad, she gone be more worried when she see your neck." LayLay smiled.

"Damn. That ain't bad, shorty." He smiled back. "But what we did right here can't neva happen again."

"Why not?" she frowned.

"Because we foul as hell and you know it. Pap a good nigga."

"And I'ma boss bitch," she countered.

"I'm lost."

"I'ma boss bitch. Meaning I only fuck wit' boss niggas. Pap is a good nigga and all. But I'm tryna see what's to you. I know you got a baby mama or whateva. But I know how to play my role and stay in my place. And I'ma down-ass bitch on whateva you on."

Star's mouth almost touched the ground when she was finished. He couldn't believe this 20-year-old girl was spitting game to him like she was a 30-year-old man. What was even more shocking was that he liked it.

"Aight shorty. Ima take you up on that… When I call, you answer." He licked the side of her face and they left—

oblivious to the surveillance team snapping photo after photo.

AT THE SAME TIME

Buddah pulled into TaeTae's driveway and killed the engine. He looked at the raggedy ranch-style house and instantly understood why TaeTae was knee-deep in the streets. He wasn't like most of the kids his age who did it because it was cool or they wanted to be accepted. He did it to feed his family.

"You sure you don't want me to help you inside?" He looked TaeTae's way.

"Nah, I got it. I'm tryin' to tell you, you don't wanna see my mama. Bad enough I got shot and gotta make up a lie. She see yo grown ass helpin' me and all hell gone break loose." He smiled, grabbing his crutches.

"Aight lil bro, whateva you say… But check it out." Buddah dug under his seat and came out with a small book bag.

"Is that what I think it is?" TaeTae smiled, unable to contain his excitement.

"Yeah it is. But I don't know why you want it when niggas runnin' 'round wit' 30 shots." Buddah passed him the book bag.

"Because I got real aim. And I got six weeks to do nothing but practice," he claimed, digging into the bag and pulling out the Night Hawk.

It was an all-black, eight-shot revolver that took .357 shells. The handle was wood while the sights were glowing green. Though it was a weapon of mass destruction, it was surprisingly light."I hope so… Now get yo lil bad ass in the house. Ion need Mom dukes on my ass."

CHAPTER 17

HOURS LATER

"I'm just glad you're okay," Kierra cooed as she wrapped the gauze around Star's neck. "Yeah, me too. I'm just mad as hell I couldn't see my son on the screen." He smiled, rubbing her stomach.

"Who said it's a boy?" Kierra fisted her hands.

She and Star decided to have a gender reveal, so neither one of them knew the sex of their unborn child. Star wanted a junior bad, while Kierra wanted a mini-me. She loved the idea of matching clothes and hairstyles.

"I said it's a boy. But truth be told, I wouldn't care either way. As long as my kids come out healthy, I'm cool."

"Kids?" She smacked his hands away from her stomach and frowned. "Fuck you mean kids with a S, nigga? TT is not havin' that baby. I will kill that bitch first."

"Aye!" he snapped, jumping to his feet. "What da fuck is wrong wit' you? You sound crazy as hell."

"Nigga, I don't give a fuck how I sound. That hoe needs to know her place! I give you an inch and you take a mile. How fuckin' hard is it to understand I don't want to share my child's father? Don't you understand?" she said on the verge of tears.

"I ain't takin' a mile…" He pulled her into his body. "You just feel like she takin' yo spot when she ain't and neva could." He kissed the top of her head.

"You say that now. Then down the line it's gone be somethin' different."

"What is it gone take for me to show you that you my number one?"

"Marry me." She looked up at him.

"What?"

"I said marry me."

"Aight. But it's gone be on my time. I wanna do it the right way," he claimed.

"How long is that gone be?"

"Not that long."

"Promise?"

"Yeah, I promise."

"EEE! I'm finna be Mrs. Cross!" she squealed. "I gotta call my momma and let her know," she added, scampering off.

THE NEXT DAY

Knock! Knock! Knock!

"Come in, Fletcher!" Waller yelled.

"Umm, you wanted to see me, sir?" Fletcher asked as he stepped in.

"Yes, take a seat." He motioned to the chairs in front of him.

"What is it?"

"I went over the case you petitioned for an arrest warrant for." He held up the envelope for emphasis.

"And?" Fletcher leaned forward on the edge of his seat.

"It's very good stuff… but I cannot submit this for a warrant. Not yet anyway."

"Why not? Did I make a mistake somewhere in the paperwork?"

"No. You just don't have anything concrete to convict all of them yet. You have their leader Cross by the balls, but you don't really have anything else on the rest of them. Sounds like your informant only has the details about Cross." He slid the envelope across his desk.

"But sir, I have shootings. I have the mob they're beefing with, and I have an ex-member of theirs who is able to identify each and every last one of them. I'm almost certain a judge will give us a warrant."

"I'm sure too. But what I'm not sure about is a conviction. Your entire case is based on the word of an informant."

"Isn't that how all our cases work?" Fletcher hissed, frustration etched in his tone.

"Yes, that's how they start. But they also are substantiated by our own surveillance and intel, which as of right now, you don't have enough of. So go back to the drawing board, bring me some damning evidence on each and every one of them—then and only then will we pursue charges." Waller stood up, signaling their meeting was over.

"Sure thing, boss." Fletcher snatched the folder up and stormed out of the office.

He was steaming on the inside, but knew Waller had a point. Fletcher was rushing and, in the process, skipping steps. He was so thirsty to retire that it made him lazy. Now he had to go back to the drawing board and start from scratch, prolonging his retirement even further.

ON 79TH

"Man, I swear to God I wish I could go wit' y'all. On Stone, I'm ready to smoke one of they brick ass," Pewee claimed, propping his leg up on the couch.

RayMoe, Tito, and 50 were standing in the middle of the kitchen loading their Glizzys, getting ready to murder a GD they caught. Well really, this was Tito's initiation. He wanted to be completely done with the GDs, and the only way to do that in his mind was to kill one of the GDs and become Black P. Stone.

"Don't even trip, Ku. Ima spill they shit for you," Tito claimed, using the Moes' slang.

"Damn, you sure you ain't been Black Stone?" RayMoe half-joked.

"Shit, maybe in my past life. Or I'm just built for this shit." He grinned, then cocked his Glock-22.

50 and RayMoe followed suit with their Glock-17 and Glock-26.

"Damn, I wish I could go wit' y'all. Y'all in this bitch lookin' like some real menaces," Pewee hissed, pissed he was about to miss the action.

"You gone be back in the mix soon. Until then, we gone put these niggas in a blender," 50 claimed, shaking up with Pewee.

RayMoe and Tito shook up with him as well, then they were out the door and into their stolen SRT Charger on the hunt.

***

Billa stepped off his porch, looked up the street both ways, then started his march to the gas station. The 3.5 grams of weed he just finished smoking had his stomach growling and his mouth cotton dry. He had to secure some snacks before he hit the block to hustle. Billa was Buddah's younger cousin, and like Buddah, he was GD crazy. Tito had killed Tre and Twan. Star needed somebody else to step up and take Tito's place. Buddah was against his cousin stepping up because he knew how loose he was, but Star was adamant about putting a person in play they could trust until Pap got out. Buddah could trust Billa but knew he wasn't as sharp as the rest of them. He loved to get high and chase pussy, which made him a liability.

Billa made his way in the gas station, swiped his favorite snacks and drinks, and was ready to make his exit when a woman entered with the fattest ass he'd seen in a long time.

"Damn," he mumbled.

She looked over her shoulder and gave him a sly smile, letting him know she heard him.

"So do that sexy ass smile you gave me mean I can have your number?" he slid next to her.

"Maybe," she giggled.

"Why maybe?"

"Because you look like trouble."

"And you look like you like trouble," he countered.

"I do." She pulled out her phone.

They quickly swapped numbers, then Billa was on his way.

As soon as he crossed the street, an all-black Charger caught his attention. Instinctively, he reached for his gun, but it wasn't there. He had left it on his dresser like he always did when he was high.

"Fuck!" he said out loud as he started speed walking.

He turned the corner and peered over his shoulder, and just like he expected, the Charger was on him. *VRRMMMM!* The engine roared, then screeched to a halt in front of him. He took off in full sprint, and Tito and 50 jumped out, running right behind him. Billa was fast, but Tito was faster. He was on top of him in a matter of seconds.

"Ah! No, please!" Billa begged as he ran for his life.

BOCA! A shot to the back was Tito's response. Billa went down in a heap and rolled across the pavement. 50 kept a lookout for any unwanted eyes while RayMoe pulled the Charger down the block.

"GDK, nigga," Tito spat as he stood over Billa.

"P-Please," Billa whispered before coughing up globs of blood.

BOCA! BOCA! BOCA! BOCA! Tito filled Billa's chest and face full of slugs.

"Fuck you, nigga!" he growled before joining RayMoe and 50 in the Charger.

CHAPTER 18

ON 57TH
TWO DAYS LATER

Crazy G and Star sat on the living room couch listening to Buddah rant about Billa. He was beyond pissed and even shed a couple of tears for his blood. For the first time since the war started, OTM had really hit home, and they were all feeling it. Tito switching sides had really given the Moes hope.

"A closed casket. My Auntie can't even send cuz off the right way. Ona G, them niggas dead! D-E-A-Fuckin'-D! Ion give a fuck who I catch. Anybody that's ova there dyin'!" Buddah vowed, wiping the lone tear that slid down his cheek.

Star didn't know what to say, so he just kept quiet. Plus, he felt guilty for putting Billa in the mix when Buddah begged him not to. Crazy G listened to Buddah rant while he stalked a couple of OTM's main faces on Facebook. He was hoping to catch one of them posting something that could help them find them. Instead, he came across Tito's live. He clicked on it and was instantly filled with rage. Tito was flanked by RayMoe and Pewee, smiling like they were best friends as they smoked Dutchies stuffed to capacity.

"Damn," Tito coughed. "That Billa pack strong than a muthafucka." He laughed, passing the blunt to RayMoe.

RayMoe pulled on it a couple times, then said, "No please don't kill me. That nigga went out like a straight bitch." He passed the blunt to Pewee.

"On Stone, you bitch ass niggas know wassup wit' us. Stop hidin' and pop out, cuz we ain't gone stop spinnin' til we smoke every one of you brick ass niggas," Pewee claimed, then ended the video.

Though Buddah and Star didn't see the video, they definitely heard it. Buddah was so angry that he bit down on his bottom lip until he tasted blood. It went without saying that Crazy G and Star felt the exact same way.

"Once we bury yo lil cuz and our brother of the struggle, it's open season on them niggas. We killin' dogs, cats, and goldfish. Mornin', day, and night. We on they ass 'til them niggas extinct. Or them niggas go into hidin'. I'on give a fuck," Star said, his voice low and full of aggression.

"It's war time," Crazy G co-signed.

DAYS LATER

"I was born by the river / in a little tent / And oh just like the river I been runnin' / Ever since."

Sam Cooke's *Change Gon' Come* blasted from the speakers of the church as everyone in attendance came up to the casket to pay their final respects.

Buddah and Star came together on all expenses, making sure Billa was laid to rest properly. Though they couldn't see what he was wearing, they had him wrapped in a silk Gucci suit with the shoes to match. His casket was rose gold with the Bentley sign engraved into the top, and instead of the traditional all black, everybody wore all white. They wanted to celebrate Billa's life rather than mourn his death. After the pastor gave his eulogy, Buddah and his Auntie Pamela said a few words, then it was time for them to go to the burial site, which was Burr Oaks Cemetery located on the far side in an area known as the Wild 100s.

Just as everybody was starting to file out of the church—*SCCCUURRRTTT!*—an all-black Charger slammed on the brakes right at the exit. RayMoe and Tito hung out of the front and back passenger, aiming their straps.

"Oh my Gawd!"

"Run!"

"He got a gun!"

A group of women yelled out simultaneously just before shots rang out.

BOCA! BOCA! BOCA! BOOM! BOOM! BOOM!

Instantly chaos erupted as people scrambled for their lives. Buddah, Crazy G, and Star were all the way at the end of the line when the shooting started, so they had to push through the crowd to make it outside. By the time they did, Tito and company were long gone. Not a word needed to be spoken between the trio. They knew exactly who did this, and exactly what time it was. Nobody was off limits. The gloves were officially off. Tito and RayMoe purposely didn't hit innocent bystanders. They shot up the building to disrespect Billa's funeral… but along with the disrespect, they'd woken the monster in Buddah.

***

Buddah, Crazy G, and Star watched the faded green two-story house from the comfort of their hijacked Ford F-150. It was just past midnight, and the block was dead still with the exception of a few cars here and there.

"You sure this her address?" Buddah asked, fidgeting with his AR pistol.

"Yeah nigga. How many times you gone ask me that shit? I told you me and Pap used to drop him right here when him and TT got into it," Crazy G explained, drumming his fingers on the steering wheel.

"I still can't believe my slim chocolate thick shake used to fuck wit' that Goofy." Star shook his head.

"Yo what, nigga?" Crazy G locked eyes with him through the rearview.

"My slim chocolate thick shake," he repeated.

"Da fuck is that?" Crazy G laughed.

"TT and Kiera… TT chocolate and thick as hell. Then Kiera slim and yellow. Put them both together, you get a slim chocolate thick shake." Star smiled.

"Hell nah." Crazy G laughed. "You funny as hell."

"If this the right spot, what we waiting for?" Buddah interrupted.

He wasn't in the mood to be laughing and joking. He was seeing red and would be until he strangled the life out of Tito, RayMoe, Pewee, and 50.

"For the lights to turn out," Star said, looking at the house.

"Why? That shit don't even matter," Buddah replied with irritation in his tone.

"Because when people are ready to go to sleep, they rush into things," Crazy G added.

"Fuck allat," Buddah spat, climbing out of the truck.

"Damn, this nigga," Star huffed, climbing out behind him. "If you see anything that don't look right, beep twice," he added before jogging up to the front door.

Buddah stood on one side while Star took the other.

KNOCK! KNOCK! KNOCK! Buddah pounded on the door like he was the police.

"Who dat?" a male voice called out.

"RayMoe." Buddah smiled wickedly, as thoughts of splattering brains all over the floor crossed his mind.

"Who you lookin' for?" the man asked.

"Tito told me to drop this money off to Yo-Yo," Buddah lied.

At the mention of Tito and money, the locks could be heard turning. As soon as the door cracked, Star put his size 10 in the middle of it, knocking the man to the ground.

"What the fuck is this shit?" he yelped as they rushed inside with their guns leveled with his face.

"What is allat noise!" Yo-Yo yelled, stomping down the stairs.

The second she locked eyes with Star and Buddah, she sprinted back up the stairs, but Star was on her. He chased after her and was able to snatch her up by her braids.

"Noo! Let me go, muthafucka!" she kicked and screamed as Star dragged her back down the stairs. "Let me go! Help! Som—"

CRACK! Star slapped her with his Glock, instantly silencing her before he tossed her next to the man who answered the door.

"C'mon now. What's this all about? I think y'all got the wrong house," the man claimed.

"Nah, we got the right house," Buddah said, then squeezed the trigger.

BLAH! BLAH! The AR pistol jerked in his hands, knocking half the man's face off.

"Oh my God, Mike! Please, no, no, no," Yo-Yo begged, but her pleas would fall on deaf ears.

Buddah yanked her head back by her braids and jammed the AR into her mouth so hard, he knocked a couple teeth out in the process.

"Mmmm!" she moaned, her eyes wide as a porn star's legs.

BLAH! BLAH! Blood and brain matter flew everywhere. Star could even make out a few teeth scattered about. It was gruesome.

"Let's go," Buddah said, licking the blood from around his cheek.

THE NEXT MORNING

"A wave of violence has rocked Chicago's East Side in what Chicago police are calling a gang war. This weekend, 68 people shot and 9 dead, with the East Side accounting for 21 of those shootings and murders. I'm Golden Davis with Fox 32."

"You see what's wrong with this picture?" Fletcher asked, pausing the news recording.

"Nah, not really," Laylow lied.

He knew exactly what Fletcher was hinting at but played dumb, hoping he wouldn't receive the blame for the casualties.

"You know exactly what the problem is here…" He got up and walked over to the dry-erase board behind him. "The problem is you haven't gave me nothing I can use except for the evidence against this Cross guy…. Sooo what we're going to do today is build a pyramid." He drew a line down the middle of the board, then wrote OTM on one side and 71st Mob on the other.

"What about me seeing my mother? You told me I was gonna be able to see her today," Laylow huffed.

"Yeah, that's going to have to wait. You should have thought about that when I asked you did you tell me everything I needed to know." He paused to let his words sink in. "Until we successfully secure an arrest warrant for these guys," he held up the stack of mugshots, "you won't be seeing mommy. So let's get to work."

If looks could kill, Fletcher would have died right there on the spot from the mean mug Laylow shot his way.

"C'mon, man. I ain't seen my OG since all this shit first started," Laylow whined.

"Well then, if I were you, I would finish these quickly. The quicker I get that warrant, the quicker you see your family."

CHAPTER 19

"Star!" TT yelled, shaking him awake.

"Wassup?" he replied with his eyes still closed.

"Can we talk?" she asked, climbing into bed with him.

"I guess. Shit, you already woke a nigga up." He turned to face her while rubbing the cold from his eyes.

"So what am I to you?" she asked, staring at her hands.

"Whatchu mean?"

"This. What am I to you… Like what are we doing here?" She spread her arms as if to say *look around you.*

"You my lady. Why you even askin' me this?" He sat up.

"No reason."

"Nah." He grabbed her chin and turned her face towards him. "Why you askin' me this? Where is all this shit coming from?"

"I'on know. It just seem since Kierra bugged up over me being pregnant, you been distant. Now she talkin' about y'all getting married. So I guess I'm just tryna figure out how I fit in all of this."

"TT," he said, pulling her into him. "You gone forever be a part of me. You carrying my baby. Just because me and Kierra talkin' marriage don't mean you gone be left out. Or that don't mean I love you any less. We locked in foreva."

"Promise?" She stared into his eyes.

"On my OG grave." He raised his right hand into the air.

"Ok, but you betta not hurt me or yo ass gone be the one gettin' shot this time." She half-joked."Whateva. Now gimme kiss so I can catch some Z's."

Unbeknown to Star and TT, Kierra was right around the corner listening to their entire conversation, and she was livid. She refused to let TT take her spot. No, she would lay down and die first.

"Hmp! I got somethin' for yo ass, bitch. Yeah, I gotchu," she mumbled, then walked away.

ON 57TH AND EMERALD

"Man, you sure about this shit, G?" Fabo asked as he pulled his car into the ditch next to the train tracks.

Fabo was and had been TaeTae's ace since the second grade. He was a tall, skinny, light-skin dude with long dreads that stopped at his lower back.

"Yeah, nigga. I do this shit all the time," TaeTae claimed, flinging his car door open.

He grabbed his crutches from the back seat and hobbled closer to the forest preserve. Fabo grabbed the bag full of targets and started sticking them onto trees.

"Now what?" he asked, joining TaeTae.

"We wait for the train. That big ass freight train be so loud. They ain't gone be able to hear us shootin'." TaeTae explained.

"Damn, yo lil ass ain't playin', is you?" Fabo smiled mischievously.

"Ona G. It's up. I'm not playin' wit' nobody no more. Them bitch ass niggas almost took me out this shit. I ain't givin' no nigga the chance to do that again."

Fabo nodded his approval. He knew when niggas got shot, it either did one of two things—turned you all the way up or turned you all the way down. In TaeTae's case, he was turnt to the max… and the only thing that could turn him down was the grave or a jail cell.

A COUPLE WEEKS LATER
COOK COUNTY JAIL

Pap, as usual, paced a hole in his tiny cell, but this time it was a happy pace. The judge had just granted him a 750-

thousand-dollar bond, which he only had to pay 10% of… $75,000. He was sure Crazy G, Buddah, and Star had twenty-five a piece. In his mind, it was only a matter of time before he was free. A smile crept onto his face as he thought about beating Lay-Lay's back in and smoking a 3.5 to the face. Now he just had to get to the phone and let the guys know what was up.

By him being in the hole, he was only allowed 15 minutes a week, which he'd already used talking to Lay-Lay earlier in the week. Now he had to wait three more days until it reset on Sunday. *"Shit, I been waiting this long,"* he thought, scooping up his urban novel.

While in seg, that's all he did—read urbans. His favorite authors were Ghost and Ca$h from Lockdown Publications. They told the streets the way the streets were meant to be told. Especially *Trust No Man* and the *Trust No Bitch* series by Ca$h.

"This bitch Treebie somethin' else. I definitely trust no bitch after seeing how this hoe get down."

MEANWHILE

ZZNNNTT! ZNNNNT! The tattoo gun buzzed, echoing throughout the entire basement.

Tito was laying flat on his back while Scooby went to work on his chest. He was putting the finishing touches on the angel with the words "R.I.P. Yo-Yo" underneath. He had already got a five-pointed star shaded red under his left eye. Next, he was getting a pitchfork dipped in the center of his neck to disrespect the GDs.

"On Stone. He snappin' on that bitch," Pewee claimed.

"On bro, that muthafucka official," RayMoe co-signed.

"Good lookin' out, y'all," Scooby said, wiping Tito's chest with the rag.

Scooby was a white dude from around the way, who was wicked with a tattoo gun. He could've made thousands of dollars if he wasn't addicted to cocaine.

"Aye, as soon as he done, we spinnin' through them fuck niggas' block. They bitch ass been hidin'. They know I'm on they back," Tito spat before chugging from the bottle of Hennessy like it was water.

"On Stone, Moe, you know they bitch ass shook. They see we got that belt out. Now they wanna play hide and seek," RayMoe added.

"C'mon now, Moe. You know them bitch ass niggas pussy anyway. They couldn't see us wit' the gunplay. So they did some coward shit and went after innocent people."

Pewee shook his head, then sparked his blunt stuffed with exotic weed.

"Man, my OG won't even talk to me behind this shit. She blames me for this shit, and it's driving me crazy, Moe. These bitch ass niggas took everything from me. On my dead sister grave, Ion give a fuck where I catch any one of them bitch ass niggas at. I'm crashing out!" Tito growled through clenched teeth.

"On Stone, you know I'm right wit' you," RayMoe vowed.

"Ku, you already know what time it is with me." Pewee balled his right fist up and slammed it into his heart the way the Black Stones did after their handshake.

"Where da fuck is 50?" Tito asked.

"I'on know. He said he was finna stop at his BM house. Then he was on the way."

"You know he love that thot ass bitch, Jasmine," RayMoe joked.

***

ARRGGHH!" Star groaned as he erupted in LayLay's throat.

She was leaned over the armrest in his Aston Martin, sucking his pole as if her life depended on it.

"SSSHIT." He threw his head back and could feel his toes curling in his boots. "Aight, damn," he huffed, pushing her head.

"Mm, I told you," she giggled, flipping down the visor and fixing her hair. "But you thought I was cappin'." She smacked her lips for emphasis.

"Yeah, you did yo shit," he mumbled, zipping his pants up.

"So what we finna do now?" she turned in her seat so she was facing him.

"Whatchu mean *we*?" He picked up his Glock and sat it in his lap. "I told you I got shit to do. So I'm finna drop you off."

"Nooo. I'm tryna chill wit' you. It ain't shit else for me to do… I promise you won't even know I'm here unless you tell me to jump on that dick." She laughed but meant every word she said.

"Lil girl, we c—"

"Grown ass woman," she interrupted.

"LayLay. You know we can't be ridin' around together like everything chicken ass. Somebody see us, this gone be the talk of the hood."

"Who da fuck gone see me behind this tint?" She tapped on the window. "What if the police pull you over? You need this pretty face to talk for you and hold yo gun." She smirked, knowing she had him right where she wanted him.

"Aight, damn. But you betta not start actin' extra and shit." He started up the Aston.

"Yay! I knew you fucked with me," she chirped, dancing in her seat.

Star eased off into traffic full of guilt. He knew he was dead wrong for carrying on with LayLay. A bomb on the head and the wettest pussy he'd ever had had him hooked, even though he didn't want to admit it. She had her claws in him like he had his teeth in her. Their sneaky fuck fest was turning into something that could turn deadly in a blink of an eye. There was a lot of hearts being broken and a lot of loyalty thrown aside. They were both so caught up in the moment that they were blinded by the harsh reality in front of them.

THE NEXT NIGHT

Pewee maneuvered his stolen Jaguar with ease. It was a speed demon, and he loved it. He pulled up in front of Jasmine's house and beeped the horn twice. Two minutes later, 50 followed by Tito came out.

"What's the demo, Stone?" Tito greeted, climbing into the passenger side.

"I'm well, Moe. What y'all on?" Pewee shot back, shaking up with Tito.

"Shit, you know us. We tryna slide," 50 claimed, jumping in the back. "This lil hoe I be fuckin' wit' say they 'posed to be havin' a little kickback tonight, and she gone drop the low after she leave."

"Wait, who 'posed to be at this kickback?" Pewee looked from Tito to 50.

"Some of them niggas' homies. But Ion think Star or none of they heavies gone show they face," Tito announced, placing his tool on his lap.

"So why we even wastin' our time?" RayMoe questioned.

"Cuz they so-called big homies put up, so we finna apply pressure to they lil guys until them niggas show they face! These bitch ass niggas killed my sister. Ion give a fuck who I catch. I'm puttin' they ass on a shirt!" Tito snapped.

No more words needed to be spoken. Pewee put the car in reverse, then pulled off into the night. They rode around aimlessly for almost two hours with Boss Man D Low's new album on repeat while they smoked back to back. Tito was geeked off the ecstasy he popped an hour ago and was starting to become restless.

"Man, I wish this bitch hurry up and drop they lo. I'm ready to kill one of these lil niggas," Tito growled through clenched teeth while he gripped his gun.

His eyes were bucked and bloodshot red, with his face twisted in a mask of anger, making him look like the monster he was. Then, as if she could hear him talking about her, 50's phone jingled in his pocket.

"Yeah?" he answered… "Aight, Ima see you lata tonight," he added before hanging up.

"So where they bitch ass at?" Tito rolled down his mask.

"They on Ashland," 50 said, slipping on his COVID mask.

"At the New Budget Motel?" Pewee asked.

"Exactly."

THE NEW BUDGET MOTEL

"I buy a Cuban and fill it wit' diamonds / Send my assistant to pick up some condoms / Instagram model at the hotel textin' me now / Want me to give her the Johnson…"

DaBaby's *Beatbox Challenge* was cranked to the max.

Weed-laced smoke filled the air while the entire kickback got their drink on. The small room was packed with 10 people—six girls, four boys. One of the boys being TaeTae. This was his first day without his cast on his leg. To celebrate, Fabo threw him a kickback. TaeTae could really care less about the party. In fact, the only reason he showed up was so he would have an alibi if any of the Moe decided to snitch on him.

"You wanna drink, boo?" a pretty thot, Lamaria, asked.

"Nah, I'm good. But thanks anyway." TaeTae smiled.

"Ok, well me and my cousin finna get out of here. Enjoy yo self." She hugged him, then left with her cousin Ari in tow.

"Damn, why they leave?" Fabo asked.

"Shit, Ion know. Them hoes be doin' dicks everywhere," he laughed.

"On Folks nem grave, Mari got a bomb on the head. I was prayin' she stayed the night," Goonie co-signed.

Goonie was Fabo's younger brother and looked just like Fabo, except with a haircut.

"I'm finna slide too, though," TaeTae said, standing to his feet.

"Nigga, how da fuck you gone leave yo own party?" Fabo looked at him sideways.

"I'm comin' back, nigga. I just gotta go check on somethin'," he claimed.

"Aight, I'm finna go wit' you," Fabo claimed.

"C'mon now, nigga, you gotta hold the party down."

"Whateva. Goonie got it. I'm finna bail wit' you."

Fabo was onto TaeTae the second he said he wanted to leave.

"Aight, c'mon man," he huffed.

"We a be right back, Goonie."

***

"Stop! That's room 107 right there," Tito pointed.

"Bet," Pewee said, throwing the car in reverse.

He backed the car up until it was a couple feet away from the room's door. Without another word, 50 and Tito slid from the car and made their way to the door, but before they could knock—BOOM! BOOM! BOOM! TaeTae's night hawk woke the neighborhood up. Fabo was tipsy and forgot his gun, so they had to circle back, making them run right into Tito and company.

"Oh shit!" Tito yelled as he ducked for cover.

BOOM! BOOM! Bullets narrowly zipped past 50's head and slammed into the motel's door. Finally able to catch his footing, Tito came up blowing. BOCA! BOCA! BOCA! BOCA! But TaeTae didn't budge. He swung his cannon in Tito's direction. BOOM! BOOM! CLICK! The revolver signaled it was empty.

TaeTae, without hesitation, pressed the eject, ducked behind Fabo's car, and stuffed a speed reload into the chamber, then snapped it closed. BOC! BOC! BOC! BOC! BOC! BOC! 50 fired recklessly at the car.

"Fuck!" Fabo yelled, ducking into the floorboard.

BOOM! BOOM! BOOM! TaeTae fired three quick ones to keep them at bay.

"We gotta go!" Pewee yelled.

BOCA! BOCA! Tito fired back as he ran to the car. 50 jumped in the car at the same time as Tito. As soon as they pulled out of the parking lot, a Crown Vic jumped behind them with its lights flashing and its sirens blaring.

"Go! Go! Go!" Tito yelled.

RRRMMMM! The Jag's engine roared to life. Pewee tried to make a hard right but lost control, and the Jag slid off the road and into a ditch. Pewee mashed the pedal, but the Jag didn't budge. He tried again, and the tires spun angrily, but the Jag still didn't move.

"Fuck that shit!" Tito opened his car door and jetted on feet.

Pewee and 50 followed suit, but 50 was slower and ended up jumping out last, giving the officer enough time to pull out his taser and line 50 up.

ZZZAANNN!

"Arrrggh!" 50 yelled as he crumbled to the ground.

He tried to get back up, but the officer was on top of him. He quickly cuffed 50. "I've got one in custody on 89th. Two other suspects are on foot heading southbound!" he barked into his radio.

CHAPTER 20

TWO DAYS LATER

"This is a collect call from an inmate at the Cook County Jail. To accept this call, press—"

LayLay pressed 1, quickly silencing the operator. She was beyond irritated and couldn't take another second of her voice.

"Thank you for using Secures. You may start the conversation now."

"Hel' lil mama," Pap said smoothly.

"Wassup?" she replied dryly.

"Damn, that's how we answering the phone now?" He looked at the receiver like it had two heads.

"Nah, I'm just blown right now. How you feeling?"

"Still in the hole. But I get out next week. Aye look though, I only got 15 minutes. Tell Bro nem I got a bond. My shit 75 though."

"75 what?"

"75 thousand. Tell them to come grab me ASAP. I'm ready to get the fuck up out of this hell hole."

"Oh my God, I can't wait," she said, her tone not matching her words.

"Man, is you good, Shawty? Like, wassup?" he asked, picking up on her tone.

"Yeah, I'm good. Why you ask me that?" she shot back, worried he knew something.

"Yo energy… It's off. It's like you don't sound too happy to talk to me."

"Psst!" She smacked her lips. "Boy, you know I'm always happy to hear yo voice. I'm just stressed out and ready for all this to be over."

"You have one minute left," the operator interrupted.

"Aight, man. I miss you. And Ima see you soon. Make sure you stand on the business so I can beat them cheeks how you like it."

"You know I'm finna do that right now," she claimed.

"Thank you for using Secures. Goodbye."

LayLay tossed her phone on the couch next to her and ran her fingers through her hair. She knew Pap would come home eventually, but not this soon. She was falling for Star head over heels and didn't know if she would be able to control herself around Pap. She still had feelings for Pap but wanted Star in the worst way. He was a boss and made her feel alive. Not that Pap didn't… Star was just more experienced in every aspect, and she loved it. She knew this day was coming. Now it was time to choose: Pap or Star.

"Damn," she huffed, picking her phone back up.

She had to deliver the news to her secret lover that her boyfriend got a bond.

DOWNTOWN

"And I'm guessing that's why Tito flipped sides," Laylow said, stepping back from the dry erase board for Fletcher to see.

Fletcher, who was standing off to the side, had to admit Laylow did a hell of a job with the pyramid. He had everything and everybody lined to a tee. He even made them all color-coordinated by position, rank, and status. He was an official rat but could care less. He wasn't spending most of—or the rest of—his life in a box.

"You've really outdone yourself this time." Fletcher gave a round of applause.

"Thanks, I guess."

"Don't thank me yet… What about these guys?" He walked over to the board and pointed at TaeTae and Fabo's picture.

"I told you, ion know who da fuck they is," Laylow shrugged. "They must be new niggas or something. That's why I got a question mark by them."

"Okay, I get that. But why do you have this guy so high up?" He tapped Pap's picture. "Since we've started surveillance on him, we haven't come up with jack shit. We even tapped his jail call, and we've come up empty. Then you still haven't told me anything about who's in charge of 57th and Shields."

"C'mon man, I told you everything I know. I keep trying to get you to understand I been in hiding for forever. A lot of this shit I wasn't around for. I just want to see my mama. I did everything you asked. It's time for me to see her."

"Except it isn't," Fletcher smirked.

"What you mean? You said once I—"

"No, I said once we secure an arrest warrant you can see your mother, which we have yet to do… I really need to figure out this situation on 57th. Then we will be ready."

"How long you think that's gon' take?" Laylow asked, frustration evident in his tone.

"Who knows? Could be weeks. Could be months… Then you're going to have to testify in front of a grand jury. So just sit tight. We're about 85% done. You'll see your mother soon enough."

HOURS LATER

50 woke up to two detectives entering the small interview room for the third time. Instantly, he sat up. He'd already told them he wasn't trying to talk, so what did they want?

"Man, I already told the last detectives I don't wanna talk, and I'm tellin' y'all the same shit. I don't speak poink," he claimed, leaning back in his seat.

"Well, it's a good thing we're not detectives," the first man said, taking a seat.

"Then who the fuck is you?"

"I'm Agent Fletcher with the F.B.I." He flashed his badge. "And this is Anthony Zere, federal prosecutor." He paused to let his words sink in. "Now let me start by saying you're in a shit storm right now." He opened up the folder and slid it to 50.

"But," Anthony chimed in, "we can help you out if you help us. You're facing multiple charges right now. Federal and State. Without a doubt, if you're convicted on one of these, you will be spending the rest of your life in prison."

50 flipped through the still shots of him, Tito, Pewee, and RayMoe in utter shock. They had pictures from Tito's Facebook showing them smoking weed and flashing guns. They even had pictures of Jasmine, his girlfriend, holding guns and flexing with pounds of weed.

"Now, I'm sure I don't have to spell it out what this means for you or your pretty little girlfriend… So what will it be? Because I promise you won't get this chance again," Fletcher warned.

"Don't throw away your life and your woman's life over some dumb street code that ain't worth two copper pennies rubbed together," Prosecutor Zere added.

"Man, I'll tell y'all whateva y'all wanna know. Just leave my girl out this shit."

THE NEXT MORNING

"*Sho me love / Treat it like we freakin' on the weekend / Show me love / I'll eat up the seconds, time, and minutes / For your love / This not the season for nobody else but us.*"

Alicia Keys' "Show Me Love" blasted from the speakers as Kierra danced around the kitchen in nothing but her bra and panties. Her stomach was oiled up and poking, while her hair was pinned up in a bun. She had just finished making scrambled cheesy eggs, pancakes, and bacon.

"Damn, you got it smellin' good in here," TT claimed as she entered the kitchen.

"When don't I do my thang in the kitchen?" She smiled, piling two plates and walking them to the table. "You gon' join me or just gon' stand there drooling?"

"Okay bitch, what's up?" TT cocked her brow and placed a hand on her hip.

"What you mean?" Kierra said through a mouthful of eggs.

"You know what I mean—all this." She waved her hand around the kitchen. "Why you being all nice and shit? What's really on yo mind?"

"Girl, ain't nobody on no bullshit wit' you. I'm just being nice, shit. I'm tired of all the fightin' and drama. If we gon' have these babies together, then we may as well do it… peacefully."

"Well… thanks. You don't know how much I needed to hear that shit." TT joined her at the table.

"Mmm," she moaned with a mouthful of food. "You definitely still got it."

"Wait 'til you taste the smoothies I made for us."

"Okay, 'cuz a bitch definitely hungry."

ON 57TH

"Sooo what da fuck we gon' do?" Buddah questioned, looking back and forth between Crazy G and Star.

They were seated in Crazy G's living room as usual, discussing Pap's bond.

"Shit, Ion know. But I know for a fact we can't just walk in the county with 75 tryin' to bond him out. He gon' have to get us all a lawyer when we done," Star said, stroking his chin.

"What the lawyer say?" Crazy G lounged on the couch.

"Say he can post the bond. Then we gotta pay him an extra 25. And Bro gon' have to sit another two weeks," Star explained.

"Damn. Them Italians don't be playin' 'bout they money," Buddah half-joked.

"Yeah, you know they gon' hustle a nigga any chance they get," Star replied.

"Sooo it sound like he waitin' for two weeks then," Crazy G rose to his feet.

"What you finna do?" Buddah asked.

"Shit, I was finna slide on Laylow's OG."

"For what!" Buddah and Star yelled simultaneously.

"To find out where she buried bro at. She owe us that much," he shrugged.

"Man, you sure that's a good idea?" Star questioned.

"I told you I was thinkin' 'bout it. I ain't really made my mind up yet."

"Aight, well let a nigga know when you do so one of us can slide wit' you," Buddah replied.

"Man, where da fuck is Taetae?" Star asked out the blue.

"Fuck if I know," Crazy G claimed.

"Shit, don't look at me. I hit his line this morning and he ain't answer," Buddah added.

"Aight, fuck it. We gon' fill him in lata. But as of right now, we need a new plug ASAP," Star huffed.

"Whatchu mean? What happened to Zoe?" Buddah asked.

"He got snatched up by the Feds. Him and his whole crew. It's been all over the news all morning."

"Damn, I ain't neva think The Diamond Family Empire would go out like that." Crazy G shook his head. "I thought they had connects."

"They did. A dirty F.B.I. agent got wrapped up wit' them in the process," Star pinched the bridge of his nose.

"I mean, we should be good on the weed and pills. I know a couple niggas from out west who got packs by the boat load," Buddah announced. "But finding a real plug to buy birds from gon' be harder."

"I'm already knowin'. Shit already been movin' slow since we switched traps anyway, so whatever we do, we gotta do it quick."

"So what about them OTM niggas?" Crazy G asked.

"I'm baking a real cake for them niggas. All we gotta do is get Tito and Pewee nem out the way. And the rest of them niggas gon' crumble," Star said.

"Cut the head off and watch the body fall," Buddah quoted.

"Exactly."

***

TaeTae pulled down the alley and killed the engine to his stolen Nissan. He pulled his ball cap down and exited the car, gun in hand. He tiptoed down the alley until he was at the backyard of the house he thought would be in the middle of the block. Effortlessly, he leaped over the 5-ft gate and crept down the side of the house. He peeked around the corner and just like when he drove past earlier, a couple of Moes were still outside. For some odd reason, Buddah's voice popped into his head.

"Breathe. This shit ain't nothing." Buddah's voice echoed in his head.

He took a deep breath, then jumped from behind the house letting his gun talk for him.

BOOM! BOOM! BOOM!

The Night Hawk thundered, making everybody scramble for cover, but TaeTae was on one.

He lined the man up that was closest to him and fired.

BOOM! BOOM!

The hollow points ripped through the man's leg and back. He spilled to the ground, then tried to crawl away… TaeTae was having none of it. He skipped over to him.

BOOM! BOOM! BOOM!

Sparks jumped up from the ground as they ripped through the man's back. Wasting no time, he reloaded the Night Hawk and made his exit as quickly as he came.

THE NEXT DAY

Tito looked around at all the men in the room and could sense mixed emotions. Some were ready to kill. Some were uncertain, while others even seemed scared. He needed to find a way to reassure his men, or the GDs would continue to pick them off. Plus, they needed somebody to take 50's general slot in his absence. Then there was the drought problem. They had already run through the drugs he'd taken from Star. He glanced Pewee's way and for the first time since he switched sides, he saw Pewee was worried.

"Aye, y'all listened up!" Tito yelled.

Instantly the room fell silent, and all eyes were on him.

"I ain't gone do too much talkin' 'cause that ain't how we move. Shit ugly right now, but we know that's what come wit' war. These niggas ain't did shit. And they ain't gone do shit but try to catch us one by one or get down on innocent muthafuckas. So it's simple—when we out on Kingston, we make sure we overstrapped, and we got somebody out there wit' us. It's the same shit when we on the 9. Y'all drawin' off that?"

"Yes sir, Ku. We drawin'," a couple of the men said together.

"Slap, you gone be the G until we can bond Vo big brother out," he added.

"When that's gone be?" Slap asked.

He was the spitting image of his brother, just a couple shades lighter.

"He got bond court at one. We gone see what they yellin'," Pewee announced.

"A shooting. Some bitch got hit in the leg in the process… He should be good. Bro ain't got a record," Pewee explained.

"We good. Let's just tighten up our defense and keep puttin' the belt on them niggas. Stone Love," Tito cheered.

"Stone Love," they yelled back.

CHAPTER 21

LANSING, IL

"Whoa! Slow down 'fore you wreck my shit," Star barked from the passenger seat.

"Boy, ain't nobody finna wreck yo car," LayLay yelled back as she pulled into the parking lot. "I know what I'm doing. Dang!"

"Man, yo lil ass almost crashed twice talkin' 'bout you know what you doin'."

"Whateva, nigga. Don't hate. You know I can drive. And who apartment is this anyway?" she asked, killing the engine.

"It's yours," he replied, opening the door.

"For real?" She smiled from ear to ear. "Don't play wit' me, Star," she screeched, climbing out of the car behind him.

"I'm fa'real… Well, it's for the both of us. So we can do our own thing without havin' to worry 'bout all the extra shit." He tossed her the key. "You in charge, though."

"Oh my God! You finna let me decorate too?" She wrapped her arms around him and squeezed.

One would think with Pap on the way home, Star would get as far away from LayLay as possible. That was the last thing on his mind. Lately, all he did was spend time with her when he wasn't in the streets. The last two weeks he'd only spent three nights at home with TT and Kierra. He was slipping. Being in control of everything made him think he could do whatever he wanted, whenever he wanted, to whoever he wanted. He was blinded by power.

***

"Man, how da fuck they gone deny bro a bond? That shit crazy. They actin' like a nigga El Chapo or some shit," Tito claimed as he, RayMoe, Slap, and Pewee left the Cook County building.

"Man, ion know. You know how them crackers is. They don't wanna see a nigga win for shit," RayMoe claimed.

"Facts. But what we gone do 'bout this lil nigga Taetae? He startin' to become a real fuckin' problem," Tito claimed.

"Shit, you tell us. You used to hang wit' them niggas. You don't know where his bitch ass hidin' out at?" Slap asked.

"Fuck you mean by that?" Tito spat, stopping mid-stride.

"Shit, I'm just sayin'—you know these niggas. So you should know how to get up on they ass, that's all," Slap claimed.

"Nah, I don't. Once them niggas figured out what was up, they changed up everything. I mean, I know they spot on 57th, but they got that bitch over-sewed up. Shit would be suicide tryin' to slide down they block."

"So what we supposed to do now? Just keep waitin' on them niggas to slide on us?" Slap asked.

"Hell nawl," Pewee interrupted. "While we waitin', we gone get our bands up. I know a couple of goofies we can take down."

"Then once we get our chips up, them niggas ain't gone be able to see us," Tito added.

"Fuck you mean, Ku? Them brick ass niggas ain't seein' us now," RayMoe laughed.

***

"Arrggh." TT sat up holding her stomach.

"You good?" Kierra asked, sitting up as well.

"Yeah, I think so… These last couple of days I been havin' like sharp pains right here." She touched a couple inches below her navel.

"Yeah, that shit happens to me on the regular. You eventually get used to it." Kierra rubbed her swollen belly.

"I can't believe we actually 'bout to be moms. Like, especially with the same baby daddy," TT locked eyes with her.

"I mean… It's not exactly what I was expecting my life to be, but I can't complain. I got a house, car, and everything I want. I just wish Star was around a little more."

"Girl, when these babies drop he a—ARRGGH!" she yelped, clutching her stomach. "A-Are you sure it's supposed to hurt this bad?"

"I don't know. How bad does it h—"

"ARRRGGHHH!" She doubled over in pain.

"Oh my God. Girl, are you okay?" Kierra asked, rolling out of bed.

"Uuugggh! C-Call an ambulance," TT cried.

Kierra scrambled to find her phone.

***

VRRMMM! VRRMMM! Star's phone vibrated on the kitchen table for the third time in minutes but wouldn't be getting an answer any time soon. He had LayLay flat on the kitchen floor while he pounded her hard and fast.

"Oooohh. Ooh-ooh-ooooh," she moaned, clawing at the floor.

"Yeah. You. Like that dick. Don't you!" he huffed as he plunged in and out of her.

"Ooooh. Y-Yeah. Yeah."

"Shhh—I'm finna cum all over this ass. Fuck!" He pulled out and dumped his seed all over her ass and back.

Like the boss freak she was, LayLay made her ass clap for him.

"Damn," he mumbled, rubbing his tip between her cheeks.

"And you wonder why a bitch be all over you," she giggled.

VRRMMM! VRRMMM! VRRMMM! His phone rattled again, stealing his attention.

"Don't answer." She reached back and grabbed his throbbing head, but she would have no such luck.

Star got up and retrieved his iPhone. The streets were crazy right now, and he knew anybody could be calling for any reason. He saw it was Kierra calling and was about to decline it until he saw the 14 missed calls.

"Wassup, Ki?" he answered, giving LayLay the shut-the-fuck-up look.

"Where da fuck are you?! I been callin' you for like 30 fucking minutes!" she yelled so loud into the phone Star had to pull it away from his ear.

Meanwhile, LayLay crawled over to him and stuffed his semi-hard dick into her mouth.

"I-I been handlin' business. I told… you, shit ova crazy right now. Wassup?" He clenched his teeth to keep from moaning out.

LayLay was giving him that slow head with extra spit.

"What the fuck are you doing!" she barked.

"Nothin'. I'm leavin' Buddah crib right now. Like what's goin' on, Ki? Why you goin' crazy?"

"Because I'm at the goddamn hospital with TT while yo yellow ass M.I.A."

"Hospital?" he repeated, pushing LayLay away. "What da fuck happened? Are y'all okay? What hospital you at?" He fired off question after question.

"I'm at St. James Olympia Fields. I'm good, but TT was havin' bad-ass stomach pains. Then she started bleedin'. She in the back now. I'm scared, Star," she whispered.

"I'm on my way." He hung up the phone.

"Call me tonight when you figure everything out," LayLay said, disappointed as she switched to the shower.

"Aight… Don't get in yo feelings. I'm comin' back here tonight," he claimed, scrambling to get dressed.

"You betta."

Forty-five minutes later, Star stormed into the emergency room and linked with a teary-eyed Kierra. They sat in silence as they awaited the doctor's arrival, each lost in their own thoughts. After almost two hours, a doctor finally came out and greeted them while simultaneously breaking the news that TT had miscarried. Star wanted to see her, but the doctor was against it. He claimed TT was heavily sedated on top of dealing with the loss of her child. Reluctantly, Star respected the doctor's wishes but promised he would be back first thing in the morning.

LATER THAT NIGHT

"They tell me don't get high and I should try to make a livin'

I tell 'em I'ma hustla and I rather make a killin'

My eyes get so wide as it rise in the skillet

I let my bitch bag it, if she steal, then I'ma kill her—"

Lil Wayne's "Sky Is the Limit" was on blast in Buddah's truck as he zoomed down the expressway. TaeTae was riding shotgun with his Night Hawk in his lap.

"Aye!" He reached over and turned down the music. "Let me get the aux. You got us ridin' to this washed-up ass nigga Wayne."

"First of all, lil nigga, never touch my aux cord. Two, don't ever fix yo mouth to get down on the greatest rapper of all time," Buddah said, shaking his head in disbelief.

"The GOAT? You callin' Wayne the GOAT?" TaeTae raised his eyebrows.

"Duh, nigga. Who did what Wayne did? Wayne had the game in a choke for nine years straight. Shorty, do yo research."

"Man, that's my point. Had. He ain't got no slide music. I wanna hear that Durk, Herb, Von. They talk that straight murda talk," TaeTae said through clenched teeth.

The Adderall he popped earlier kicked in and was in full effect.

"Nigga, that's you lil niggas' problem nowadays. Everybody wanna be a killer instead of playin' the part they was meant to play," Buddah schooled.

"Man, all that—you just sayin' that 'cause you ain't no slider," TaeTae teased.

"You right, I'm not… That's the difference between me and a lot of these niggas. I chase the money. Then when I gotta slide, I'ma slide. Or if a nigga swerve in my lane, I crash 'em. Catchin' bodies just to be catchin' bodies is goofy shit. The game was made to create opportunities for people of poverty to get rich and be able to provide for they loved ones." He glanced TaeTae's way, and just like he thought, he had his full attention. "Anything outside from that is in the way. So you can keep all that slider and stepper shit," he added before turning the radio back up.

"Turn right onto exit 294, and your destination will be on the left in a quarter mile," the GPS screamed through the speakers.

"Aye, look," Buddah said as he jumped onto the exit. "I been fuckin' wit' these niggas on and off for a couple years now. But I don't trust these niggas as far as I can throw 'em. These niggas is as cutthroat as they come. So if these niggas blink wrong—"

"Start blowin' they ass down," TaeTae finished his sentence for him.

"You have reached your destination," the GPS announced.

Buddah parked in front of a shabby two-story house with boards on the windows and front door. Off back, both men knew it was a trap house.

"Stay focused, Folks. These ain't yo average out West niggas. This the Austin area," Buddah shot back, scrolling down his contact, then pressing call.

Unlike the majority of the West Side, which was known for fly dressing and drug dealing… the Austin area was known for its violence. From murders to robberies and even kidnappings, the Austin area was a far cry from the rest of out West. They even held the murder rate for the city some years.

"Yoo!" Whiteboy answered in his usual raspy tone.

"I'm out here," Buddah replied.

"Aight, gimme one minute, foe, and I'm on my way."

"What I tell you 'bout all that 'foe' shit? You'd have a heart attack if I called you G."

"Hell nawl," he laughed. "As long as you know," he added, then disconnected.

Whiteboy was a 4 Corner Hustler—a deadly gang that dominated the majority of the West Side and part of the East and South. They were under the five-pointed star and black diamond, making them the sworn enemy of GDs, but in today's time that hardly mattered. In today's game, cliques ran the city. Same gangs killed each other on a regular basis, and the only thing that really mattered was where you were from—and how many bodies you had. Or in Buddah's and Whiteboy's case—how much money you had.

Whiteboy emerged from the back of the house flanked by two men, and instantly TaeTae tensed up. He gripped his tool and grabbed the door handle.

"Easy, lil bro. He always come like that," Buddah cautioned.

"What you on?" Whiteboy smiled, leaning in Buddah's window.

He was exactly what his name spelled—high yellow with shoulder-length dreads.

"Not shit. You ready? You know it's hot as hell out here. The Jakes been ridin' all through this bitch," Buddah claimed.

"Yeah, I'm already knowin'." He tossed a shopping bag onto Buddah's lap.

Buddah nodded at TaeTae, who passed Whiteboy a manila envelope filled with money.

"And you sayin' I can put this shit on anything?" Buddah asked.

"Duh. Shorty, that's a hunnit percent fentanyl," Whiteboy bragged.

"Aight, bet. I'ma get at you." He shook hands with Whiteboy.

"Aye, look," he said, pulling out a cheap touchscreen phone. "Use this when you wanna get at me. Feds hot as hell. And don't call nobody else off this. My new number already locked in." He passed Buddah the phone.

"Say less. I'ma get at you."

Buddah eased off into traffic, jumping straight back onto the expressway.

"Ona G, big bro—you was right. I could feel the grimy comin' off that nigga," TaeTae claimed, checking their rearview mirror.

"I told you them ain't yo typical out West niggas," Buddah laughed.

"I see." He turned the music up.

CHAPTER 22

A DAY LATER

TT opened her eyes and instantly clutched her stomach. She still had some lingering pain, but the pain inside her heart was ten times worse. She'd lost her first baby and couldn't help but blame herself.

"Am I unworthy? Why did this happen to me? Did I do something to deserve this?" she questioned herself as thoughts of Star leaving her consumed her mind.

"Oh good, you're awake," the nurse cheered as she entered the room.

"Yeah," TT grumbled, mugging the pretty blonde-haired, blue-eyed woman.

"How's your pain?" She made her way to her bedside.

"It's not that bad. Just a little throbbing, that's all."

"Good." She scribbled on TT's chart. "Any nausea? Constipation? Or dizziness?"

"Nah. I feel pretty good physically," TT shrugged.

"Trust me, I know how you feel. It's going to be just fine. What God has for you is for you." She rubbed TT's leg, then smiled. "Now since you're doing fine, we should be releasing you… but the doctor wants to speak with you first."

"Ok… um, did anybody come to see me?" TT raised her brow.

"Yes, actually your boyfriend and girlfriend said they're on the way." She gave her a knowing look.

"Oh… ummm, ok thanks." TT's cheeks turned red.

With that, she left TT to her thoughts. Almost ten minutes later the doctor tapped on the door, then entered. He was a short, slim Arabic man with a zillion greys surrounding the top of his bald head. A pair of wire-rimmed glasses sat on the edge of his beak-like nose.

"How are we feeling?" he asked, his Arabian accent thick.

"I'm good. A little sore, but other than that I feel pretty good," TT countered.

"That's what your nurse told me. But I wanted to see you to ask a few questions." His face turned serious, and it instantly made her uneasy.

"Have you been taking any type of medications, pills, or anything like that?"

She shook her head.

"What about birth control or anything in that nature?" He stared into her eyes as if he was searching for the truth.

"No… why do you ask?" She looked up at him.

Her nerves were on edge, and she unconsciously started biting her nails.

"Well, we found two substances in your bloodstream. One is consistent with birth control. And the other is consistent with a pill known as Plan B."

"What the fuck! Are you serious?" Her eyes narrowed into slits.

"Yes… are you sure you haven't taken anything?"

"Yes, I'm fucking sure!" she snapped.

"I'm sorry. I know how difficult all this may be for you." He paused to let his words sink in. "But please understand I'm only doing my job while trying to help you get to the root of this catastrophe."

"I just don't understand," she whined, her voice shaky and her eyes teary. "I haven't taken anything," she cried, allowing her tears to fall freely.

"Ok, ok. I believe you, sweetie… What about eating out? Have you eaten anywhere that you usually don't?"

"No. I've only been eating at my—" she trailed off.

The shocking reality of what really was taking place choked her. Now she understood why Kierra was being so nice to her and bringing her smoothies every day… But could Kierra really be that low down and conniving? Then her thoughts shifted to Star. Was he in on this? Or was this his plan to begin with? A small part of her wanted to blame the doctor. She wanted so badly to tell him he didn't know what the fuck he was talking about or tell him he did this, but deep in her heart of hearts she knew this was Kierra's doing.

"Umm, Doc," she whispered.

"Yes?"

"I don't want any visitors right now. I just wanna be alone. Clear my head until I'm released. Okay?" She looked up at him.

"Absolutely. I'll get right on it." He walked out of the room.

As soon as the door shut, TT jumped out of bed. She yanked the I.V. from her arm and shed the hospital gown. She was getting ghost. She didn't want to see Star or Kierra. At least not until she cleared her head.

30 MINUTES LATER
AT ST. JAMES

"What da fuck you mean she left!" Star roared, slamming his fist onto the receptionist desk. "How y'all just let one of your patients walk away without y'all knowing!" He was pissed.

Not only was TT missing in action, but she wasn't accepting his or Kierra's calls. Then to add fuel to the flame, the hospital staff had no answer for him either.

"Look sir, I understand your frustration, but a patient who isn't psych can leave any time they want. This is not a prison, you know." The mean-mugging receptionist looked Star up and down.

"Yeah bitch, you keep doin' allat eye rollin', prison is exactly where da fuck Ima be goin'," Kierra snapped. "Let's just go, baby. We can figure this out at home." She hooked her arm into Star's.

"Look, if you or any of the other staff see her or she comes back, call me." He turned and left with Kierra.

"What the fuck? Like why would she just run out without sayin' shit?" Star said as soon as they were inside the car.

"I don't know… Maybe she just wanted to clear her head. I mean, she is going through a lot. The loss of a child can put you in a crazy space mentally," Kierra responded.

"Sounds like you speaking from experience."

"I am… That's why I've been so focused and determined to keep this one." She rubbed her swollen belly. "Just give her time to figure everything out. She'll be hittin' us up in no time."

"I hope so. I hope so," he claimed, starting the car.

LATER THAT NIGHT

TT curled up in the middle of the bed crying her eyes out. She couldn't believe she'd been so dumb. She knew firsthand how jealous Kierra could be, and she still thought they could be one big happy family. After she left the hospital, she went to her apartment, emptied one of Star's safes, then ducked off in a motel to plot her next move.

Vrrrmmmm! Vrrrmmmm! Her phone vibrated again. She didn't even have to look at the screen to know it was Star calling. He'd been blowing up her phone for six hours straight.

"Fuck you," she mumbled, turning off her phone. But she knew in her heart she still loved him and wanted to believe he had nothing to do with Kierra's diabolical plan to kill her baby. Yet she knew it would be impossible to convince Star she did it… unless...

CHAPTER 23

A COUPLE DAYS LATER

Pap dragged his matt and property onto his new deck, which was Division 102 C. Half of the deck was already out for dayroom, so immediately all eyes were on him.

"Aye, where you from, my boy?" a dark-skinned dude with short dreads asked as soon as the CO closed the foyer door.

"Where you from?" Pap countered.

"I'm from 68th and Hoyne… Where you from?" he reiterated.

"I'm from 71st and East End," Pap stated proudly.

"Oh yeah, it's a couple of y'all floatin' through the county. What they call you?"

"Pap… What they call you?"

"Kilo. What cell they got you goin' in?"

"13 cell. Who in there?"

"Ion know the nigga name. He on the new. I think he one of the Moes though," Kilo shrugged.

Instantly, alarm bells rang in Pap's head, but on the outside he was calm, cool, and collected. As soon as he was about to respond, someone calling his name from one of the back cells stole his attention.

"Who is that?" he yelled walking up on the cell.

"This JG, nigga!"

Pap looked through the chuckhole and instantly started smiling. JG was from Jeffery, two blocks from East End. He even hustled with Buddah a time or two, and he was GD.

"Man, bitch ass Django hawked a nigga down, caught me wit' a switch," he claimed, shaking his head.

"Damn, how long you been booked?"

"Three weeks… Oh yeah, just so you know, one of them OTM niggas in cell 13," JG whispered.

"Yeah, that's the cell I'm goin' in. What's his name?"

"50… You know him, or he on the knock off?"

"Nah, that's a real opp. I'm finna kill him as soon as I step in that bitch," Pap claimed, his smirk turning into a real mean mug.

"Man, wait 'til med line so we can kill his ass together." JG pounded his fist into his palm.

"Aye, look, I'm finna use this phone real quick. Cuz soon as that door roll, I'm smokin' him."

Pap shook up with him, then went to use the phone. Kilo, knowing what was going on, was player and let Pap use the rest of the time left on his phone line. He called Crazy G, Star, and LayLay, but she didn't answer. He ended up talking to Star and Crazy G the entire time. By the time he got off the phone, he was seeing red and ready to kill 50 with his bare hands. The hood was wilding out, and he needed to get back ASAP.

"Ona G! I'm finna fuck this nigga up," he thought as the CO escorted him to his cell.

50 was in his cell sitting on the desk watching the visitors come and go, so he was completely off guard when the door was unlocked, and Pap came rushing in. He turned around the same time Pap swung.

Clap! Pap connected squarely with his jaw, staggering him.

"Oh shit! 10-10! 10-10!" the CO yelled into his radio.

Pap could care less though. He swung two more times, connecting with a vicious straight right, straight left that sat 50 on his back pockets.

"Stop or I'm going to fuckin' spray your ass!" the CO warned.

"Kill that bitch, G!" JG yelled.

Pap couldn't hear either one of them; he was in the zone. He grabbed the top bunk and started stomping 50 clean out.

"Aight! You got me! Aight! Aight! C'mon man!" 50 begged, balling up in a fetal position.

"Shut yo bitch ass up! OTMK, nigga! OTMK!" Pap barked, using him as a trampoline.

By now, backup from the other COs came, and Pap was sprayed with mace, cuffed, and dragged right back to the hole.

MEANWHILE

TaeTae cruised through the streets listening to Lil Wayne's *I Am Not a Human Being* mixtape. Since he been hanging with Buddah, that's all he listened to was Lil Wayne, and now that's all he listened to. He glanced in his rearview and instantly gripped his Night Hawk. The all-black Charger had been following him since he'd left the gas station on 71st.

He made a left turn, then ran the stop sign. The Charger did the exact same. He glanced in the rearview again and spotted Tito leaning out the window, aiming a Draco at him.

"Fuck!" He ducked low and mashed the gas pedal.

BRRDAT! BRDAT! BRDAT! BRDAT! 7.62's slammed into the Impala, shattering the back window.

Sccuuuuurt! TaeTae made a wild right. He slid into oncoming traffic and stomped the gas again, but Pewee was a pro behind the wheel and stayed with him the entire way.

BRRDAT! BRDAT! BRDAT! Tito let the Draco roar again. Bullets rocked the Impala, narrowly missing TaeTae's head.

Boom! Boom! Boom! TaeTae fired back blindly. Bullets danced up the hood of the Charger and cracked the windshield, forcing Pewee to slam on the brakes. TaeTae made a quick left, then a hard right, and ended up back on 71st. He flew all the way to the end of the street and parked in their old headquarters apartment complex. Wasting no time, he jumped out, gun in hand and murder in his eyes, but the Charger never turned the corner.

Once he was sure they were gone, he started walking in the opposite direction while he called Buddah.

***

"Why do you keep callin' the bitch? It's clear she don't want to be found, so fuck her. She left us, remember?" Kierra spat as she stomped after Star. "You need to be focused on our baby shower tomorrow instead of that bitch." She was beyond heated.

She was positive that once TT miscarried, Star would be done with her, especially since she'd run out of the hospital without telling them anything. She had clearly underestimated how much love he had for TT, and it had her seeing red.

"Why the fuck you think I'm callin' her? The same way I would be callin' and lookin' for yo ass." He flopped onto the living room couch, found the TV remote, and turned on the WNBA game. Angel Reese was playing Caitlin Clark for the season opener, and he wasn't trying to miss it for a petty argument.

"Like you would for me?" she repeated, standing directly in front of the TV. "So what you sayin'? You love that bitch?" She gave him the nastiest look she could muster.

"Could you gone." He craned his neck trying to see the game.

"Answer my fuckin' question before I break that stupid ass TV!"

"Kierra." He pinched the bridge of his nose. "What you got goin' on that you suddenly care if I love TT or not? A week ago it was just 'you didn't give a fuck about her as long as I married you.' So what's the problem?"

"The problem is you treatin' this bitch like she me. Now answer my fuckin' question. Do you love that bitch?"

Truth be told, she already knew the answer but wanted to hear him say it.

"Yes, I got love for her, but I'm not in love wi—"

SLAP! Before he could finish his sentence, Kierra slapped DNA out of his mouth. He slowly rose to his feet with rage in his eyes.

"Now I know you havin' one of your pregnant moments, so I'ma let you have that. But if you ever slap me again, I'ma slap yo ass back." He slid to the kitchen, swiped his keys, and was out the door.

He was getting ready to hit the hood, but another idea popped into his mind. Thirty minutes later, he found himself in LayLay's apartment complex parking lot. He dialed her.

"Heeyy, Big Daddy!" she answered on the first ring.

"I'm downstairs," he replied.

"Okay, you got a key… so why you ain't just come up?"

"I told you this yo spot. And I'ma respect yo privacy. Neva know when you might have company.""Boy, please. Ain't no niggas ever comin' here if that what you hintin' at. So just come up.

"My girl Porsha here," she said, then hung up.

Star made it up to the apartment in two minutes. He found LayLay on the couch talking to who he assumed was Porsha.

"Baby!" she cheered, running over and jumping in his arms.

"You missed me?" he laughed.

"You know damn well." She climbed down. "This my bestie Porsha. Porsha, this Big Daddy."

"Wassup," Star greeted.

"Okay, now I see why she so crazy ova you. It's always the Eastside ones." Porsha smiled.

"Is that where you from?" he asked with a cocked brow.

"Yup. 79th and Kingston. Colfax—I'm all through there," she bragged.

"Damn, I know a couple of they ass from right there. Who yo people is?"

"My cousin is RayMoe."

"Big swole ass RayMoe? Get the fuck outta here. That's yo cousin? Like, blood cousin?" he said, feigning disbelief.

"Yeah, I'm dead ass. I just left my auntie house on Colfax," she claimed.

"The yellow house on the corner?"

"Nah, she stay in the brick house in the middle."

"Dayum, that's crazy. It's a small ass world. Next time you see cuz, tell him I said wassup."

"I will. What's your name?"

"Star… Look, lil mama, I gotta handle something. I was just stoppin' by to give you this." He dug in his pocket and came out with a wad of bills.

"Psst! I thought you was here to spend the night." LayLay smacked her lips and poked her lip out.

"Depending on what time I get back tonight, I'ma slide through." He smacked her ass.

"Nah, ion care what time it is. I'ma be up waitin'."

"Aight, say less, lil mama. Say less."

FORTY-FIVE MINUTES LATER

"Slidin' through the streets, took off my cleats and got some peace from it / I been in it since I was sellin' water zips for 300 / First time I hit somethin' wit that Blic I had a weak stomach."

EST Gee's *Water Zips* blasted from the speakers of Crazy G's Charger as he glided through the streets, drunk as ever. He had his R.I.P. Laylow shirt on while he gripped his 1911. His trigger finger was itching, and he was ready to let it squeeze at the drop of a dime.

OTM was becoming a real thorn in his side since Tito switched sides and put them on. Then his thoughts shifted to Laylow's mother; he wanted to confront her so bad about the whereabouts of Laylow's body, but he knew he probably wouldn't be able to control himself. Yet he still wanted answers.

"Fuck that shit," he said out loud.

He made a right turn on 71st, then a left on Jeffery. He came to a crawl in front of Laylow's house, then parked two houses down. Just as he was about to climb out of the car, an all-white Chevy Malibu zoomed down the street and into Laylow's driveway.

Crazy G watched in disbelief as Laylow climbed out of the car and jogged to the front door. He peered around sneakily, then knocked on the door. The door was pulled open by his mother, and Laylow disappeared into the house. Crazy G shook his head in shock. He even picked up the empty Hennessy bottle and looked at it sideways, but ultimately he knew he wasn't that drunk, nor was his mind playing tricks on him.

If Laylow's death was a lie, then Crazy G knew that could only mean one thing. He wiped the single tear that slid down his face with the back of his hand, snatched his mask off the passenger seat, and slid from the Charger, gun in hand.

After making sure his mask was on straight, he sprinted to the front door and kicked it.

BOOM! It came splintering in with ease. A wide-eyed Laylow and his mother watched the nightmare known as Crazy G step through the door in terror.

CRACK! With cat-like speed, he smacked Laylow in the mouth with the steel, folding him like a lawn chair.

"Nooo!" his mother screamed.

BLOCKA! BLOCKA! A shot to the chest and neck sent her spinning to the ground right next to Laylow.

"Please! No! Don't do this! Don't do this!" Laylow begged, covering her body with his.

"Fuck you, rat ass nigga!" Crazy G spat.

Laylow locked eyes with him, instantly recognizing the voice. He tried to find the right words to speak to his old friend—words that would save his life—but knew there were none.

BLOCKA! The force from the .45 snapped his head back, forcing his body to fall on top of his mother's lifeless body. But Crazy G wasn't done yet. He aimed his Colt again and squeezed.

BLOCKA! BLOCKA! BLOCKA! BLOCKA! BLOCKA!

Bullets ripped through both their bodies, tossing them this way and that. Satisfied with his handiwork, he bolted out the front door and into his Charger and zoomed off the block.

Had he waited 30 more seconds, he would have been swarmed by Fletcher and his F.B.I. motorcade.

The second Fletcher found out Laylow slipped from witness protection, he rallied the troops and headed for the one place he knew Laylow would be… but he was too late and knew it once he jumped from his car and saw the front door off the hinges. He drew his Glock and stepped into the house, flanked by multiple agents.

"Fuck!" he spat, holstering his weapon and rushing to Laylow's side, but the blank expression on his face told Fletcher exactly what he already suspected.

"We need EMS to 7131 Jeffery Street immediately!" he barked into his radio.

He knew with Laylow gone, his chances of convicting Star and the GDs were slim to none. His entire case was built on Laylow's word; now he was back to square one.

HOURS LATER

"No suspects have been identified in the slaying on 71st and Jeffery. Authorities believe this to be gang-related. If you have any information, contact your local authorities or visit CrimeStoppers.net."

Star pressed pause on the news recording Crazy G had sent him, and the car grew dead silent. Buddah, TaeTae, and Star looked at each other wide-eyed. When Crazy G first called saying he killed Laylow, Star dismissed him as being drunk. But when he sent them the news clip, it left their heads swirling. Just like Crazy G, they all believed Laylow to be dead. Not only that, they'd all let their tools bang in his honor only to find out he was—and had been—a federal informant for years.

"On the G, this shit still seem fake to me," Buddah finally spoke.

"Man, I ain't even tryin' to think 'bout that rat ass nigga." TaeTae shook his head.

"We'll figure out allat shit in the A.M. Right now, let's focus on smokin' this bitch ass nigga RayMoe," Star said, turning his attention back to the brick house.

Thanks to LayLay's motor mouth friend, they were parked outside RayMoe's mama's house awaiting his arrival.

"But what if that bitch was on some fan shit and he don't even stay here?" TaeTae stated.

"That's what we here to find out. Either way, what we got to lose? We catch his ass, then we winnin'. If we don't, we ain't trippin'."

No sooner than the words left his mouth, an all-red Toyota pulled into the driveway. The tension in the car was so thick you could cut it with a knife. As the passenger side door swung open, none other than RayMoe stepped out smiling from ear to ear. He bid the cutie in the driver's seat farewell, then headed for the front door.

Without any hesitation, Star bolted from the car with TaeTae hot on his heels. Just as RayMoe was sticking his key in the lock, Star put his Glock to the back of his head.

"I ain't got shit on me. Y'all robbin' the wrong nigga," RayMoe claimed, raising both hands high in the air.

"Naw nigga. You got exactly what I want. Fuck OTM!" Star spat, then squeezed the trigger.

BOCA! The Hydra-Shok ripped through his skull with ease, spraying his brain matter all over the door and front porch.

BOOM! BOOM! TaeTae dumped two more into him for all the trouble RayMoe caused—and for trying to kill him twice.

"Oh my gawd! Somebody shot Ray!" a woman screeched from inside the house.

Knowing what time it was, TaeTae and Star zoomed back to the car, and Buddah zipped off into the night.

CHAPTER 24

THE NEXT DAY

Pap was jolted awake by someone kicking his cell door.

"What!" he barked, peeking from under the sheet.

"Get dressed. You have a legal call," the officer claimed.

"Gimme a second. I gotta get my shit together."

"I'll be back in five minutes," he said before walking away.

Pap quickly washed his face and brushed his teeth. As promised, the officer came back in five minutes. By him being back in the hole, he had to be shackled from arms to legs before he could go anywhere. Once that was done, he was on his way.

Instead of going in the visitor room direction, he was being put on the elevator.

"I thought I had a legal call," he said as they stepped on the elevator.

"Outside agency," the CO replied.

"What the fuck is outside agency?"

"Meaning, like, sheriffs or detectives from an outside agency want to speak with you."

Pap shook his head with a million thoughts running through his head. There was no telling who wanted to see him and what they wanted to see him for. He truly was living life on the edge when he was free.

They stepped off the elevator and maneuvered through the halls until they came up on a room with two detectives in it. Pap was escorted in and cuffed to a chair. He glanced around the room and locked onto the fingerprint machine and instantly knew it wasn't good.

"Hi, how are you?" the female detective spoke first.

She was brown-skinned with light eyes and the thickest thighs Pap had seen. The skin-tight jeans she wore made it impossible not to stare.

"Can we just skip allat? I'm tryin' to figure out what this is about." Pap got right to it.

"Well, young man, this about you savagely beating a man into a coma yesterday," the male detective spoke up.

He was tall and lanky with a salt-and-pepper beard.

"What?" Pap said barely above a whisper.

He knew he'd did a number on 50, but he didn't think he did him that bad.

"What is right. What were you thinking? And what was that about?" the woman asked.

Pap remained silent.

"So that's the route you want to take. All we're trying to figure out is what really happened."

"Just a simple fight," Pap shrugged.

"Just a simple fight made you stomp a man's head for a full minute?" the woman asked.

Pap didn't respond.

"No answer for that, huh?" The man smiled.

"Aye, am I being charged with something?" Pap looked back and forth between them.

"I'm afraid you are being charged with aggravated battery with great bodily harm."

The woman uncuffed him and waved him to the fingerprint machine.

"Aight," Pap said coolly, but on the inside, he was boiling.

He had less than 72 hours before Frank, his lawyer, was bonding him out. Now he would have to wait until he went to court for his jailhouse, which would probably be another 3 to 4 weeks. Though it was only a Class 2, which carried 3 to 7 years or probation, it was a major setback that he would have to explain to LayLay and the rest of the Moes.

***

"Motherfucker!" Fletcher roared, knocking over his entire desk with one swipe.

He'd just received the news that 50 was in a coma. Now both his informants were gone, and he would have to start from square one or find something concrete. In all his years working law enforcement, he'd never encountered anything like this.

It wasn't like the GDs or OTM were outsmarting him… In fact, they were reckless as hell, but they were extremely lucky. It was driving him mad. He turned around and looked at the pyramids Laylow built for him.

He knew there was a chance one of them would flip informant if the right amount of pressure was applied, but at the same time, if they didn't, his entire investigation would be compromised—which Laylow almost already did.

"Dammit," he huffed, sinking into his chair.

He knew there was a gap in the castle wall somewhere… He just had to find it. He scooped up the files from the floor and started organizing them in chronological order. He wasn't letting them slip through the cracks, even if it meant spending the rest of his career.

ACROSS TOWN

Star opened his eyes and instantly went into panic mode. His hands were tied behind his back while something was wrapped tightly around his neck. Underneath his feet was a stepping stool, letting him know exactly what was planned for him. He could hear shuffling behind him, but the rope around his neck restricted him from looking back.

"Did you think I forgot about you?" a familiar voice asked.

The figure came into view and instantly sent chills down his spine. It was his sister. Her eyes were glowing red as if on fire, and her entire face was covered in blood. He tried to speak, but the rope tightened immediately.

"You're a scum of the earth. A snake in the grass, sleeping with thy neighbor's wife." She shook her head. "The flames of eternity await you." She kicked the stool from under him.

"Oh shit!" Star gasped, sitting up in bed.

"You okay?" LayLay sat up as well.

"Yeah… I'm Gucci," he claimed, checking his throat for rope marks.

The nightmare felt so real it had shook.

"Another nightmare? You been havin' a lot of those lately. You sure you good? You know you can talk to me 'bout whateva." She rubbed his thigh.

Star looked around the room, still trying to collect his thoughts. The sunlight was starting to sneak through the blinds, reminding him how important today was. It was his baby shower and gender reveal.

"Yeah, I'm straight… I'm finna take a shower and slide," he looked at her over his shoulder.

"Shit. You ain't gotta tell me twice." She jumped out of bed and followed him.

After an hour fuck session and a fifteen-minute shower, Star was in his Aston Martin and on his way to pick up a couple last-minute gifts and items for the shower.

VRRMMM! VRRRMMM! VRRRMMM! His phone buzzed in his pocket.

Truth be told she already knew the answer but wanted to hear him say it.

"Yes, I got love for her but I'm not in love wi—"

Slap! Before he could finish his sentence, Kierra slapped DNA out of his mouth. He slowly rose to his feet with rage in his eyes.

"Now I know you havin' one of your pregnant moments so I'ma let you have that. But if you ever slap me again I'ma slap yo ass back." He slid to the kitchen, swiped his keys, and was out the door.

He was getting ready to hit the hood, but another idea popped into his mind. Then 30 minutes later he found himself in LayLay's apartment complex parking lot. He dialed her.

"Heeyy Big daddy!" she answered on the first ring.

"I'm downstairs," he replied.

"Okay you got a key…so why you ain't just come up?"

"I told you this yo spot. And Ima respect yo privacy. Neva know when you might have company."

"Boy please ain't no niggas ever comin here if that what you hintin' at. So just come up.

"My girl Porsha here," she said then hung up.

Star made it up to the apartment in two minutes. He found LayLay on the couch talking to who he assumed was Porsha.

"Baby!" she cheered, running over and jumping in his arms.

"You missed me?" He laughed.

"You know damn well," she climbed down. "This my bestie Porsha. Porsha, this big daddy."

"Wassup," Star greeted.

"Okay now I see why she so crazy ova you. It's always the Eastside one." Porsha smiled.

"Is that where you from?" he asked with a cocked brow.

"Yup 79th and Kingston. Cofax I'm all through there," she bragged.

"Damn I know a couple of they ass from right there. Who yo people is?"

"My cousin is RayMoe."

"Big swole ass RayMoe? Get the fuck outta here. That's yo cousin. Like blood cousin?"

"Yeah I'm dead ass. I just left my Auntie house on Cofax," she claimed.

"The yellow house on the corner?"

"Nah, she stay in the brick house in the middle."

"Dayum that's crazy. It's a small ass world. Next time you see cuz tell him I said wassup."

"I will. What's your name?"

"Star…Look lil mama I gotta handle something. I was just stoppin' by to give you this." He dug in his pocket and came out with a wad of bills.

"Psst! I thought you was here to spend the night." LayLay smacked her lips and poked her lip out.

"Depending on what time I get back tonight. Ima slide through," he smacked her ass.

"Nah ion care what time it is Ima be up waitin'."

"Aight say less lil mama. Say less."

BACK AT THE PARTY

The shower was packed with most of Kierra's friends and family, with the exception of Buddah, TaeTae, Crazy G and LayLay. Unbeknownst to Star who still hadn't showed up yet. LayLay called Crazy G claiming she needed to get out of the house knowing he was headed to Star's baby shower. She really wanted to see what Kierra looked like, and if she had anything on her. Of course in her mind she didn't.

"Okay y'all it's time for the gift opening. Then we'll do the gender reveal!" Ms. Lewis cheered.

"Nah let's do the gender reveal first," Star said strutting in the building.

Today he put on his best. He had on a pair of white washed Amiri jeans with a tight fitting black Balmain shirt. A pair of all-white Jordan 11's were on his feet. A gold Cuban link was wrapped around his neck with a six point Star medallion that hung to the middle of his chest. Immediately all eyes were on him.

"Where da fuck have you been!" Kierra leaned over and whispered harshly.

"C'mon now. It take time to get this fine. Ain't that what you always tell me." He half smiled.

She was beyond irritated, but had to admit her man looked good, especially with his hair freshly lined and taped.

"Okay now for what these two have been dying to find out these last couple of months," Ms. Lewis brought Star the pop can. "Shake it and open it baby."

Star did exactly as he was told and when he pulled the top. Poof! Pink dust flew everywhere.

"It's a girl!" Everybody cheered.

"Yay!" Kierra clapped.

Star was salty he wasn't having a boy, but he really wasn't mad about it either. In fact what really was on his mind was what TT told him. He wanted so badly to say she was wrong, or it was some type of mix up, but he couldn't argue the facts. He looked up and locked eyes with LayLay and almost had a heart attack, but she quickly looked away as if she didn't even know him. After they opened up the gifts, they ate, drank, and danced until everybody parted ways. Keyanna, LayLay, Buddah, Star, Crazy G stayed back to clean up the hall.

"You so fuckin' fine right now. I can't wait to ride that dick," LayLay whispered as she swept the floor.

Star peeked around to make sure nobody was listening. "I'm cum all over yo face tonight," he whispered back.

"Say what nigga?" Buddah said walking up.

He looked from Star to LayLay.

"What you mean?" Star replied, but Buddah had heard him loud and clear, and the look on his face spoke volumes.

"Nothin' I'm' get at you lata. I'm finna head out," he said giving LayLay the nastiest look in the world.

Star looked at LayLay and shook his head. They were caught and if Buddah spilled the beans…

CHAPTER 25

LATER THAT NIGHT

Star tiptoed into his bedroom and checked to see if Kierra was still asleep. Once he was sure she wasn't getting out of bed anytime soon, he swiped her purse and darted into the bathroom. After a careful search, he came up empty-handed. He returned her purse, then started checking her dresser drawers. After making it halfway through, he was about to call it quits—until an aluminum-like package sticking out from under her pants caught his eye.

He lifted the pants, and there were five of them, with each package holding 12 pills—except for one that was missing nine tablets. He looked at the name on the label and was instantly filled with rage. It read a name he couldn't pronounce, then "generic birth control."

He looked at a sleeping Kierra with pure disgust. He couldn't believe she could be so low. Even he wouldn't kill a baby, and he was a stone-cold murderer.

He stomped over to the bed and shook her by the shoulders violently.

"What the fuck!" she yelled, her eyes wild.

He didn't respond. Instead, he slapped her with the birth control tablets, then dug in his pocket and shoved TT's hospital labs in her face.

"Muthafucka, have you lost your mind!" she growled, knocking the papers aside. "Don't you ever put yo hands on me!" she screamed.

"Nah, bitch, you lost *yo* mind!" he yelled back. "How fucked up you gotta be to poison yo pregnant friend?"

Instantly, Kierra's face flushed, and her head dipped. Only then did she realize what Star had slapped her with. Then she scooped up the papers and knew she was caught red-handed.

"Aw, no, yo triflin' ass get it. When TT first got at me with that shit, I almost choked the life outta that bitch. But when she showed me those papers, I thought they made a mistake. But then I remembered all them threats you made 'bout not lettin' her have my baby."

He mean-mugged her with murder in his eyes.

The only thing that was stopping him from strangling her to death was his daughter in her stomach.

"Well, what the fuck did you expect me to do!" she slammed the papers on the bed and got in his face. "You think I was just gon' let that bitch ride off into the sunset with you? I already let the bitch share our bed because I knew you couldn't stop fuckin' the hoe behind my back. And what you do after that? You move the bitch in. I let that shit go as long as you put me first. Then you get the bitch pregnant. No matter what the fuck I did, it wasn't gon' be enough. So yeah, I did what I had to do. I ain't proud of it. But that bitch need to know her place."

"Get da fuck out," he mumbled.

"Nigga, I ain't goin' no muthafuckin' where. You got me fucked up. All the shit you put me through. Yeah, you got me fucked up."

"Aight bet. Stay." He snatched two empty duffel bags from the closet and started piling his clothes into one.

Kierra knew he was serious when he started emptying his safe.

"Are you fuckin' serious? So what—you done? You gon' leave to be wit' that bitch because of this shit?" She stood right behind him with her arms folded defiantly.

Star ignored her. He just kept packing his money. Right now, he couldn't stand the sight of her and had to get away, or he would surely kill her tonight. Once he finished packing, he snatched up his bags, but Kierra stood in his way.

"Where the fuck you think you goin'!" she screamed at the top of her lungs.

"Kierra, just watch the fuck out," he said calmly.

"So you just gon' walk out on us for that bitch?" She placed both hands on her stomach.

"Kierra, what da fuck did I just say!" he snapped, brushing past her. "Ain't nobody said they done. I just need time to clear my head," he said, never looking back.

"With that bitch, right?"

"If that's what you think. But I ain't stayin' wit' her either." He jogged down the stairs and out the front door without another word, leaving Kierra on the porch heated.

"Ooooooh! Ima kill this bitch!" she roared, stomping back into the house.

ON 57TH

"Man folks, that new shit you been puttin' out here got the hypes going crazy. I mean, they ass been findin' all type of shit to sell for that dope." Crazy G smiled.

He and Buddah were in his apartment finishing their nightly count, which was almost double what they normally made. Since Buddah mixed their heroin with the fentanyl he got from White Boy, they virtually took over the South Side's heroin game overnight.

"Wassup wit' you? You been quiet since the baby shower," Crazy G pointed out.

"Do Star and LayLay know each other?" Buddah gave Crazy G a knowing look.

"Nah, why you ask that?" Crazy G leaned forward, giving Buddah his undivided attention.

"Man… I walked up on him at the baby shower, and he was tellin' her how he was gon' nut on her face tonight."

"What! Hell naw, is you sure?"

"Nigga, on Larry Bernard Hoover, I'm sure." He threw up the pitchforks for emphasis.

"So you think that nigga fuckin' on Pap's girl? That's some snake-ass shit."

"I mean, can we really put it past him? Look at the shit wit' Tito and TT."

"What was she doin' when he was sayin' that shit?"

"She was smiling. They was lookin' dead at each other."

"Damn. That thot-ass bitch. That nigga Pap really look up to that nigga. Shit, that nigga was best friends with Buck Wild before he got smoked… We gotta tell bro," Crazy G claimed.

"Yeah. But we gotta make sure that's what it is first."

"Fuck you mean we gotta make sure? If they talkin' to each other like that, they already fuckin'."

"Yeah. But you gotta look at this shit from every angle before we jump straight to that conclusion," Buddah countered. "What if he was drunk, tweakin'? Then we front our move on false accusation. Now he on our ass by law."

"Yeah, that nigga definitely gon' try to play catch 22."

"Exactly… But Ima slide to the crib. We'll figure this shit out in the A.M." Buddah stood up.

"Say less." Crazy G shook up with him.

Buddah drove home thinking about Star and LayLay the entire drive. The more he thought about it, the more convinced he was that they were messing around. When he and Crazy G picked her up, she was too excited to go to a baby shower for some people she didn't know. Then the entire ride, she talked about Star as if she knew him.

"Yeah, that lil pussy fuckin'," he mumbled, pulling into his driveway.

He looked at the house, and all the lights were out except his bedroom. He climbed out of his truck, hoping Lita, his baby momma, was asleep. It had been two days since he'd been home, and he knew she was going to let him have it.

He opened the door and was met by something hard across the side of his face.

"Fuck," he cried as he dropped to his knees.

CRACK! This time he was struck in the back of the head so hard he almost blacked out. Quickly, his hands were zip-tied behind his back along with his feet. He was so dizzy he couldn't fight back if he wanted to. The lights were turned on and his attackers came into view. There were three of them. All of their faces covered with ski masks, and all of them had Dracos. What really rattled him was Lita and his 8-year-old daughter zip-tied as well.

"Do whatever y'all gotta do to me. Just let them go." He strained his neck to look up at his captors.

"This shit is as easy as you make it, fat boy," the shortest one spoke first; his voice was low and raspy.

Instantly Buddah recognized the voice, but what puzzled him was how he was able to find out where he lived… Then it clicked—the phone.

"You might as well take that mask off. I know yo voice anywhere, White Boy," Buddah mugged him.

"Congratulations!" White Boy laughed, then stomped Buddah in the back. His chest bounced off the ground, instantly knocking the world out of him. "Now you can tell us the code to that big-ass safe you got up there, and where you put my phone. And your daughter and BM gon' be okay."

Buddah took one look at his family zip-tied and gagged on the floor and knew what he had to do. Even though he was sure White Boy would kill him anyway, he could care less. He would die for them a thousand times over. He quickly told them the code and let them know the phone was inside the safe. White Boy and one of the other goons went to empty the safe. Buddah looked for a way out of his certain death, but there was none. White Boy and company came back in a flash, and just as Buddah predicted, he aimed his Draco at Buddah's dome and squeezed. The deadly 7.62s ripped through Buddah with ease and sent his lifeless body skidding across the living room.

"MMMM!" Lita cried through the sock that was taped in her mouth.

Then the same way they came, they were gone, leaving Buddah in a pool of blood.

***

The next morning Crazy G's apartment was so quiet you could hear a mouse piss on cotton balls. TaeTae, Star, and Fabo were on one couch while Crazy G paced the floors with a bottle in hand. They had been there since they left the hospital with Lita. Buddah was so twisted that Star and Crazy G had to confirm his body for her. No words needed to be spoken; each and every man knew exactly what time it was. Today they would mourn their brother, but tomorrow they would paint the streets red with the enemies' blood.

"Them niggas from out West gone be hard to catch," TaeTae broke the silence once Lita explained the story to them. TaeTae instantly knew exactly who was responsible for Buddah's death. Them asking for a phone that wasn't Buddah's was a dead giveaway.

"Nah they ain't. Once the jakes release Buddah's phone, we got they number," Star said.

"Then they life," Crazy G added.

CHAPTER 26

DAYS LATER
BURR OAKS CEMETERY

"From ash to ash you shall return," the pastor whispered as he dumped dirt onto RayMoe's casket.

The entire OTM plus a few of the other Black P Stones from various hoods came out to pay their respects. RayMoe was an outstanding member and had mad love throughout the entire South Side. His funeral spoke for itself with over 120 people in attendance.

"I love you forever, boo," Dreah, RayMoe's baby mother whispered, tossing a red rose onto the casket.

"Look Mommy." Rain tugged at Dreah's leg. "Angels for Daddy," she pointed.

Dreah peeked over her shoulder and was instantly paralyzed with fear. Three men in white ski masks were jumping the gate with guns in their hands. Dreah opened her mouth to scream, but it was too late.

Boca! Boca! Boca! Boom! Boc! Boc! Boc! Boom! Boom! The masked men opened fire on any and everybody in sight. People screamed, ran, and knocked each other over in an attempt to escape the hellfire being unleashed upon them. Some of the Moes even tried to return fire, but the innocent bystanders rushing their way made it almost impossible. The masked men let their tools bang again before jumping back over the gate. They sprinted back to their stolen Dodge Durango. Before they could jump all the way in, Fabo mashed the pedal. The hemi roared loudly as they zipped up the block. He made a couple of quick turns and was about to bring the Durango to a halt when a police cruiser popped out of nowhere with its lights and siren blaring.

"Oh shit!" Fabo yelled, stomping the gas again.

Sccuurt! The truck fishtailed before it took off, but the police cruiser was a Charger and stayed with them.

"Aye we gotta lose this muthafucka before backup come!" Star snapped from the passenger seat.

"I'm trying!" Fabo yelled, panic etched in his tone.

Crazy G gave TaeTae a nod, and they both spun around aiming their straps.

Boom! Boom! Boca! Boca! Boca! Boom! Bullets danced up the hood of the cruiser and ripped through the windshield. The cruiser instantly swerved in an attempt to dodge the hail of bullets and crashed into a parked car head-on.

"Damn! We just clapped 12!" Fabo yelled, panicking.

"Aye pull over. We gotta bail out on foot. They gone be all over this car," Star instructed.

"You sure? I can g—"

"Just pull the fuck over!" Crazy G snapped.

"Aight. Aight." Fabo navigated the Durango to the side of the street.

Star wasted no time stuffing his ski mask into his pants and wiping off anything he may have touched with the sleeve of his hoodie. Crazy G and TaeTae followed suit before they all jumped out on foot. Sirens blasted in the distance letting them know it was crunch time. They cut through a backyard and ended up in an alley. Star made a beeline for the dumpster and slid behind it. TaeTae slid behind it with him, while Crazy G and Fabo jumped inside of it. Knowing their time was limited, Crazy G pulled up the Uber app and ordered one.

"Uber on the way in six minutes," he whispered.

Star would be lying if he said he wasn't scared. No, he was terrified. All he could think about was going back to Menard forever. He knew he probably only had a couple of shots left after all the shooting he did at the cemetery, but that was more than enough. He would hold court right then and there and die in the streets before he went back. He just hoped like hell he didn't have to die today.

"Man y'all think we gone be straight? This some crazy shit," Fabo said.

"Shut up!" They all whispered harshly.

***

At the County Jail "So how long until I get the fuck outta here? I'm sick of all this extra goofy shit. I'm ready to get out," Pap claimed, cupping his hands around the glass so Frank could actually hear him.

"Well, as of right now your original case bond is already paid. Once you receive a bond tomorrow, we'll figure everything out," Frank replied.

"Aight cool. But how much you think it's going to be? It shouldn't be that much since it's only a Class Two, right?"

"It shouldn't be, no. But since you picked up these charges on the inside, the judge might try to make an example out of you. Even still, it shouldn't be that much." Frank scooped up his papers and stuffed them into his briefcase. "Any questions for me?"

"Nah. We all good, Frank. We all good." Pap smiled.

HOURS LATER

"17 wounded, 6 dead, and two in critical condition in what authorities are calling the Burroaks Massacre—"

Fletcher paused the news recording and pinched the bridge of his nose in frustration. If only Waller had listened when he'd begged him to have undercovers at the funeral, then none of this would have ever happened. Now six people were dead with one of them being a cop. Then on top of it all, Waller and the mayor were on the verge of cutting funding for his investigation if he didn't come up with something solid soon. All his hopes and dreams of retiring as one of Chicago's and Illinois' top agents were going right down the drain—and all because of dumb luck.

He flicked through all the still shots he had of 71st Mob and OTM.

"Useless. Nothing. Garbage," he mumbled, flinging pictures across the room one by one, until he landed on one that got him out of his seat. He thumbed through the ones behind it, and they were just as useful.

"How did I miss these?" he whispered, a sly smile spreading across his face.

This was exactly what he needed. He was 85% sure this would help him turn the tables and secure the evidence he needed to put Star and the G.D.'s away for life.

ON 57TH

"Man, what the fuck?" Fabo said, peeking out of the blinds for the hundredth time in minutes. "You think they on to us?"

TaeTae, Crazy G, and him were held up in Crazy G's apartment. Star had TT come scoop him so he could lay low at her place. The Burr Oaks Massacre was being broadcast on every news station in America. The only thing they had working in their favor was that Burr Oaks Cemetery was located in the Wild Hundreds, which was almost thirty minutes away from them and on Chicago's South Side.

"What da fuck is you sayin'? If they was on us, they woulda been smacked this bitch," TaeTae said, irritated Fabo was acting so paranoid.

"Plus, lil Folks nem on S. Anything that look wrong, they gone blast first and figure allat other shit out lata… You goo, my dude? It sound like you panicking." Crazy G looked Fabo's way.

"Nigga, hell yeah I'm panicking. The fuck. Nigga, we just clapped the jakes. The streets is on fire. Fuck you mean, is I'm panickin'," Fabo repeated.

"Them people don't know shit. And ain't gone know shit as long as you keep it cool and don't say shit." Crazy G stood up and mugged him.

"Nigga, I ain't no rat, so watch that shit." Fabo started in Crazy G's direction, but TaeTae blocked his path.

"Y'all niggas chill. Ain't no tellin' what's going on right now. We all we got. Right now can't be tryin' to kill each other." He pushed Fabo one way and Crazy G the other.

Fabo looked as if he wanted to try Crazy G but knew he would have to go through TaeTae, which was an impossible task. If nobody else knew, Fabo knew firsthand how TaeTae was with the hands. He was a stone-cold knockout artist, and once he turnt up, there was no turning down.

CHAPTER 27

MEANWHILE ON 79TH

"Man, is you sure about this?" Tito asked, loading his 50-shot drum to the max with hollow points.

"Fuck, is you scared or somethin'?" Slap pulled the slide on his AK-47.

"Neva that. Nigga, the city on fire. Every police in the world want they get back for whoever smoked that police," Tito shot back.

"That shit was all the way in the Hunnits." TaeMoe co-signed as usual. He also had a Draco equipped with a 75-round drum.

"The fuck that mean? The streets ain't hot?" Tito looked at both men like they were stupid.

"So what if they is!" Pewee spat. "Them hoe-ass niggas put our brother in the dirt. Then came and shot up any and everybody at his funeral. Them niggas ain't give a fuck 'bout shit then, so why should we give a fuck now?" He stood up with both his 30-shot Glocks in hand and murder in his eyes. "You ridin' or not?"

Tito understood Pewee's pain but didn't agree with his plan to shoot up 57th. Not only did Crazy G have Shields on smash, but he knew firsthand how the police got when one of their own was touched. They would be out harassing and arresting anybody they could until the culprits responsible were brought in or killed. Right now, Pewee was moving with his heart instead of his head, and he wanted no parts. He knew how this story ended, but for some reason he still felt obligated to ride.

"Yeah, I'm slidin'," Tito claimed.

"Say less." Pewee turned on his heels and headed for the door with Slap, TaeMoe, and Tito in tow.

Twenty minutes later, they were parking their van two blocks from Shields on Troop. It was a breezy afternoon with the sun setting in the sky, so there was barely anybody out with the exception of a few fiends here and there. They cut through a backyard which led to an alley, then they jumped a gate and came out on Shields.

"Aye!" one of the G.D.'s on security yelled, reaching for his gun, but he was too late.

Tito kicked it off, letting his Glock speak. BOOM! BOOM! BOOM! Instantly, the men on the porch ducked for cover, but Slap was on them, finger-fucking his K like his life depended on it.

DOCKA! DOCKA! DOCKA! One of the five men was ripped to shreds by the deadly 7.62's, but the others managed to slip off the porch unscathed. Just as they were about to return fire, TaeMoe and Pewee let their tools bang.

BRRDDDT! Pewee's twin nines were drowned out by TaeMoe's Draco. Two more of the men dropped like flies, crying out in the process.

BOC! BOC! BOC! BOC! Tito slammed on his trigger relentlessly as he walked the men down. Slap was weaving in between the parked cars trying to get an angle on the men, so he never saw TaeTae, Crazy G, and Fabo exit the building with their guns aimed high.

BOOM! BOOM! BOOM! TaeTae got off first, catching Slap twice in the back and once in the neck. Slap tried to yell out but coughed violently with blood flying from his mouth. Then he went still.

BLOCKA! BLOCKA! BLOCKA! BOCA! BOCA! Fabo and Crazy G sent a barrage of shots Pewee and TaeMoe's way, but the bullets sailed harmlessly over their heads.

DOCKA! DOCKA! DOCKA! DOCKA! DOCKA! TaeMoe let his AK do all the talking for him, immediately forcing them to scramble for cover. The unmistakable sound of police sirens and engines revving let them know what time it was, but Pewee could care less.

BOCA! BOCA! BOCA! BOCA! He squeezed over and over again, completely clueless to TaeTae aiming at his dome.

CLICK! CLICK! CLICK! The revolver signaled it was empty. He never reloaded after the cemetery. Wasting no time, he tucked his gun and sprinted up the street.

"We gotta go!" Tito yelled, still letting the men on the side of the house have it.

TaeMoe was the first to make his way back through the cut they originally came through, followed by Tito, then Pewee. Fabo was about to give chase when—BLOCKA! A bullet from Crazy G's 1911 ripped through his skull. He fell face-first in the grass with his eyes wide open, confusion etched into his face. Crazy G knew how much he was panicking—that he couldn't be trusted. He could only imagine what he would do and say if the police put any type of pressure on him… so he had to go.

Quickly, Crazy G bolted back into his building and locked his apartment door. He wasn't worried about any of the neighbors snitching. They knew exactly who he was and how he got down. To snitch on him would be a death sentence.

THE NEXT MORNING

Pap paced the length of the bullpen as he waited for his name to be called. Today was his bond hearing for his jailhouse case. Frank had already spoken with the State, who claimed they wouldn't pursue an excessive bond, so Pap was on cloud nine. His name was called, and he was escorted in front of the judge. A huge smile spread across his face when he saw Laylay seated in the back. She was dressed to impress, with her lips extra glossy the way he liked it.

"What do we have?" the judge asked.

He was an older white man with glasses that sat on the tip of his nose and a bald head.

"A bond hearing for a Class Two Aggravated Battery with Great Bodily Harm," the State's attorney announced.

She looked to be mid to late thirties and reminded Pap of the actor Jennifer Lawrence.

"Any background?"

"No. But the defendant does have pending charges for two separate unlawful use of a weapon," the State replied.

"Bond will be set at sixty-five thousand. So you will need to post ten percent of that. Any questions for me?"

Pap shook his head and was escorted back to the bullpen with the biggest smile on his face. All he needed to do was sixty-five hundred more dollars and he would finally be free.

BACK ON 57TH

Crazy G scanned the block from his apartment window, and nothing had changed. The block was still crawling with police cars and detectives.

"Bitch-ass shit," he spat, yanking the curtain closed.

The heavy police presence was making it impossible to set up shop. He had already missed the early morning rush, which was the most profitable time of the day. Now it was going on ten and they were still showing no signs of leaving. He pulled his phone out and tried TaeTae again but got his voicemail again.

"I hope this nigga ain't booked," he thought.

DING! His phone chimed, letting him know he had a text message. It was from Star, telling him to meet him on 71st ASAP.

"What da fuck now?" he mumbled, tucking his gun under the couch and snatching his keys. He wasn't risking walking past a thousand cops with a gun that had multiple murders on it.

IN FRANKFORT
HOURS LATER

Kierra called Star for what had to be the thousandth time since he left and received the same result… he declined.

"I cooked breakfast," Keyanna sang as she entered the room.

"It's one o'clock," she sniffled.

"Bitch, I know you ain't tryin' to call that lame-ass nigga of yours." Keyanna cocked her brow and folded her arms across her chest.

"Please don't start." She tossed her phone on the bed and wiped her eyes.

"No, I'm gone start. You need to be worried 'bout havin' this baby. If that nigga ain't thinkin' 'bout you, then you not thinkin' 'bout him, period."

Now her frown turned into a smile.

"Do you want to know what I cooked?"

DING-DONG! DING-DONG! The doorbell echoed throughout the house.

"You invited Zach?" Kierra huffed.

"No, I didn't invite Zach. I don't know who that is. Maybe it's that sorry-ass nigga of yours coming to beg for forgiveness." She stomped off to answer the door.

She pulled the door open and was met by a smiling Agent Fletcher flanked by Prosecutor Zarc. "Uuummm, can I help y'all?" Keyanna wrinkled her face as if they were beneath her.

"You sure can. I'm Agent Fletcher with the FBI." He flashed his badge. "This is federal prosecutor Zarc. We're here to have a chat with Kierra."

"Do y'all have a warrant? And is she in some kind of trouble?"

"Depending on how this conversation goes, she might be," Zarc claimed.

"Kierra!" she yelled. "Some people down here wanna talk to you." She stepped to the side, letting them enter.

ON 71ST

"Sooo you want all of us to go on vacation? What about the block? What about Buddah's funeral?" Crazy G spoke while looking at Star like he was crazy.

"Nigga, don't you think I wanna be there when they put Folks in the ground? You think I don't wanna get money?"

Star shot back. "Use yo head for once. You know we hot as hell right now wit' all this shit goin' on. Why not get out the way before we even get in the way?"

Crazy G finally took a seat in TT's living room armchair, stroking the few chin hairs he had. He knew Star had a valid point, but he also knew there was a chance he was overreacting. In his mind, if the police knew anything remotely close about who was responsible for killing one of their own, they would've been under the jail already.

"G ball, I hear where you comin' from and appreciate the offer. But ima pass. Take TaeTae wit' you. Ima grab a couple extra soldiers from Jeffery and hold down the fort. Ima see you niggas when y'all get back." He stood back up.

"Where is TaeTae? I been tryin' to get at him and Fabo since last night," Star claimed, oblivious that Crazy G whacked Fabo.

"I don't know where TaeTae is. I been lighting his shit up too. But as for Fabo—checked in that bang out. Caught one to the dome." He gave Star a knowing look.

"Probably for the best. That nigga was a panic button." Star gave him a sly smirk.

"Naw G. I'm thuggin'."

BACK IN FRANKFORT

"Like I said, you really need to think about this shit before you play it that way… I mean, tax evasion and money laundering is some serious shit. Ki, you can end up doin' ten years in a federal prison. And for what? A nigga that don't give two fucks about you. Because if he did, he would be here to protect you when the Feds rolled up. You 'bout to be a mama. You don't need this shit."

Keyanna preached as she shuffled through the still shots of Star with Laylay and TT. "I mean, look at this dog-ass nigga. You deserve better, Ki."

"I just… I just don't know what to do. If I snitch on him, then I gotta worry 'bout the rest of them niggas tryna kill me," Kierra claimed. "This—this still is the father of my… Ah! Shit!" She grabbed her stomach.

"Are you okay?" Keyanna stood up.

"Oh my God. I think my water just broke." She leaned back on the couch, scrunching up her face in agony. "C-call Star. AAAhh!"

HOURS LATER

Star stepped off the plane and into the airport with TT in tow. They had packed zero luggage because Star planned on balling out of control the entire trip. Las Vegas was the city of sin, and he planned on doing just that. This was his first real vacation, and he was charged.

"So what we doin' first?" TT asked, taking his hand in hers.

"Shit, ion know. I wanna see all their casinos and strip clubs. Shit, I wanna see everything." He smiled.

VRRMMM! VRRMMM! DING! DING! VRRMMM! His phone went crazy in his pocket. While in the sky, he had lost signal. Looking at his screen, he had to do a double take. He had so many missed calls and texts, but the one that snagged his attention was from Keyanna. It read: *You dog-ass nigga. You couldn't even be here for the birth of your daughter.* Instantly, his heart sank to the pit of his stomach. Did he really miss the birth of his daughter?

"What's wrong?" TT asked, reading him like a book.

"We gotta go back. Kierra is having the baby," he replied, heading for the front desk.

"Are you sure she ain't doin' this to get you back in the house?" she questioned, following closely behind him.

"Yeah, I'm sure. Let's go. After this shit done, we gone come back."

DOWNTOWN CHICAGO MCC

"Aye, can somebody tell me what da fuck is going on?" TaeTae yelled, kicking the holding cell door.

"Look, if you don't cut that shit out, I promise you I'm putting your ass on suicide watch!" the guard warned.

"Man, fuck you and suicide watch. I'm tryna figure out what da fuck is going on, and why y'all brang me here!"

"Just sit tight. Someone will be to speak with you in the morning."

"The mornin'?" he repeated, scrunching up his face as if something stunk. "I been here since last night, and ain't nobody gave me a phone call or shit. I don't even know where I'm at."

"You're in the M.C.C.—federal holding. An agent will be in, in the morning, to speak with you," he said before walking off.

CHAPTER 28

THE NEXT MORNING

Star pulled up to the hospital with his mind running wild. He knew for a fact that Kierra was about to snap the second he entered her room. Then to make matters worse, her sister and mother were present, so without a doubt, it would be three on one. When he finally made contact with Keyanna, he tried explaining why he was in Vegas, but she wasn't trying to hear none of it. Even though he had a legit reason for missing his daughter's birth, he still felt low. He tried to make it back last night, but Las Vegas had a record-breaking sandstorm, which delayed all flights. Now here he was, trying to find the right words to say when he saw Kierra, who he knew hated him. Quickly, he climbed out of the car and made his way into the lobby. A white lady who looked like she wasn't a day over 21 occupied the desk.

"Hi, how can I help you?" she sang, flashing her pearly whites.

"I'm here for Kierra Johnson… she had gave birth to our daughter yesterday." He smiled back.

"Oh… um, one second." She picked up the phone and started dialing.

Almost a full minute later, two heavyset security guards stomped his way.

"Sorry sir, but we're going to have to ask you to leave," the receptionist said.

"Da fuck you mean you need me to leave? You ain't just hear me tell you my lady is havin' our baby?" Star mugged each and every single one of them.

"Ms. Johnson has asked us not to let you up… I'm sorry, but we have to respect her wishes," the receptionist claimed.

"The fuck you mean? Aye look, just call her room and tell her I'm down here."

"Sir, I think it's best if you just leave," one of the security guards stepped his way.

"I promise you, if you touch me, Ima stretch yo bitch ass out in this bitch," he growled with murder in his eyes.

"Sir, you need to just leave," the receptionist begged.

"Ima leave right now. But Ima be back tomorrow. So I suggest you talk to Ms. Johnson and let her know that when I come back, I betta be able to see my daughter, or I'm gon' wreck this bitch." He turned on his heels.

"Is that a threat?" the security guard asked.

"I said what I said," he replied over his shoulder.

Knowing the games white people played when threatened, Star made his way to his car with some pep in his step, then burned rubber out of the parking lot.

Vrrrmmm! Vrrmmm! Vrrmm! His phone rang.

"Wassup?"

"I need you to come see me ASAP," LayLay claimed.

"Aight, wassup though?" he questioned.

"I'll tell you when you get here."

ON 57TH

Crazy G peeked out his apartment window and couldn't help but smile. The police activity was finally dying down, and they were back to making money hand over fist… but there was another problem. They were running out of the work that Buddah put together. Plus, the majority of the fiends were spooked after the shootout and all the police activity.

Vrrmm! His phone vibrated on the windowsill. The caller ID read *Scam Likely*, so instantly he declined it. Vrrmm! Vrrmmm! It read *Scam Likely*, so again he declined it. **Vrrm!** It was *Scam Likely* again, but this time he answered.

"Man, who da fuck is—"

"This is a collect call from Pap, an inmate at—"

Crazy G immediately pressed 1 to answer.

"What's the word, G?" he greeted.

"Shit, tryna figure out why you niggas ain't came to scoop a nigga yet?" Pap half-joked.

"Fuck you mean? We sent the lawyer to bond you out. But he said you caught a new case."

"I did, but I got a bond for that two days ago. LayLay ain't tell y'all? She was at my court date."

"Hell nawl, she ain't say shit," Crazy G claimed.

"Fa real? Fuck type of time she on? My shit only seventy-five hunnit," he said with irritation etched in his tone.

"Man, ion know what's to her. Maaan, her lil ass… but you sure yo shit seventy-five hunnit?"

"Yeah, and what you mean her lil ass? Let me know somethin'."

"Nah, it ain't shit. I'm finna come scoop you right now though. We need you back out here. Shit ain't been the same without you," Crazy G said truthfully. "They finna let my nigga out. It's finna be a fuckin' movie."

"You know that." Pap laughed. "But fa real though, my nigga, what was you finna say 'bout LayLay? Don't have me lookin' like a goofy. If she out there fuckin', then let a nigga know somethin'," Pap said seriously.

"Ima tell you when I come scoop you."

"Bet," Pap said, then hung up.

Crazy G swiped his keys and headed for the door, debating on whether or not he should tell Pap what Buddah heard.

"Fuck it," he thought.

If the shoe was on the other foot, he would want Pap to tell him.

AT THE M.C.C.

"That's all I know," TaeTae huffed.

He spent the last three hours explaining 71st's whole operation, including the Burr Oaks Massacre. Though he initially seemed solid, he was far from it. Without putting any pressure on him, he told Fletcher everything he wanted and needed to put Star, Crazy G, and a few of the other GDs under the jail. He even snitched on Fabo and Buddah. He could care less. All he wanted was not to spend the rest of his life in jail. In his mind, he was still a gangster and would get right back out doing the same thing, while the stand-up members would rot in jail. He was the scum of the earth; he was what you called a killer rat. He would kill you if he got the chance, then snitch at the same time. There was only one place for people like TaeTae… and that was the grave.

"You sure this is it?" Fletcher asked, sliding the ten pages of TaeTae's written statement over to him with a pen.

"Yeah, I'm sure."

"I need you to sign and initial every page." Fletcher smiled, unable to contain his excitement.

This, with Kierra's help, would certainly bury the 71st Mob for good.

"Are you sure I'm only going to get five years?" TaeTae asked as he signed every page.

"Isn't that what the prosecutor agreed upon, right?"

"As long as I testify," he said, signing away.

"Then you have nothing to worry about."

IN LANSING

"I don't understand why you so mad about it. I thought I was givin' us more time to figure shit out," LayLay claimed, grabbing Star's hand, but he snatched away.

"That ain't no shit you do. You don't leave a righteous nigga to rot in a cell," he snapped.

"Oh, you just fuck his bitch," she countered with a raised brow. "Like let's be honest, allat righteous shit went out the window the second we started doin' us. You try to act like we just fuck buddies. But you really fuck wit' me, Star. And

I really fuck wit' you. So why not just say fuck what everybody else think and be together?"

Star pinched the bridge of his nose in frustration. He was hearing LayLay but knew it would never be that easy. He was already catching hell from Kierra for a big misunderstanding. Then if word got out that he was fucking his dead best friend's little brother's girl, people would lose all respect for him—especially TT. That was something he couldn't afford right now, especially with them being in the middle of a war.

"Look, I fuck wit' you. But right now this shit gotta stop." He grabbed all his bags and headed for the door.

"Where da fuck you goin'?"

"To bond Pap out."

"Why da fuck would you do that? All I gotta do is break up wit' him and we can start doin' us. You know that, right?" she followed behind him.

"Shit still ain't gon' look right. Just give a nigga some time to figure they own shit out, then we can figure the rest out lata," he claimed as he stepped out of the door.

Star quickly loaded his money and clothes into the trunk of his car. He didn't want to risk riding around with almost a million in cash, so before he went to bond out Pap, he was going home to drop it off.

ON 79TH

Tito and Pewee were in Pewee's basement plotting their next move. Well, Pewee was doing all the plotting while Tito listened.

"Them niggas' spot on 57th is a gold mine if we can hit that bitch… we a be ova up and standin' on them niggas at the same time," Pewee claimed before picking up his rolled-up twenty-dollar bill and sniffing the rest of the crushed Percocet.

"Nigga, is you crazy? You think we gon' actually be able to hit they shit? Look what just happened the first time we went down there. We would be better off blitzing them every day so they can't make no money. It take money to war," Tito said.

"Nah, fuck that." Pewee pinched his nose and leaned his head back. "We hittin' them niggas' pockets my way. Them niggas gon' know I mean business."

Tito looked at Pewee with pure disgust. Gone was the street-savvy leader that he looked up to, and in his place was a pill-sniffing, trigger-happy goofy.

"Aight, bet. But I ain't gon' be a part of that shit. Niggas is gon' be dyin' for yo pride. And I can't get wit' that." Tito stood up to leave.

"Pssst!" Pewee scoffed. "It ain't like yo pancake ass know what pride is anyway."

"Fuck you just say, nigga!" Tito stared him down.

"I say y—"

BOC! BOC! BOC! Bullets ripped through Pewee's chest. He looked up at Tito with wide eyes. He tried to reach for his gun on the table, but Tito swiped it onto the floor. Pewee gasped for air as blood began pouring from his mouth. Tito was about to make his way upstairs when the light bulb went off. He quickly ran back down the stairs and removed Pewee's stash from under the couch. He locked eyes with Pewee, who was still fighting for his life.

Boc! A shot to the dome snapped Pewee's head back, killing him instantly. Sure he was done, Tito jogged up the stairs and bolted out the door.

CHAPTER 29

AT THE COUNTY JAIL

Pap stepped through the county's double doors and smiled from ear to ear. Even though he'd only been in for a couple of months, it felt like eternity. He spotted Crazy G leaning on his Charger and bopped his way.

"What's up, nigga," he greeted.

"Same shit," Crazy G shot back.

They shook up G.D., then embraced thug style.

"Damn, nigga. You been workin' out." Crazy G thumped his chest with a closed fist.

"Ain't shit else in that bitch to do."

"C'mon, nigga. Let's get da fuck outta here. You know I got my blic on me." He smiled, hopping in the driver's seat. "Where you wanna eat at?" he asked once they were both in the car.

"Shit, it don't even matter as long as it ain't no whack-ass McDonald's."

"Aight, bet. I know this slick spot on 63rd."

IN FRANKFORT

Star pulled into his driveway and killed the engine. He stared at his house thinking about his situation with LayLay. He tried to come up with a good reason as to why he did it but came up blank every time. He had no reason at all except for his lust and disloyalty. With Tito, he owed him no loyalty and knew he was a fuck nigga.

Pap was the complete opposite in every aspect. He was dead wrong and knew it. He popped the trunk, grabbed his money, and slipped inside. He quickly loaded the money into the safe with the exception of thirty thousand. He planned on bonding Pap out for seventy-five hundred and giving him the rest. He shed his clothes and slipped into the shower. He turned the water off just as he turned it on. He could have sworn he heard banging. He listened for a full minute before turning the water back on. The second he did—

Boom! The front door came flying in.

F.B.I.

Lock Down Publications and Ca$h Presents Assisted Publishing Packages

Due to an increase in the price of services we have increased our prices. The prices below reflect the price increase as of 11/1/24.

BASIC PACKAGE	UPGRADED PACKAGE
$699 Editing Cover Design Formatting	**$1000** Typing Editing Cover Design Formatting Upload eBooks to Amazon Upload Paperback to Amazon
ADVANCE PACKAGE **$1,400** Typing Editing (line editing/content) Cover Design Formatting Copyright Registration Proofreading Upload eBooks to Amazon Upload Paperback to Amazon	**LDP SUPREME PACKAGE** **$1,700** Typing Editing (line editing/content) Cover Design Formatting Copyright Registration Proofreading Set up Amazon Account Upload eBooks to Amazon Upload Paperback to Amazon Advertise on LDP's Amazon and Facebook Page

***

Other services available upon request.
Additional charges may apply

Lock Down Publications
P.O. Box 944
Stockbridge, GA 30281-9998
Phone: 470 303-9761
Email: lockdownpublications@gmail.com

Submission Guideline

Submit the first three chapters of your completed manuscript to ldpsubmissions@gmail.com. In the subject line add **Your Book's Title**. The manuscript must be in a Word Doc file and sent as an attachment. Document should be in Times New Roman, double spaced, and in size 12 font. Also, provide your synopsis and full contact information. If sending multiple submissions, they must each be in a separate email.

Have a story but no way to send it electronically? You can still submit to LDP/Ca$h Presents. Send in the first three chapters, written or typed, of your completed manuscript to:

LDP: Submissions Dept
P.O. Box 944
Stockbridge, GA 30281-9998

DO NOT send original manuscript. Must be a duplicate.
Provide your synopsis and a cover letter containing your full contact information.

Thanks for considering LDP and Ca$h Presents.

NEW RELEASES

BLOODLINE OF A SAVAGE 1-3
THESE VICIOUS STREETS 1-3
RELENTLESS GOON 1-3
BY PRINCE A. TAUHID

THE BUTTERFLY MAFIA 1-3
BY FUMIYA PAYNE

A THUG'S STREET PRINCESS 1&2
BY MEESHA

CITY OF SMOKE 3
BY MOLOTTI

GET IT IN SLUGS 1 &2
BY B. STALL

STANDING ON HER BUSINESS 1&2
BY DG SANTANA

STEPPERS 1,2&3
THE REAL BADDIES OF CHI-RAQ
BY KING RIO

THE LANE 1&2
BY KEN-KEN SPENCE

THUG OF SPADES 1&2
LOVE IN THE TRENCHES 2
CORNER BOYS
BY COREY ROBINSON

TIL DEATH 3
BY ARYANNA

GANGSTERS BLEED BLUE | GUTTA

THE BIRTH OF A GANGSTER 4
BY DELMONT PLAYER

PRODUCT OF THE STREETS 1-3
BY DEMOND "MONEY" ANDERSON

NO TIME FOR ERROR
BY KEESE

MONEY HUNGRY DEMONS 1-2
BY TRANAY ADAMS

HUB CITY MENACE 1-3
BY J. WHITE

A THUGGISH PASSION 1&2
LAND OF DA HOOLIGANZ 1-4
KILLAZ ON STANDBY 1&2
BY IRA B.

FO'EVA ROLLIN 1&2
BY ASSA RAYMOND BAKER

THE LEVEL UP 1&3
BY LUXURY KING

Coming Soon from Lock Down Publications/Ca$h Presents

IF YOU CROSS ME ONCE 6
ANGEL V
By Anthony Fields

A THUGS STREET PRINCESS 3
By Meesha

CORNER BOYS 2
By Corey Robinson

THA TAKEOVER
By Keith Chandler

BETRAYAL OF A G 2
By Ray Vinci

SAVAGE FAMILY EMPIRE 1&2
SOULLESS GOON 1,2&3
THE DIRTY SIDE OF MONEY 1,2&3
By Prince

FOR MY ENEMY'S SAKE
AMBITIONS OF A SLIDER
FRESH OFF DA PORCH
By IRA B.

THE TRUCKLOAD 1-4
TIPPIN' THE SCALES 1-3
BAD BITCHES WIT GUNZ 3
PROBLEM SOLVED 2
By Christopher "Diesel" Hornezes

Available Now

GANGSTERS BLEED BLUE | GUTTA

BLOODY COMMAS I & II
SKI MASK CARTEL I, II & III
KING OF NEW YORK I II, III IV V
RISE TO POWER I II III
COKE KINGS I II III IV V
BORN HEARTLESS I II III IV
KING OF THE TRAP I II
By **T.J. Edwards**

WHEN THE STREETS CLAP BACK I & II III
THE HEART OF A SAVAGE I II III IV
MONEY MAFIA I II
LOYAL TO THE SOIL I II III
By **Jibril Williams**

A DISTINGUISHED THUG STOLE MY HEART I II & III
LOVE SHOULDN'T HURT I II III IV
RENEGADE BOYS 1-4
PAID IN KARMA 1-3
SAVAGE STORMS 1-3
AN UNFORESEEN LOVE 1-3
BABY, I'M WINTERTIME COLD 1-3
A THUG'S STREET PRINCESS 1&2
By **Meesha**

A GANGSTER'S CODE 1-3
A GANGSTER'S SYN 1-3
THE SAVAGE LIFE 1-3
CHAINED TO THE STREETS 1-3
BLOOD ON THE MONEY 1-3
A GANGSTA'S PAIN 1-3
BEAUTIFUL LIES AND UGLY TRUTHS
CHURCH IN THESE STREETS
By **J-Blunt**

CUM FOR ME 1-8
An LDP Erotica Collaboration

GANGSTERS BLEED BLUE | GUTTA

BLOOD OF A BOSS 1-5
SHADOWS OF THE GAME
TRAP BASTARD
By **Askari**

THE STREETS BLEED MURDER 1-3
THE HEART OF A GANGSTA 1-3
By **Jerry Jackson**

WHEN A GOOD GIRL GOES BAD
By **Adrienne**

THE COST OF LOYALTY 1-3
By **Kweli**

BRIDE OF A HUSTLA 1-3
THE FETTI GIRLS 1-3
CORRUPTED BY A GANGSTA 1-4
BLINDED BY HIS LOVE
THE PRICE YOU PAY FOR LOVE 1-3
DOPE GIRL MAGIC 1-3
By **Destiny Skai**

A KINGPIN'S AMBITION
A KINGPIN'S AMBITION II
I MURDER FOR THE DOUGH
By **Ambitious**

TRUE SAVAGE 1-7
DOPE BOY MAGIC 1-3
MIDNIGHT CARTEL 1-3
CITY OF KINGZ 1&2
NIGHTMARE ON SILENT AVE
THE PLUG OF LIL MEXICO 1&2
CLASSIC CITY
By **Chris Green**

A GANGSTER'S REVENGE 1-4
THE BOSS MAN'S DAUGHTERS 1-5
A SAVAGE LOVE 1&2
BAE BELONGS TO ME 1&2
A HUSTLER'S DECEIT 1-3
WHAT BAD BITCHES DO 1-3
SOUL OF A MONSTER 1-3
KILL ZONE
A DOPE BOY'S QUEEN 1-3
TIL DEATH 1-3
IMMA DIE BOUT MINE 1-6
DYING FOR LIKES
By **Aryanna**

A DOPEBOY'S PRAYER
By **Eddie "Wolf" Lee**

THE KING CARTEL 1-3
By **Frank Gresham**

THESE NIGGAS AIN'T LOYAL 1-3
By **Nikki Tee**

GANGSTA SHYT 1-3
By **CATO**

THE ULTIMATE BETRAYAL
By **Phoenix**

BOSS'N UP 1-3
By **Royal Nicole**

I LOVE YOU TO DEATH
By **Destiny J**

I RIDE FOR MY HITTA
I STILL RIDE FOR MY HITTA
By **Misty Holt**

LOVE & CHASIN' PAPER
By **Qay Crockett**

TO DIE IN VAIN
SINS OF A HUSTLA
By **ASAD**

BROOKLYN HUSTLAZ
By **Boogsy Morina**

BROOKLYN ON LOCK 1 & 2
By **Sonovia**

GANGSTA CITY
By **Teddy Duke**

A DRUG KING AND HIS DIAMOND 1-3
A DOPEMAN'S RICHES
HER MAN, MINE'S TOO 1&2
CASH MONEY HO'S
THE WIFEY I USED TO BE 1&2
PRETTY GIRLS DO NASTY THINGS
By **Nicole Goosby**

LIPSTICK KILLAH 1-3
CRIME OF PASSION 1-3
FRIEND OR FOE 1-3
By **Mimi**

TRAPHOUSE KING 1-3
KINGPIN KILLAZ 1-3
STREET KINGS 1&2
PAID IN BLOOD 1&2
CARTEL KILLAZ 1-3
DOPE GODS 1&2
By **Hood Rich**

THE STREETS ARE CALLING
By **Duquie Wilson**

STEADY MOBBN' 1-3
THE STREETS STAINED MY SOUL 1-3
By **Marcellus Allen**

WHO SHOT YA 1-3
SON OF A DOPE FIEND 1-4
HEAVEN GOT A GHETTO 1&2
SKI MASK MONEY 1&2
By **Renta**

GORILLAZ IN THE BAY 1-4
TEARS OF A GANGSTA 1/&2
3X KRAZY 1&2
STRAIGHT BEAST MODE 1&2
By **DE'KARI**

TRIGGADALE 1-3
MURDA WAS THE CASE 1-3
By **Elijah R. Freeman**

SLAUGHTER GANG 1-3
RUTHLESS HEART 1-3
By **Willie Slaughter**

GOD BLESS THE TRAPPERS 1-3
THESE SCANDALOUS STREETS 1-3
FEAR MY GANGSTA 1-5
THESE STREETS DON'T LOVE NOBODY 1-2
BURY ME A G 1-5
A GANGSTA'S EMPIRE 1-4
THE DOPEMAN'S BODYGAURD 1&2
THE REALEST KILLAZ 1-3
THE LAST OF THE OGS 1-3
By **Tranay Adams**

MARRIED TO A BOSS 1-3
By **Destiny Skai & Chris Green**

KINGZ OF THE GAME 1-7
CRIME BOSS 1-4
By **Playa Ray**

FUK SHYT
By **Blakk Diamond**

DON'T F#CK WITH MY HEART 1&2
By **Linnea**

ADDICTED TO THE DRAMA 1-3
IN THE ARM OF HIS BOSS
By **Jamila**

LOYALTY AIN'T PROMISED 1&2
By **Keith Williams**

YAYO 1-4
A SHOOTER'S AMBITION 1&2
BRED IN THE GAME
By **S. Allen**

TRAP GOD 1-3
RICH $AVAGE 1-3
MONEY IN THE GRAVE 1-3
CARTEL MONEY 1&2
By **Martell Troublesome Bolden**

FOREVER GANGSTA 1&2
GLOCKS ON SATIN SHEETS 1&2
By **Adrian Dulan**

TOE TAGZ 1-4
LEVELS TO THIS SHYT 1&2
IT'S JUST ME AND YOU
By **Ah'Million**

GANGSTERS BLEED BLUE | GUTTA

KINGPIN DREAMS 1-3
RAN OFF ON DA PLUG
By **Paper Boi Rari**

THE STREETS MADE ME 1-3
By **Larry D. Wright**

CONFESSIONS OF A GANGSTA 1-4
CONFESSIONS OF A JACKBOY 1-3
CONFESSIONS OF A HITMAN
CONFESSIONS OF A DOPE BOY
By **Nicholas Lock**

I'M NOTHING WITHOUT HIS LOVE
SINS OF A THUG
TO THE THUG I LOVED BEFORE
A GANGSTA SAVED XMAS
IN A HUSTLER I TRUST
By **Monet Dragun**

QUIET MONEY 1-3
THUG LIFE 1-3
EXTENDED CLIP 1&2
A GANGSTA'S PARADISE
By **Trai'Quan**

CAUGHT UP IN THE LIFE 1-3
THE STREETS NEVER LET GO 1-3
By **Robert Baptiste**

NEW TO THE GAME 1-3
MONEY, MURDER & MEMORIES 1-3
By **Malik D. Rice**

CREAM 2-3
THE STREETS WILL TALK
By **Yolanda Moore**

THE STREETS WILL NEVER CLOSE 1-3
By **K'ajji**

LIFE OF A SAVAGE 1-4
A GANGSTA'S QUR'AN 1-4
MURDA SEASON 1-3
GANGLAND CARTEL 1-3
CHI'RAQ GANGSTAS 1-4
KILLERS ON ELM STREET 1-3
JACK BOYZ N DA BRONX 1-3
A DOPEBOY'S DREAM 1-3
JACK BOYS VS DOPE BOYS 1-3
COKE GIRLZ
COKE BOYS
SOSA GANG 1&2
BRONX SAVAGES
BODYMORE KINGPINS
BLOOD OF A GOON
By **Romell Tukes**

CONCRETE KILLA 1-3
VICIOUS LOYALTY 1-3
BLOODY MONEY BAGS
By **Kingpen**

THE ULTIMATE SACRIFICE 1-6
KHADIFI
IF YOU CROSS ME ONCE 1-3
ANGEL 1-4
IN THE BLINK OF AN EYE
By **Anthony Fields**

THE LIFE OF A HOOD STAR
By **Ca$h & Rashia Wilson**

NIGHTMARES OF A HUSTLA 1-3
BLOOD AND GAMES 1&2
By **King Dream**

GHOST MOB
By **Stilloan Robinson**

HARD AND RUTHLESS 1&2
MOB TOWN 251
THE BILLIONAIRE BENTLEYS 1-3
REAL G'S MOVE IN SILENCE
By **Von Diesel**

MOB TIES 1-7
SOUL OF A HUSTLER, HEART OF A KILLER 1-3
GORILLAZ IN THE TRENCHES
OOPS CRY TOO 1&2
THE DAUGHTER OF A CARTEL BOSS
By **SayNoMore**

BODYMORE MURDERLAND 1-3
THE BIRTH OF A GANGSTER 1-4
By **Delmont Player**

FOR THE LOVE OF A BOSS 1&2
By **C. D. Blue**

KILLA KOUNTY 1-5
TENDER
By **Khufu**

MOBBED UP 1-4
THE BRICK MAN 1-5
THE COCAINE PRINCESS 1-10
STEPPERS 1-3
SUPER GREMLIN 1-4
A GANGSTA'S SON
By **King Rio**

MONEY GAME 1&2
By **Smoove Dolla**

A GANGSTA'S KARMA 1-5
By **FLAME**

KING OF THE TRENCHES 1-3
By **GHOST & TRANAY ADAMS**

BAD BITCHES WIT GUNZ 1&2
PROBLEM SOLVED
By "Christopher Diesel" Hornezes

QUEEN OF THE ZOO 1&2
By **Black Migo**

GRIMEY WAYS 1-3
BETRAYAL OF A G
By **Ray Vinci**

XMAS WITH AN ATL SHOOTER
By **Ca$h & Destiny Skai**

KING KILLA 1&2
By **Vincent "Vitto" Holloway**

BETRAYAL OF A THUG 1&2
By **Fre$h**

COUNTDOWN OF A KILLA 1&2
SEX, MURDER AND GOD 1&2
GUNS DOWN, BOTTOMS UP 1&2
By Lo-Life

THE MURDER QUEENS 1-7
By **Michael Gallon**

FOR THE LOVE OF BLOOD 1-4
By **Jamel Mitchell**

HOOD CONSIGLIERE 1&2
NO TIME FOR ERROR
By **Keese**

PROTÉGÉ OF A LEGEND 1,2&3
LOVE IN THE TRENCHES 1&2
By **Corey Robinson**

THE PLUG'S RUTHLESS DAUGHTER 1&2
By **Tony Daniels**

BORN IN THE GRAVE 1-3
CRIME PAYS
By **Self Made Tay**

MOAN IN MY MOUTH
By **XTASY**

TORN BETWEEN A GANGSTER AND A GENTLEMAN
By **J-BLUNT & Miss Kim**

LOYALTY IS EVERYTHING 1-3
CITY OF SMOKE 1-3
By **Molotti**

HERE TODAY GONE TOMORROW 1&2
By **Fly Rock**

WOMEN LIE MEN LIE 1-4
FIFTY SHADES OF SNOW 1-3
STACK BEFORE YOU SPLURGE
GIRLS FALL LIKE DOMINOES
NAÏVE TO THE STREETS
By **ROY MILLIGAN**

PILLOW PRINCESS
By **S. Hawkins**

GANGSTERS BLEED BLUE | GUTTA

THE BUTTERFLY MAFIA 1-3
SALUTE MY SAVAGERY 1&2
By **Fumiya Payne**

THE LANE 1&2
By Ken-Ken Spence

THE PUSSY TRAP 1-5
By **Nene Capri**

DIRTY DNA
By **Blaque**

SANCTIFIED AND HORNY
by **XTASY**

BOOKS BY LDP'S CEO, CA$H

TRUST IN NO MAN
TRUST IN NO MAN 2
TRUST IN NO MAN 3
BONDED BY BLOOD
SHORTY GOT A THUG
THUGS CRY
THUGS CRY 2
THUGS CRY 3
TRUST NO BITCH
TRUST NO BITCH 2
TRUST NO BITCH 3
TIL MY CASKET DROPS
RESTRAINING ORDER
RESTRAINING ORDER 2
IN LOVE WITH A CONVICT
LIFE OF A HOOD STAR
XMAS WITH AN ATL SHOOTER

www.ingramcontent.com/pod-product-compliance
Lightning Source LLC
LaVergne TN
LVHW020709110826
845149LV00012B/2174